# RIPTIDE

## Eric E. Wright

**RIPTIDE**

**COPYRIGHT 2013 by ERIC E. WRIGHT**

Contact Information: titleadmin@pelicanbookgroup.com

Cover Art by *Nicola Martinez*

Harbourlight Books, a division of Pelican Ventures, LLC
www.pelicanbookgroup.com PO Box 1738 *Aztec, NM * 87410

Harbourlight Books sail and mast logo is a trademark of Pelican Ventures, LLC

Publishing History
First Harbourlight Edition, 2014
Paperback Edition ISBN 978-1-61116-301-8
Electronic Edition ISBN 978-1-61116-300-1
**Published in the United States of America**

# Dedication

This book is dedicated to all those who struggle with the fallout of divorce in a manner consistent with the standards of Scripture and the grace of God. May God enable them rise above pain and trauma. It is also dedicated to their friends who seek to comfort and support them and also to the innocent victims of divorce, the children.

I want to acknowledge my indebtedness to the Revision online critiquing group, the Warkworth Writers' Group and the Brighton Writers' Group for their invaluable and very encouraging input.

The books, *Shrimp* by Jack and Anne Rudloe and *An Unreasonable Woman* by Diane Wilson have contributed greatly to my understanding of shrimping and appreciation for those who quest for pink gold.

I am grateful to M. Jamie West and Nicola Martinez of the Pelican Book Group for applying their editing skills to the story. They helped immensely in improving the manuscript.

I'm thankful for my agent, Les Stobbe's belief in the value of my scribbling.

I'm awed by the love of Mary Helen, my bride of fifty-two years, and God's grace has led us through the years.

# Praise

"*Riptide's* twists and turns kept my emotions on high alert! Great read!" Brenda J Wood, author and speaker.

"*Riptide* draws the reader immediately into the exotic world of St. Simons Island where Ashlyn Forsyth is dumped by her husband into his secret life involving high level criminals, FBI, and Russian mafia. This suspense driven plot engages the reader's mind and heart as we follow Ashlyn's unwitting adventure towards a new life." Pat Calder, author.

"*Riptide* engages the reader as we see Ashlyn develop her relationships with her daughter, the people she meets on St Simons Island and Remy. She ends up a stronger character after all her adventures—and there are many of those. The pace is fast." Felicity Sidnell, writer

# 1

Craig and I were standing in the congregation at First Baptist Church on St. Simons Island, Georgia, singing when he stopped and handed me a sealed envelope.

"What's this?" I whispered as I turned to him, but he was already striding up the aisle towards the exit.

My stomach knotted, the bulky envelope growing heavy in my hand. I stared at it, unthinking, and then glanced at the heavy oak doors. Craig was gone.

Forcing my mind to focus on something other than the confusion and dread swimming through my head, I realized that the music had stopped and I was the only one standing. With a flush creeping up my neck, I grabbed my purse and fled. Fortunately, this wasn't our home congregation in New York where everyone knew us.

Outside, I caught sight of Craig getting into a silver sedan. I peered at the driver. A woman. Marlee, one of the investment advisors in his firm? What was she doing here?

Marlee stared at me over her shoulder, grimaced, and then hit the gas. The wheels kicked up gravel as she accelerated out of the parking lot.

I stared after them with my mouth open until the fluttering clouds of Spanish moss hanging from the ancient oaks hid them from view.

I gazed at the envelope, and then jammed it in my

purse. No need to read it—yet. Instinct told me what it contained.

*Sorry, Ashlyn, but this is not working. I've tried, but I just don't love you anymore. I want a divorce. Blah, blah, blah.*

Our attempt to recover what we'd lost by spending two weeks on romantic St. Simons Island had failed. Was this it, then? Twenty-one years and two kids meant nothing? How would I explain to Tiffany and Tyler?

Something black and terrible began to gnaw at my insides as I searched the parking lot for our car. Tears coursed down my face. At least he left the car.

I fumbled in my purse for the keys, opened the door, and jumped in. Skidding out of the parking lot, I drove with one hand and pounded the dashboard with the other. The arrogant brute. A dear-John letter during a church service. Real macho. Well, two could play at that game. If he thought I'd just roll over and play dead, he was sadly mistaken. I'd make him regret this day.

Gritting my teeth and swiping at the tears I couldn't quell, I drove without thought while rage ricocheted inside me. When I ran out of road, I screeched to a halt, slammed the door and set off down the beach. Oblivious of cruising terns and diving pelicans, I walked aimlessly on the hard sand kicking every shell I saw, imagining it was Craig's vaunted manhood.

In spite of my attempts to avoid softer patches, the heels of my Sunday pumps sank into the sand, and I tumbled backwards. For a few minutes I lay there, not caring about the effect ocean water would have on my best dress. Then I sat up, slipped off my pumps and stared at them.

*Aren't heels archaic anyway; as archaic as marriage? As outmoded as promises—'til death do us part, for better or worse, in sickness and in health? Is that what I am, prehistoric? The model Christian wife; gentle, obedient, faithful? Well if I get my hands on him again, I'll show him how gentle I am—and how faithful.*

Tears began to stream down my face anew. I thought of all the advice I'd given clients in my family therapy practice. Just be patient with one another. Hah. Forgive one another. Double hah. Not so easy now to spout glib clichés about being forgiving.

As I sat there in the damp sand feeding my rage, the scrape of a beach chair on a deck made me aware of how strange I must appear from the cottages fronting the ocean. Grasping my shoes in one hand, I leapt to my feet and set off barefoot down the beach.

I must have walked for miles, oblivious to my surroundings until I found myself on a wooden pier staring at the water swirling at my feet. How had my life come to this? The face that stared up at me looked otherworldly, a phantom with red-rimmed brown eyes, wild fawn-colored hair, and a brooding mouth. I reached up to touch the mole on my left cheek—to see if it was really pulsating or just a trick of light. I shivered.

"Are you all right, ma'am?" The shout woke me from my brooding.

I became aware of the reek of fish and the shrieks of seagulls wheeling overhead. I frowned as other sounds pierced my consciousness: the creak of ropes, the scrape of metal, the lapping of waves. I turned towards the voice. "What?"

Two piercing, sapphire eyes set in a leathery face looked down on me from the deck of a shrimp boat.

My mouth fell open. What was I doing here?

"Please ma'am, move back from the edge of the dock. It's dangerous with the tide coming in so strongly."

I stared at my bare feet. They curled over the very edge of the dock. I swayed. A hand reached out and grabbed my arm, pulling me back from the brink.

I turned towards the man who had jumped down on the dock to keep me from falling.

"I'm sorry. I was distracted...thank you."

The man who held my arm in his massive, calloused hand had bushy brows and a stubbly, creased face. He wore a captain's hat perched on sun-bleached hair. My nose wrinkled at the pungent odor of fish that wafted from his boat.

He dropped my arm and moved back a step. "I thought you'd fall. The water here in the sound is treacherous."

I reached up and patted my windblown hair. "My mind was on some...some bad news."

He cocked his head to one side and squinted at me. "Are you sure you'll be all right? I can drive you back to your hotel."

"No, no, I'm fine." I grimaced. "Although I must be a sight."

He crossed his muscled arms over his faded gingham shirt. "A sight? You are that; right perty."

I looked down, and then turned away and headed back up the pier as a flush began to creep up my neck for the second time that day.

Riptide

# 2

Back at the beach house I tossed my ruined patent leather shoes onto the porch and collapsed into a lounge chair. My head throbbed. I should've eaten something, but I couldn't bear the thought of food.

My purse hid incendiary cargo—Craig's letter. But instead of opening the purse and extracting the letter, I reached down to finger a broken toenail. My feet were a mess. My barefoot ramble along the beach had left them stinging from scratches and cuts where I'd stepped on shells and caught a sliver from the dock. So much for the expensive pedicure I'd had in high hopes of weaving together the tattered strands of our marriage.

Three days of effort, that's all he'd given it before taking off with that tart in her silver Lexus. And I'd thought Marlee was not only one of his business partners, but a friend. A couple of years earlier, we had even been close. She babysat my kids; we had girls' nights out. Craig and I had included her in our family barbecues.

I felt the rage build up within. Looking back, I could see that they'd been too chummy, sharing private glances when they thought I wasn't looking. How could she?

Was I overreacting? But what other reason could she have for being here on the island—

waiting to pick up Craig—unless they were having an affair?

I'd trusted her, loved her as a Christian sister, and she'd stabbed me in the back. Stolen Craig. Or was Craig responsible? Had it all started the time he drove her home when her car broke down? I'd been right to worry about his wandering eyes.

I opened my purse, took out the bulky envelope, and tore it open. A legal document, a note, and some hundred-dollar bills held together with a paper clip fell into my lap. I tossed the money aside. Did he think he could buy me off? The legal document, as I'd feared, was notice that he was filing for divorce. I tossed it after the money and turned to the handwritten note.

*Ashlyn,*

*Our marriage is just not working out. No matter how often we've tried, it remains a shell. Spending more time talking—arguing—isn't going to help. This holiday has only made it clearer. Except for the kids we have little in common anymore.*

*Don't bring up the Bible and talk about an eternal covenant and all that stuff. I'm sure God doesn't expect me to keep on living a lie.*

*I don't blame you. We're just not in love anymore. It happens all the time, so please accept it. You don't love me either, or you wouldn't freeze me out.*

*I've applied for a divorce. Please don't contest it. And please understand that I never wanted to hurt you. You've been a great mother to Tiffany and Tyler. Blame me if you like, but I just can't continue with the kind of armed truce we've negotiated over the last five or six years. The kids are independent now and very resilient. They'll get over it.*

*I've enclosed $700 to cover any bills I may have*

*forgotten. The beach house is paid for until the end of September. Oh, and Tiffany's tuition is paid through the end of next term. I've sent a money order for Tyler to pick up when he gets to Melbourne.*

*I'm dropping out of sight for a while so you won't be able to contact me.*

*Craig*

I threw the note after the money and bit my lip in an attempt to smother the storm rising within. Not even a *Dear Ashlyn* or *Love, Craig*. This was the work of a cool-headed financial consultant, cutting his losses. The creep must have been planning his exit for some time; never meant to use our time at the beach to sort things out. No wonder people gave him money to invest. How could I have been so blind, so naïve?

My lips trembled. I was determined not to cry again. But despite my efforts to swallow my grief, tears gushed down my face as I remembered some of the good times we'd had.

A couple walking hand in hand on the beach road glanced my way. I fled into the beach house where I slipped off my dress and tossed it over a chair. In the bathroom, I washed my face with water as cold as I could stand. Taking a deep breath, I collapsed onto the toilet seat and looked around.

Craig's toothbrush was gone along with his toiletries. His robe no longer hung on the hook behind the door. Out of the corner of my eye, I caught sight of something under the sink. I reached down and picked up a small fragment of hard plastic.

Someone had cut up a credit card. All I could make out were the first two letters of a name, a

"C" and an "r". Craig? Why would he cut up one of his cards?

I marched into the bedroom and flung open the closet door. Empty hangers mocked me. His bureau drawer was also empty. I scanned the room. Gone were his cell phone, his travel alarm, the book on offshore investments he'd been reading, his briefcase, and suitcase.

All that remained of him was an indentation on the bed-sheets and the mug in which I'd brought him his morning coffee.

So cold and calculating! Blast! He must have arranged for Marlee to pick up everything while we were in church.

*Craig, I hate you! And Marlee, I despise you.*

I stared at my image in the full-length mirror. Red circles rimmed my eyes. My shoulder length brown hair looked mousy and dull. Even sucking in my breath I couldn't hide the thickening waist and the slight bulge of my tummy. Nothing could disguise the stretch marks from two pregnancies.

I picked up the mug he'd left and hurled it at the mirror. It bounced twice and rolled intact under the bed while the mirror shattered into a thousand silvered pieces. How ironic. He had waltzed away to start a new life while I was left to pick up the pieces.

I stood there looking at the scattered fragments and thinking how useless mirrors were to reflect what I'd actually contributed to this marriage. Thousands of rides to and from school, ten thousand meals prepared, a hundred thousand dishes washed.

With a sigh, I avoided the shards of mirror on the floor, pulled on a pair of jeans and a T-shirt, and ran a hand through my hair. Then, slamming the bedroom door, I went into the kitchen to put on the kettle for a cup of tea.

While the kettle was coming to a boil, I rummaged in the cupboards for teabags and something to eat. Crackers. A can of soup. Another of spaghetti sauce. And no tea bags. But there was a box of chocolates.

I grabbed the box, turned off the element under the kettle, and strode into the living room. Flopping on the sofa, I opened the box. Chocolate truffles, almond nougats, and coconut clusters stared up at me seductively. With a deep sigh, I closed the box and set it on the floor beside me.

How many times had I welcomed distraught women into my office and prayed with them about bingeing on chocolate, or wine, or shopping? Now it was my turn.

Ashlyn Forsyth, the esteemed family counselor, needed counsel; the dedicated Christian savoring a corrosive rage, plotting revenge.

I forced myself to stop acting like a jilted teenager. To grow up. To remind myself that I'd seen this coming for a couple of years.

One thing was clear, I wouldn't be going back to my practice for some time. How could I face more marital sob-stories and spout more platitudes. I'd have to get my secretary to cancel all my appointments— give her some time off.

What about the kids? No need to call Tiffany yet. Break it to her slowly. Let her enjoy the first few weeks of her new term. Tyler, hiking in the outback, wouldn't call in for a week or so. That left me a couple of weeks to figure out what to do with the wreckage of my life.

I got up and wandered around the living room; gazed out the picture window at the turquoise ocean and the cloudless sky. A couple of terns wheeled and dived for fish. Why couldn't the sea reflect the storm within?

My stomach rumbled. I frowned. How could I be hungry when my world had shifted on its axis? True, I hadn't eaten since the night before; we'd slept too late to grab some breakfast before dashing off to church.

I wouldn't give Craig the satisfaction of turning me into another middle-aged excuse for a woman. I'd attend to the basics. Take it one step at a time. Get some food. Read a good book. Go for a long walk. Life would go on—eventually.

In the bathroom I brushed my hair and dashed on some fresh makeup. Then I grabbed my purse and headed out the door. As I turned to lock up, I noticed the divorce papers and money I'd tossed on the veranda.

I tucked the money into my purse and threw the divorce papers inside the cottage.

With a grim smile I tore Craig's note into tiny pieces and tossed them into the air. Littering? So what.

In the village, I parked in front of the Shrimpboat Café, where I could be fairly sure not to run into any of the Sunday church crowd. Inside, I paused and glanced around. Four tough looking men occupied a table to the left of the door. A net decorated a wall to the right. On every other free space hung a requisite, but bewildering array of fishing paraphernalia.

A chunky blonde with weary eyes and too much make-up smiled. "Lots'a choice, darlin'. Pick yuhself a table."

I selected a table off to the right in a corner.

The waitress passed me a menu. "Tea?"

"Uh, no, do you have coffee?"

"Do we have coffee? Darlin', you came to the right place."

She left to fetch coffee, while I turned to the menu. The original prices had been covered with white-out and new prices written in.

Having settled on the shrimp dish with hush puppies, fries, and coleslaw, I set down the menu and glanced around in an attempt to distract my mind. The café-style checkered curtains that framed the lower half of the front windows looked clean, but faded. Beyond the four men, a couple with two children occupied another table. The boy tried to stuff a fist-full of fries in his mouth. His sister laughed. A decade ago, that could have been us.

Lottie Jane, according to her nametag, set down a mug of coffee and some creamers on the table. "What'll it be, darlin'?"

I gave her my order and sat back to see if her promise of a good cup of coffee was just whistlin' Dixie. I'd learned from Craig to enjoy bold coffee and turn down the insipid stuff.

How long before thoughts of Craig would quit popping up in my mind? I sat back sipping the coffee and trying to purge him from my thoughts.

The tinkle of the bell over the door interrupted my reverie. Three men entered wearing stained jeans and heavy work-shirts open half-way down their chests. Two of them wore baseball caps advertising some obscure product. The third sported a weathered captain's cap at a jaunty angle. It was the burly shrimper who'd grabbed my arm to keep me from falling off the pier.

I quickly picked up the menu and pretended to peruse the meal selection.

Lottie Jane arrived with a huge platter of food. "So, what's the verdict?"

Stunned by the quantity of food in front of me, I stuttered. "Pardon?"

"The coffee…thinking of switching to tea?"

"No, the coffee is wonderful. The best I've tasted since leaving home."

She folded her arms. "Our customers think so. None of that dishwater those other guys serve."

I tried to smile, but only succeeded in grimacing.

"Just visiting?"

"Ah, yeah."

"So where're yuh from?"

I speared a shrimp with my fork. "Uh, New York."

"I can still hear a Carolina drawl. Good, them Yankees haven't gobbled yuh up yet. Well, enjoy the food, dearie. I'll be back with more coffee."

The food definitely outdid the décor. It was delicious, but I quickly lost my appetite.

Lottie Jane returned to fill my cup for the third time. "Not hungry, honey?"

"There's enough there for a—a sea captain. It's just that I'm not used to so much. But the food is delicious. My compliments to your cook. I'll certainly be back."

She smiled. "I'll tell Claude. He'll be pleased."

I handed her my credit card.

A few minutes later she returned with the card. "I'm sorry dearie, but this card is coming back invalid."

"What? That can't be."

"I tried three times."

I frowned as I passed her another card. "OK, put it on my other card."

My gaze followed her as she returned to the cash register. After several tries she turned towards me and shook her head.

I felt a bead of sweat trickle down my back. This couldn't be happening. I grabbed some bills from my wallet, seeing the bundle of bills he'd left me beside it. I tossed a couple of bucks on the table and strode to the cash register. After retrieving my now useless card and paying cash, I hastened from the café.

The Southern benediction, "Y'all come back now," followed me out the door.

Had he cancelled our cards and taken out new ones without my knowledge?

I couldn't imagine Craig stooping so low.

# 3

I drove to the beach house in a daze. When I stopped, I found I'd been gripping the steering wheel so tight that it took me a few minutes of wiggling my fingers to restore feeling.

I sat there in the car taking deep breaths and trying to stuff down the panic rising within. This couldn't be happening: far from home with no plastic to pay the bills. How could both of my credit cards be invalid at the same time? I'd just used them on the trip down from New York. Fluke?

No, more like a deliberate act of my callous husband. Ex-husband? But would he be so vindictive? My mind went to the morning's scenario, and I shook my head. Scheming and devious, yes, but I couldn't see him as actually malicious...or could I? The piece I'd found in the bathroom showed he'd cut up at least one of his own cards.

Opening my purse, I took out the bundle of bills he'd clipped together. I flipped through them. Yes, $700, as he'd said. He must have known I'd be in trouble, and left me some cash to tide me over. *How thoughtful!* Was that what I was worth, $700, the price of a worn-out car, an old clunker that didn't actually run? I pounded the steering wheel with my fists until a sharp pain in my right hand made me stop.

Well, my friend Julie was right; I was too gullible. Dumb. My trust in Craig had blinded me to reality.

Swiping at the tears that began to well up, I

grabbed the purse and exited the car. Fumbling through the bag, I found the key to the beach house, but my fingers were trembling so much it took me a couple of minutes to get the key to work.

Inside I took out my cell phone and dialed the customer service number for one of my credit cards. The disembodied voice led me through myriad options.

Finally, a female operator came on the line and after authenticating my identity said, "I'm sorry ma'am, but this account has been frozen."

"Frozen. What do you mean frozen?"

"Credit facilities have been suspended."

"But that's impossible. We always pay our bills...on time."

"I can see that, ma'am."

"Well, then why?"

"I don't have that information. We've been instructed by head office to suspend usage on this account. That's all I know."

"But...but."

The woman's voice mellowed. "I'm sorry, ma'am, that I can't give you a fuller explanation. Is there anything else, then?"

"No, I guess not."

"Thanks for calling us. And have a good day."

"A good day. Yeah."

I flicked off the cell phone and collapsed onto the sofa. No use calling the other credit card company. I'd get the same run-around.

Have a good day?

Before I could stop myself I was laughing uncontrollably: snorting, wheezing, hiccupping. Tears streamed down my cheeks. Have a good day, indeed.

Enough of this. I got up, went to the bathroom, rinsed my face in cold water, dried it off, and returned to the living room.

Taking my wallet, I emptied all the contents on the dining room table. The seven hundred from Craig plus seven twenties, two tens, twelve dollars in ones, and an assortment of change. Total, $872. Two useless credit cards. My debit card from Riker's Bank. My driver's license and insurance card plus a couple of worn business cards. A copy-center card, some lint, and assorted junk. The only credit card in my own name was from a department store. *Could I buy gas and meals there? At least I could get cosmetics.*

What kind of financial mumbo-jumbo had Craig worked to freeze me out?

I grabbed my cell phone and punched in his number.

After ringing a couple of times another disembodied voice came on the line. "The number you have dialed has been discontinued. The number you..."

I bit my lip. Out of touch, just as he'd said in his note. But to discontinue his cell phone? Did he think I was going to pester him with teary appeals to seek counseling? I nodded. Probably. Six months ago I'd gone down that road—and humiliated myself.

*Well, Casanova, I'll get along without you.*

I went over to the picture window where I stood gazing down at the beach. A couple of sandpipers waddled along the shore beneath a cloudless sky. A sailboat cut through the turquoise water. Another perfect day where—as the hymn proclaims—every prospect pleases, and only man is vile.

At least I had my bank card. When funds got low, I could always use a bank machine.

A sudden premonition hit me in the stomach. I turned back to the table, returned everything to my wallet, dumped it in my purse, and dashed out the front door. My fingers trembled as I started the car and backed out of the driveway.

I tore down Ocean Boulevard taking deep breaths to ease the bands of steel that squeezed my chest. When that didn't work, I ground my teeth.

At the island's luxury hotel I blasted my horn at a sports car that pulled out in front of me. Seeing the hotel again, my heart gave a lurch. Memories of the intimacy we'd enjoyed there a decade earlier came flooding back. The walks on the beach. Counting dolphins. Collecting sand dollars. The laughter. The plans we'd made. The showers we'd taken together. Waking in the middle of night to make love a second time.

I stared straight ahead.

*Enough of that, Ashlyn. Your life has become a soap opera.* I turned right on Mallory, and then Demere Road where I sped past the airport. Parking at the Coastal Bank, I braked to a stop, turned off the engine and sat there. Did I really want to find out?

Finally, I took a deep breath, got out of the car, and tried to saunter into the bank as if I didn't have a care in the world. I smiled at a young woman turning away from the single bank machine. As I fumbled in my purse for my bank card, the door behind me opened; an old gentleman wearing a planter's straw hat entered. I nodded to him as he came over to stand behind me.

Turning back to the machine, I inserted the card and with barely usable fingers punched in the password. The machine beeped once then ejected the card. I frowned. *No wonder, I should have keyed in 2314 not 2341.* Retrieving the card, I turned to the man behind me. "Sorry, I'm always forgetting my password. Why don't you go ahead?"

The gentleman touched his hat and smiled. "I'm in no hurry, ma'am. These new-fangled machines make me so nervous, it takes me half a day to get up my nerve to use one. I prefer to use a teller, but can't today. Besides, my son says it's time I embraced the twenty-first century."

My attempt at a smile turned into a grimace. "Isn't it the truth?"

"Take your time," he smiled. "I've got nowhere to go."

I turned back to the machine and inserted my card a second time. This time I keyed in the correct password. A few moments passed before it ejected the card a second time and registered a generic message. *Funds not available. Please contact your branch.*

I stared at the message with my mouth open for a moment, and then inserted the card a third time. I held my breath as the machine beeped and whirred. It ejected my card once again and displayed the same message.

Retrieving my card I stared at the floor. No!

"Is there a problem?"

I turned back to the man and gestured at the bank machine. "It's refusing to access my account."

The lines on his face deepened as he frowned. "Knew it. Can't trust these contraptions."

He opened his wallet and took out a twenty, which he thrust towards me. "Young lady, do you need something to tide yuh over?"

"No, no," I replied as I moved to one side. "But thanks...thanks a lot. That's very thoughtful."

He tipped his hat to me as I hurried out of the bank.

In the car, I sat pressed back against the seat, gnawing my lower lip, and staring at gently fluttering wisps of Spanish moss on the gnarled oaks lining the road. This couldn't be happening to me.

Somewhere a horn blew, a person laughed, a seagull squawked.

It had to be a dream. I'd soon wake up.

A yellow Japanese car went by sporting the decal of a daisy on the door and a red kayak on the roof.

*Must be a dream.*

A European convertible pulled into the parking lot of the restaurant next door. The man went around and opened the passenger door allowing a woman dressed in a sporty top and capris to get out. He put his arm around her waist as they threaded their way through the parking lot to the restaurant.

I shook my head.

This was no dream, but a living, breathing nightmare. After twenty-one years of marriage, I'd been abandoned.

The $872 wasn't going to last very long and I had no way of getting more.

Could Craig have closed our joint accounts, moved the money to some new account? And what about my retirement savings, my 401K?

I sat clenching and unclenching my fists until my nails left indentations in my palms. Finally, I started the car, and joined the stream of traffic heading towards the pier. The muscles of my face tightened. If Craig and Marlee had been in the car in front, I would have rammed it.

∂∽

Sunday passed as a blur. I know I picked up some groceries from a grocery store, including a quart of gourmet ice cream.

I ended up at the pier to watch the sunset and get a grip on my panic. I found a parking spot facing west, leaned back and tried to relax. The sinking sun gilded a layer of clouds with gold, and then coral that gradually shaded into fuchsia and lavender. Soon that changed into streamers of the darkest purple. A returning shrimp boat stood out as an inky black silhouette trailing silvery streamers on the indigo waters.

While the sun sank into the ocean and the streetlights came on I continued to stare into the darkness.

What was that verse I'd used so often in talking to women who grew up in abusive situations? …*Though my father and mother forsake me, the Lord will receive me.* I leaned over the steering wheel and poured out my anger and frustration to the Lord.

Somewhat comforted, I pondered my options. I'd have to call my home bank on Monday; see what was going on. If only I'd brought the card for my business account, I could have used that. It would tide me over until I could pay it back.

What to do? If my parents were still living, I could

stay with them. The logical thing to do would be to return home. But what would I face there? A big empty house.

Curious neighbors. Mr. Wzenkowski, sweet but nosey, would come over with the Village Recorder and any other community newspapers that had been delivered. He'd want a blow by blow description of our vacation. And then there'd be Julie, a wonderful friend, but such a blabbermouth. No, best to stay here a few days — sort things out.

And sort them out I would. I'd proven my independence and resilience. I rehashed the successes of the last decade.

Even though my dad had said I had no business sense, my counseling practice had developed into one recommended by pastors all over the area. At the beginning, I'd faced lean times when I could hardly pay the rent on the office, but those days had become a memory.

Craig, when he wasn't complaining about me never being home, had commented more than once about my success.

Whatever happened, I would survive...wouldn't I?

I decided to contact Martin Reitman, the lawyer I'd recommended to clients. Let him sort out this mess. At least he knew what confidentiality meant.

Fifteen minutes of ruminations must have gone by before I rummaged in the glove compartment for a plastic spoon. Ripping the seal off the gourmet ice cream, I scooped up a spoonful of the softening pralines and cream. I remembered

Craig claiming that ice cream tasted best just after bringing it home from the store—when it was soft and gooey. At least he got something right.

Before I knew it, I'd polished off half the container. *Yikes.*

Back at the beach house, I put away the groceries—pushing the ice cream container to the very back of the freezer.

I looked around. The beach house that had seemed so cheery when we arrived, now felt like a cloister. Silent. Isolated. Cold. I shivered. What I needed was a cheery fire to banish the chill I felt. I stooped to gather some kindling when my eye caught sight of a pile of charred papers on the grate of the fireplace.

Kneeling down, I stirred the pile with a stick. Although they crumbled into sooty fragments, I could tell they had been spreadsheets of some kind. At the back of the fireplace I spied a crumpled piece of paper that had escaped the fire. When I had smoothed it out, I could clearly read, scrawled in red capitals; FORWARD THE MONEY TO OUR ACCOUNT IN THE CAYMANS BY TUESDAY OR ELSE!

Stunned, I stood there staring at the message with its implied threat. What could it mean? One of Craig's clients? Was his business in trouble? Was that why he'd insisted on coming to St. Simons Island—to get away from someone—to drop out of sight? But why hadn't he just told me? Didn't he know I'd support him all the way? And where was Marlee in all this mess? The divorce papers were real enough.

The vacation I'd naïvely thought of as a tryst destined to rekindle the smoldering embers of our romance must have had, in Craig's mind, a much more sinister purpose. Could he have been protecting me?

But from what: the extent of his affair with Marlee, the scope of his financial troubles?

I wandered around the cottage kneading my forehead, plumping up cushions, straightening a painting here, moving a knickknack there. At the bedroom door, I paused. The tangle of sheets where Craig and I had lain stared at me. The shards of the shattered mirror still lay scattered on the floor.

Leaving the mess, I grabbed a blanket, a pillow, and a couple of sheets out of the linen closet and returned to the living room where I made up the couch.

After making a cup of coffee, I settled down to try to read the novel I'd brought. When my mind kept wandering, I turned on the TV and flipped through channels until I came to a reality show. As I sat listening to a couple describe the tragedy that had befallen them and the inadequacy of their home, I wondered if their marriage would remain strong when they settled into the unaccustomed luxury provided by the remodeling team.

Part way through the program, still restless and distracted, I turned off the TV, and went to the veranda where I began to pace.

What would tomorrow bring?

# 4

I groggily reached over to embrace Craig, only to encounter something rough and unyielding. One eye blinked open and I tried to focus on my hand exploring an expanse of fabric. What! I jerked upright and looked around. A blanket lay tumbled on the floor along with one of the pillows I vaguely remembered tucking against my chest the night before. My toes poked out from below the rumpled sheet.

The sofa. I groaned. I'd been caressing the back of the sofa as if it was Craig nestled beside me. The detritus of sleep clung to my blinking eyelids. My head pulsed like an African drum. I sat up, rubbed my eyes, and ran my fingers through my hair. How long before my arms would stop aching for Craig? I shook the guilty arm as if I could free it from the pattern woven into its cells by years of marriage.

The dim light of early morning danced off a cobweb on the window. I grabbed the fallen blanket and wrapped it around me to ward off the chill that had settled into my bones. With a sigh, I got up and stumbled into the bathroom where I popped a pain pill and splashed my face with cold water. A red-eyed, wild-haired gargoyle stared back from the mirror. I patted my face dry, brushed my hair, and retreated to the kitchen for coffee.

While I waited for the coffee to perk, I took a shower and put on a comfortable pair of sweats. Passing the door to the bedroom, my eye caught the glint of scattered mirror fragments. Sigh. With a broom and dustpan, I swept up the shards and dumped them in the garbage. Francisca, the housekeeper provided with the beach house, could make up the bed. I'd ask her for fresh sheets and pillowcases, even if it wasn't in the contract.

Coffee in hand, I settled into a chair on the veranda to watch the sun rise over the ocean. Streamers of Spanish moss on the gnarled live oak beside the house fluttered in the breeze. Golden filaments of sunlight danced from wave to wave in the gentle swell. Tranquility reigned outside. Inside, a typhoon of emotions tore at the foundations of my psyche.

What to do? If in doubt, go for a run. I drained the last of the coffee, donned my sneakers, and set off down the beach. Quickly winded, I soon returned to collapse on the steps of the veranda. I'd no sooner relaxed than the cell phone I'd left there rang.

I snatched it up. "Hello."

"Mom, I've been calling and calling."

Tiffany sounded anxious. Had she heard?

I tried to control the tremor in my own voice. "Oh, hi Tiff, honey. I've been jogging on the beach."

"Mom, what's going on?" She'd heard, then?

"Well...your dad and I...Uh, you'd probably better hear it from him."

Her voice rose. "What'd he do to get the house seized?"

I grabbed the counter for support. "Our house?"

"Yeah, our home." Her words tumbled out. "I

came down to pick up some things. Sealed by the FBI...wrapped in police tape...big black SUV in the driveway...wouldn't let me in..."

"Whoa, slow down, sweetheart. You say the FBI is at the house?" My stomach contracted into a tight ball as I interrupted her.

"I think it's the FBI. A man in a black suit and one of those ugly ties met me at the door. Stopped me."

"Did you see his badge?"

Tiffany's voice quavered. "Badge? I was too shook up to ask to see one."

I collapsed onto a sofa. "What did the man say?"

"Say? He asked who I was...I told him I lived there and asked what he was doing there." She sobbed before continuing. "Mom, this is terrible! He said he was there under some federal warrant or something and pointed to a notice pasted on the door."

The tight grip of an ache built in my head. "What did the notice say?"

"I...I didn't read anything but the title. Something about this property being seized as part of a criminal investigation."

I massaged my head. "Criminal investigation?"

"Where's Dad? Let me talk to him."

"Uh, Tiff, honey, your Dad's not here."

"Where is he? I've been calling his cell phone, but I get a message that it has been discontinued. Did Dad get a new number or something?"

"Well...I don't really know his new number."

"You don't know?"

"He didn't give it to me, uh, before he left." I squeezed the bridge of my nose to try and ease the pain. "Tiff, your dad left...permanently."

"What?"

"You know we haven't been getting along too well lately. Well, he left me yesterday...with...with Marlee. I was going to wait to tell you, but you may as well know. He's filed for divorce."

"Left with Marlee?" Tiffany's voice became a whisper. "No way. Must be a misunderstanding?"

Tiffany and Craig were close. I rushed on before she could take his side. "We came down here thinking—well, I thought—we could revive our marriage. Your dad obviously didn't intend anything of the sort."

Her voice rose. "You're blaming him?"

"Tiff, honey, he didn't give me a chance...left in the middle of a church service...left nothing but a note."

"That doesn't sound like Dad...If you'd only stay home more, I'm sure he—"

"Sweetheart, I've tried. I'm afraid this time he's serious."

"What's happening to our family?" Tiffany sniffled. "I thought you guys were different. You're a marriage counselor!"

I paused before answering. "As soon as I get your dad's new number, I'll try to iron things out. That's all I can do."

"Does Tyler know?"

"No," I said. "He's in the outback somewhere. Out of contact."

"This is terrible...and I need my winter stuff."

I massaged my forehead as I thought about all my records, my business banking card, everything. "Honey, can you get along for a while without getting into the house? I'm sure this is all a mistake and it'll be cleared up soon."

"I'm OK for a month or two. I was going to pick up my winter coat, skates, that kind of stuff."

"According to his note, your dad has paid up your tuition, residence fees, and so on until the end of your year. So you should be OK that way."

"This is unreal. So, are you driving back?"

"I haven't decided what to do. With the house seized, where would I stay?"

"Julie would take you in."

"I can't face her yet…I'm going to get a lawyer to look into what's happening."

"A lawyer?"

"Martin Reitman, the lawyer I recommend to clients. He'll be able to find out what the FBI is doing at our house."

Tiffany's tone softened. "Mom, will you be OK? Should I come down and stay with you?"

I paused before answering. "Thanks sweetheart, I appreciate the offer. I'm sad and scared, but it'll work out. I'll be OK, but you need to think of your classes, your career."

"But—"

"I'll call you tomorrow. Let you know if I've found out anything." My voice caught. "Tiff, you know I love you very much."

"I love you too, Mom."

I shut the phone, leaned back on the couch, and stared at the ceiling. It could use a coat of paint. Why do we notice the most irrelevant details during times of crisis? Is it a defense mechanism?

What was I going to do?

# 5

After Tiffany's phone call, I sat on the couch staring into space.

Nothing. That's what I felt like doing. Nothing. Well, maybe throwing things.

*Was it only yesterday*, I thought, *yesterday when Craig left? Seems like eons ago. Another life.*

With a great sigh, I heaved off the couch and forced myself to eat a bowl of cereal. Then, unable to put it off any longer, I turned on my laptop and began composing an e-mail to Tyler. Whether it would catch up with him or not, I needed to try.

Now that Tiff knew, I couldn't take a chance he'd hear about his dad's desertion from his sister before I could talk to him. Next I tried to write an e-mail to Martin Rietman. I must have sat there ten minutes trying to conjure up some of the professional objectivity that I'd projected to my clients. Not easy when one is on the other side of the equation. Had I been empathetic enough to jilted spouses? Or had I been complacent and a bit self-righteous?

*Tell it like it is, Ashlyn.*

So I composed a message for Martin laying out the dismal facts of my splintered marriage and appealing for his professional help. I concluded the e-mail:

*Personally, I do not want a divorce, even though I assume Craig has been unfaithful and I have legitimate* grounds. I'm willing to try again. You know how I feel about marriage—it is a lifelong covenant. But this mess is complicated by other problems.

Yesterday, when I went to use my credit cards I found they had been frozen, in spite of the fact that we've always paid our balance off every month. On top of that, I tried to use my bankcard to access our bank accounts—they have a healthy balance—but my card was rejected.

Could Craig have drained our accounts and cancelled our credit cards? Everything has been held jointly, except my business account.

Worse, my daughter called to tell me that the FBI seized our house as a result of some criminal investigation. As you may know, Tiffany is in college in Illinois but she came home to get some winter clothing. Fortunately, her tuition and board have been paid to the end of the year.

Martin, what is going on here? Can Craig act without my consent? And what has the FBI got to do with it? Can you look into it quietly?

I'm very worried.

కాలు

Next, I phoned my bank about not being able to access my account. A teller immediately transferred me to Gordon Eller, the manager. We'd known him for decades.

"Gordon, it's Ashlyn Forsyth."

"Good morning Mrs. Forsyth. How can I help you?"

Strange, addressing me as *Mrs. Forsyth*, not *Ashlyn*. "Uh, well, I called to find out about our accounts."

He coughed. "Ah, yes, your accounts."

I rushed on. "I tried to access them, but my card

was rejected."

His voice took on a chill. "I'm afraid there's a problem."

My voice rose. "But we always keep a large balance!"

"You do. The problem isn't the size of your balance, but..." He hesitated. "Haven't you received notification?"

"Notification, about what?"

"Well, I'm sure your husband is aware of the...uh...seizure. Have you asked your husband?"

"My husband is not here." My hand felt clammy where it gripped the phone and I could feel beads of perspiration break out on my forehead. "What do you mean seizure?"

"The FBI has seized your accounts."

"What?" I shrilled. "They can't do that...can they?"

"I'm afraid they can, and have." His voice sounded glacial, as if he was talking to me from Antarctica. "As part of a criminal investigation."

He obviously thought that an accusation was enough to indicate guilt.

"But...but, you know us. You've known us for years. I'm not a criminal."

His voice warmed slightly. "Mrs. Forsyth, it may be that your accounts got swept up as collateral damage from some other investigation. I suggest you contact your lawyer. There's nothing I can do until the FBI releases the accounts."

"Thank you," I turned off the phone.

What had Craig been involved in? Had he been dragged into something by a third party?

Had the millions he managed blunted his moral sense? Or was it all a big mistake?

❧❧

On Wednesday or Thursday, I'm not sure which; I realized that I couldn't continue to pace the beach house mulling everything over again and again.

I grabbed my purse, jumped in the car, and drove down to the fishing pier hoping that I could lose myself in the bustle of tourists that thronged the area with all its restaurants and little shops. But as soon as I parked, the sight of a couple walking arm in arm gave my heart a lurch. I quickly looked away to a lighthouse that towered over the park.

Craig had discouraged me from climbing to the lookout, calling it a waste of time. In fact, he'd pooh-poohed anything that smacked of tourism. Well that's just what I needed to do—become a tourist for a day or two.

I walked across the park and somewhat reluctantly plunked down $8.00 for a ticket to the lighthouse. Before ascending the cast-iron spiral staircase, I forced myself to read a description of its history.

I got through the first paragraph which informed me that it had been built in 1807, but I couldn't go on without pausing. Tiffany would have loved it. She was a history buff, but I found it boring. I'd never scored well in history. Still I took a deep breath and compelled myself to continue.

I learned about the destruction of the lighthouse by the Confederates when they abandoned the island in 1862, and the construction of a new lighthouse in

1872. Maybe this was what I needed; something to read that required my full attention. At least, for a few minutes it had taken my mind off my own troubles.

When I finished the account, I ascended the staircase, counting each step to continue distracting my mind. I paused to catch my breath and gaze through a tiny window far out to sea.

A couple of teenagers squeezed by me as if the ascent was something they did every day.

I finally mounted the 129th step and joined others on the platform that circled the lighthouse. The view was spectacular. At another time, I might have taken a score of pictures and sent them to my kids by iPhone.

A waist-high railing ensured the safety of most adventurous boys, but it wouldn't be impossible to climb over and throw oneself off the lighthouse, falling to the pavement, 102 feet below. Was 102 feet high enough to kill a person? I wondered if they'd ever had a suicide attempt. Could I become the first?

I shuddered and turned away, sobered at the morbid tone of my thoughts. Hurrying down the staircase, I sought out my car. How quickly my attempt to banish thoughts of my predicament had unraveled.

Now, as I glanced at it, the lighthouse became a symbol, a reminder of all the signs I'd ignored, warnings of shipwreck ahead.

# 6

After my morbid episode at the lighthouse, I knew I needed to keep moving to avoid more fatal introspection. Leaving the village proper, I drove past the Sea Island Golf Course, and then north on Sea Island Road past Epworth by the Sea, the Methodist retreat center with its museum of Wesley memorabilia.

Now there was a kindred spirit. John Wesley. Came to St. Simons Island full of hope and idealism; left it in hopelessness and despair.

Would I, like Wesley, find hope in God's grace or be doomed to wander through life from this point on stigmatized as Craig's cast-off wife?

I kept on through aisles of gnarled oaks. The streamers of Spanish moss that had seemed so charming now struck me as depressing. They swayed as I went by, like macabre bunting erected along the route of some tragic funeral.

I pulled into the parking lot at Christ Church and sat for some time staring at nothing. Finally, I got out and wandered through the graveyard that surrounded the church. For some reason I'd always found cemeteries soothing, especially those in rural communities. The absence of crowds. The silence. The final resting places of so many lives usually brought me a sense of perspective.

I'd search for unusual epigraphs engraved on the stones; like, "She did the best she could." Well, I had done the best I could — hadn't I?

For ages, I meandered the aisles of moss-covered stones past blooming camellias. I found no peace. I gained no perspective. Eventually, I slipped into a pew near the back of the church. I was alone, which was fortunate, since tears began to stream down my face. I batted them away as I gazed around.

A woman came in and began to arrange a vase of flowers on a pedestal at the front. As she came down the aisle towards me, I eyed her through lowered eyelids. Her grey hair was cut short and she wore a white long-sleeved blouse over a dark knee-length skirt. As she approached I looked down, willing her to pass me by and leave me to my melancholy—but she stopped.

"Beautiful, isn't it?" she asked.

I looked away, as if examining the stained glass windows. "Yes, very beautiful."

"We're very fond of this church. It has such a wonderful history."

I didn't reply.

"You seem troubled. Is there anything I can do to help?"

Startled, I turned towards her, my face still wet with tears. "Help?"

"I'm sorry if I've intruded on some private grief. But I noticed you walking in the graveyard. Did you recently lose a loved one?"

I snorted as I wiped my eyes. "Lose a loved one? Not by death. He dumped me for a younger woman!"

"Oh, I'm so sorry."

"You wouldn't understand."

"Perhaps not, but I'm a good listener; and I

know what abandonment feels like."

I sighed deeply. Abandonment...yes that was a good description. I looked up into her soft, brown eyes, eyes that seemed liquid with feeling.

Before I knew it I was pouring out bits and pieces of my sordid story.

"You poor child," she said with sympathy.

I wiped my eyes with a tissue and blew my nose. "And that's not the half of it. It looks like he's cancelled my credit cards, and now...and now." I looked up at her. "You said you know what abandonment feels like?"

"My mother abandoned our family when I was fourteen. Just up and disappeared."

I moved over to give her room to sit down on the pew. "Did your mother ever explain?"

"Oh, she sent me a long note a couple of years later explaining about falling out of love with my father. As if love is something you fall into and out of."

My mouth fell open. "Why that's almost exactly what Craig said. Craig is my husband. He wrote, 'I just don't love you anymore.' As if my commitment to raise his children, cook his meals, wash his clothes, and laugh at his stupid jokes wasn't love."

She nodded. "Love is such a misunderstood word. I'm Valerie, by the way."

"Ashlyn. I'm Ashlyn Forsyth....did you ever get over your mother leaving?"

"The pain lasts a long time," she said. "And the guilt. For years I felt I'd done something to cause her to leave."

I grimaced. "I know what you mean about guilt. I was too busy building my career. One minute, I blame myself, the next minute I remember all the missed dinners I cooked, his excuses, his coldness, and I want to kill him."

"It's always hard to apportion blame when a couple breaks up."

"And that's not the half of it." I went on to tell her about our bank accounts and our home being seized by the FBI for some undefined financial fraud. "What did he get himself into? He's always prided himself on his integrity. He's a deacon at our church, for pity's sake!"

Valerie reached over and touched my arm. "You poor soul. Did you have any inkling there was a problem?" Her question twigged something in my memory. Was it a strange phone call, a letter he hid from me...what was it?

"One thing did seem odd at the time. He loves expensive cars and he'd been talking up the benefits of a German luxury sedan. Well he'd recently arranged to buy one from a church friend who is a dealer. Then suddenly, he cancelled the order. No explanation, except to say that market conditions were bad. But I knew he'd prepared for the market downturn and had large reserves in his own personal and business account. It was unlike him."

"Maybe it's all a mistake that will get sorted out."

"I hope so...but running off with a female colleague is hardly a little mistake." I shook my head. "I keep imagining them in bed together. I don't see how that can get sorted out."

"Sometimes men come to their senses; return to their wives. It's possible."

"I don't see how I could welcome him back,

after what he's done...even if I wanted him back, which I don't right now." I threw up my hands. "Oh, I don't know what I want. I'm just so miserable."

"You need time," Valerie said, taking both of my hands in hers.

"Did time help you—eventually help heal the memories of your mother's abandonment?"

"Gradually," she said, "I learned to forgive and forgiving brought peace."

"Forgive! How can I ever forgive Craig for such treachery? No, it's not possible."

Here we were in a church.

I expected her to reach for a Bible from the pew in front and turn to a couple of Bible verses. Somehow she understood that what I needed first was a listening ear and a friend. Instead of preaching at me, she said, "Do you have a place to stay? I have room."

"That's very kind," I said, "but my philandering husband at least paid rent for the beach house where I'm staying."

The catharsis continued. I poured out my soul about our marriage, our kids, my counseling practice—on and on.

Finally, I got up to go

"Whenever you feel the need, I'm here with a listening ear and a cup of coffee." She stood in the doorway and waved as I drove away.

On my way back to the beach house, I marveled at her empathy and kicked myself for pouring out my story. Never again. Time to get a grip.

But her question about whether there had been any inkling of financial fraud nagged at my mind. Something was buried in my memory. What was it? There had been enough signs of our deteriorating relationship, but fraud?

# 7

I parked in front of the beach house, and went around to sit on the porch.

What had Valerie's question twigged in my memory? Something that seemed puzzling at the time, but I'd shrugged off. It wasn't just Craig cancelling the order for his expensive car—although that had been out of character.

I thought back through the last year trying to recall anything that could have given me some inkling that Craig's business was in trouble. He'd stayed late more evenings than usual—but that had happened also when he'd originally started the company. Actually, I'd had to work late almost as much as he had. No, that wasn't it.

What about his trip to the Caribbean? Three weeks before we'd come to the island, he'd called me from the airport to say he had to suddenly fly down to Bermuda on business. That had been puzzling. On his return he hadn't given me any details, just said it was a banking problem he'd had to deal with in person. It could have been a get-a-way with Marlee, but I doubted that. On return, his eyes had taken on an almost hunted look. He'd been gloomy and uncommunicative for days—not that unusual in our marriage lately.

But there was something else that bothered me just below the surface of my mind.

I got up and went inside. The décor was typical beach kitsch. Bright chintz couches and armchairs. A predictable collection of reproductions and beach artifacts: a painting of the St. Simons Lighthouse, another of sandpipers, still another of cruising pelicans, a collage of shells, and an arrangement of bulrushes and sea oats.

If I'd owned the place, I would definitely redecorate. First, I'd throw out the chintz couch. I'd buy a genuine oil from one of the talented local artists. Without warning, I laughed. *Here you are, abandoned and almost penniless, and you're thinking of redecorating! How ridiculous can you get?*

That's when I remembered the black foreign sedan that had pulled into our driveway a couple of days before we left New York for the Island.

Craig had rushed out to meet the occupants of the car before they had a chance to come to the door. There had been two. One short, dressed in a baggy suit, the other, stocky and wearing a T-shirt. Craig had led them away from the house to the sidewalk where they'd talked for some time.

From what I'd seen through the living room window, the short one had done most of the talking. A couple of times he'd pointed in my direction.

When he came in, Craig said it was nothing, just a misunderstanding.

I'd assumed they were from the car dealership, trying to persuade him not to cancel his order. But remembering it now, I realized that the pair didn't look like car salesmen. They had seemed more threatening than overeager to make a sale. Nor had the car looked like a dealer's model. It had been dusty; as if it needed a wash.

Craig had been covering up some real

problems with his business. Why hadn't he felt he could share them? Well, we hadn't shared very deeply for some time.

But who were those two men?

And strangely enough, later that same day, Craig had suggested our trip to St. Simons Island. He'd talked about trying to make a go of our marriage. He'd been lying about that. What else had he been lying about?

∂∽

On Friday—I think it was Friday—I went into the village to stock up on groceries. After getting what I needed from a local food mart, I drove to the Shrimpboat Café. Pulling my Yankees' baseball cap low over my eyes, I sauntered to a booth in a dark corner. Peering around from beneath the cap, I surveyed the clientele.

The same trio of men in jeans and checkered shirts, who'd arrived during my first visit, occupied a table to the left of the door. Except for a businessman reading a newspaper and an elderly couple, I was the only other customer.

I glanced at my watch. Eleven twenty-five. Too early for the lunch crowd. Good. I leaned back and told myself to relax.

"Coffee, honey?" Lottie Jane, the waitress who'd waited on me before, stood there with a coffeepot in one hand and a cup in the other.

"Uh, yeah, that'd be great."

She filled the cup and fished in her apron for three or four creamers. "Thought you'd headed back to New York, or didn't like our coffee."

"N...no." I stuttered. "Your coffee was great."

"So, enjoying your stay, then?"

"Uh..." I didn't want to talk to her. I was feeling a little embarrassed about my spouting off to Valerie at the church, but I could see she wouldn't leave me be, so I tried to brighten up. "St. Simons is wonderful. I love the island."

She cocked her head to one side and her eyes narrowed. "Who was the pig?"

In the process of taking a sip of coffee I jerked and some coffee dribbled down my chin. "What?" While I mopped it up with a napkin, I stared at her with my mouth open.

She put down the coffeepot and stood with her hands on her hips. "Husband? Boyfriend?"

Unbidden, tears began to leak from the corners of my eyes. I turned away. "It's nothing, nothing."

"Honey chile, I can see it written all over your face. I've been there. Let me tell you, they're not worth it. Just a bunch of snorting pigs. Interested in one thing, and one thing only."

I grabbed my purse and stumbled to my feet. "It's really none of your business."

She stepped back and held up her hands. "Whoa. I'm sorry. You're right; it is none of my business." She glanced away. "Been dumped once too often, that's all."

Biting my lip, I dropped my purse, sat back down, picked up the menu, and pointed. "I'll have that same dish I had before—this one, the shrimp dish...please."

As soon as she left, I took out my compact. Puffy brown eyes stared back. Stray hairs straggled from my ball cap. Fresh wrinkles marked my forehead and my cheeks looked pasty. I got up and headed to the washroom. On the way, I kept my face averted as I passed the group of men by the door. After trying to repair the obvious signs of my wrecked life, I returned to my table.

A few minutes later, Lottie Jane silently set down my order. Wondering if my outburst had driven her bubbly persona underground, I avoided looking at her.

The fare was better than I remembered. After devouring every morsel on the plate: shrimp, hush puppies, fries, and coleslaw, I leaned back and sighed.

I felt better. How could that be? Had I been too miserable to notice how ravenous I'd become?

Lottie Jane raised her eyebrows as she picked up my empty plate and refilled my coffee.

"That's either the best shrimp I ever had," I said, trying to make up for my earlier reaction, "or, I've never been so hungry."

"Oh, it's the best shrimp," she said, nodding her head towards the men by the door. "Remy Jeandeau delivers them fresh every day."

"Oh, they're shrimp fishermen?"

"Yeah, Remy, the one with the captain's hat—is the best shrimper on the coast." Turning towards the men, she shouted, "Hey, Remy, you've got another fan."

Startled, I saw that it was the man who had kept me from falling off the pier.

He brought his hand to his cap in a smiling salute.

I barely nodded, took a sip of coffee and looked away. My gaze caught activity out the front window.

A tow truck stopped behind the cars parked there. The driver got out, walked over to one of the cars, and with a fluid action, jimmied open the door. What was he doing breaking into…a red car?

It was my car!

I jumped up and raced out the front door.

# 8

I shouted at the tow-truck operator as I ran out of the café. "Hey! What do you think you're doing?"

He looked up, but said nothing.

I waved my hands at him. "That's my car!"

Instead of answering, he shrugged, plopped down on the driver's seat, and began to fiddle with the steering column.

I pounded on the roof. "Get out of my car!"

He frowned at me. "Look lady, I have a court order to seize this car."

My chest tightened. "What? That's crazy."

"You need help, ma'am?" I looked up to see the captain of the shrimp boat standing there, with his two friends behind him.

"This man is taking my car." I wailed.

Remy—the waitress had called him Remy—reached through the driver's door and tapped the tow-truck operator on the shoulder. "What d'yah think you're doing, buddy?"

The tow-truck operator swore. "Get your hands off me. I've been empowered by the U.S. Marshal's Service to seize this car. The owner has obviously been involved in illegal activity." He made to get out of the car, but Remy kept him boxed in.

"Is this any way to treat a lady?" Remy asked. "Just pull up and seize her car? Look at her. Does she look like she's a criminal?"

"You'd be surprised. But that's irrelevant. Let me

continue or I'll call in help." The tow-truck operator reached into his pocket and pulled out a cell-phone.

Remy knocked the phone out of his hands. "Get out of the car and show us your authority."

The operator swore again as he came out of the seat in a rush with his fists doubled up. He bared his teeth as he stared at Remy and his two burly friends. Then slowly, his fists relaxed and he muttered. "OK, OK, let me get the court order."

Remy followed him over to the truck and watched as he reached in to grab a clipboard.

Remy pointed in my direction. "Show it to the lady."

I stood there gaping during the whole episode. While my gut still felt like lead, warmth had begun to spread through my chest. I hadn't realized how alone I'd felt until these fishermen came to my aid. Just to have someone stand up for me gave me a shot of adrenaline. I took a deep breath as I reached out to take the clipboard.

Nodding my thanks to the three men, I scanned the court order, skipping all the legalese. Sure enough it was my car. Red, 2006, with a VIN number...owners, joint, Craig and Ashlyn Forsyth. *Joint. Like everything else in our messed up marriage?* Pursuant of court order blah, blah, blah... proceeds of a federal crime....case pending in Federal Court....money laundering....Plaintiff: Craig Forsyth.

I handed the clipboard back and turned away. Money laundering! Craig? How could he?

"Is it legit?" Remy said.

I nodded and collapsed onto one of the

benches along the sidewalk.

The tow-truck operator doffed his Braves ball cap and looked from Remy back to me. "Look, ma'am, I'm really sorry about this. It's not like I enjoy doing this—especially seizing a car from a lady. It's just a job. I have to do my job."

I looked up at him, but didn't answer.

Remy eyes narrowed. "Ma'am, is the car financed?"

Looking up, I was startled by how blue Remy's eyes were, like the ocean in early morning.

"No, I own it outright."

Remy ran his hands through his windblown hair. "Buddy, can't you see what this is doin' to the lady? She needs her car. Why don't you give her a day or two to arrange a rental?"

The operator tapped the clipboard in his hand. "No can do. Really sorry. If it was up to me I would, but my boss would blow a gasket. The car's got to be in the impound yard by today."

I stood up. "Well, I want a copy of that court order...and instead of hot-wiring the car I may as well give you the keys."

I went into the café and retrieved the keys from my purse. When I returned I saw that the tow-truck operator had put the two bags with my groceries on the sidewalk along with my laundry bag.

"Here," I said, offering him the key.

"Thanks, Ma'am. Any other personal effects you need to retrieve?"

Ten minutes later the car was gone and all I had to show for the three years in which it had become my home on wheels was a road atlas, a dealer's umbrella, a pack of gum, a pair of sunglasses, and a copy of the court order. My heart gave a lurch as I watched it being towed away.

"Ma'am."

I turned towards Remy and held out my hand. "Ashlyn, my name is Ashlyn. I want to thank you and your two friends. I'm extremely grateful for the way you came to my aid. Most people wouldn't have gotten involved."

"No problem," he said, shaking my hand. "My name is Remy, and this is Gaston and Ches." He pointed first to an older man with a grizzled mustache who was short and bald, and then to a slender young man with spiky black hair and pimples.

I nodded my thanks as I turned to gather up my belongings.

Remy reached down and picked up the groceries. "Here, let me help you."

Inside the café, I dumped my stuff under the coat rack, thanked Remy and his pals again, and returned to my table to ponder what to do.

Remy followed me over and stood there frowning. "Ma'am we'd be happy to drop you off anywhere you want to go. But first, you need something to settle your nerves. Let me go next door and get you a shot of bourbon or a glass of wine."

A shot of bourbon?

My attempt to smile turned into a grimace. "Thanks, you're very kind...another cup of coffee would be good."

He signaled to Lottie Jane, who was already heading my way with a pot of coffee.

"Land sakes, child, what a hullabaloo." After

refilling my cup, she continued to stand there. "Behind on payments?"

Without looking up, I methodically stirred cream into my coffee. "No, nothing like that."

I'd quickly categorized Lottie Jane as a sympathetic soul who would happily listen for hours to tales of woe. And if she got me started, I'd be hard put to stop. I'd shown that when talking to Valerie at the old church. Her sympathetic ear had come just when I needed it, but I didn't feel like dumping on anyone else.

After seeing my car towed away, I was afraid I'd completely lose it and collapse into a puddle of emotions all over the floor. Besides, rightly or wrongly, I wondered if she was the type to spread the word far and wide. I didn't need people staring at me wherever I went.

Remy must have sensed my reticence because he motioned towards his table. "Lottie, we could use some more coffee, too."

Across the lip of my cup, I smiled my thanks.

Before Remy returned to his friends, he stood by my table a moment longer, frowning. "Now, ma'am—Ms. Ashlyn—you give me a signal when you're ready to go and we'll take you anywhere you want to go."

"Thanks again, Mr…"

"Jeandeau," he said. "But call me Remy. It's a lot easier."

"I'm really grateful for your offer, Remy…but I'm sure I'll be all right."

I looked down at the court order to avoid him seeing the moisture threatening to pour down my face.

"Just give us the word, yuh hear, if we can help."

I nodded as he returned to his table.

All right? Who was I kidding? Everything was going to be just peachy keen! No credit card, no bank card, no home to return to…and my daughter almost hysterical. My bank manager thought I was a criminal. My son was somewhere in the outback.

My loving husband, the defendant in a pending case of money laundering, had left me to be the collateral damage. Had he been planning this for months? Or was he a victim?

Who were the men in the black sedan who came to see him last week? The FBI must be searching for him.

How long before they came looking for me?

# 9

I sat in the café taking occasional sips of coffee, trying to control the panic that had turned my insides to jelly. My car—gone. I'd loved that car.

I looked down at the court order. The legal mumbo-jumbo looked impenetrable. It named some judge of a New York court. It identified the car and Mr. Craig Forsyth. Then followed something about court ordered seizure pursuant to probable cause...probable cause of what?

That the above named individual is engaged in criminal activity.

I pondered the phrase, probable cause. What evidence did they really have of Craig being involved in criminal activity? If true, how could I have been so blind? It didn't seem possible.

Did the FBI need solid evidence or could they act on nothing more than a suspicion? What ever happened to "innocent until proven guilty?" No, they must have something.

*Breathe deeply. Think positively. Pray. This must be a misunderstanding. Tomorrow is bound to be better. The bank will apologize. The FBI will return the house. Craig will come back and beg my forgiveness. And I'll...I'll slam the door in his face.*

"May I sit down?"

I looked up to see Remy standing there with his coffee cup in his hand.

Not trusting my speech, I gestured to a chair.

"Ma'am...Ms. Ashlyn, I know it's none of my business." He held up his hands to forestall any response.

I stared at his hands, not wanting to lift my gaze to his face. The palms looked cracked and callused, and his ring finger—on which there was no ring—ended in a stub. A workman's hands. As far removed from the manicured, slender fingers of my erstwhile husband as could be imagined.

He paused for a moment before continuing. "No one should have their car seized like that. It's not right what happened to you."

I looked up.

His face, tanned the color of old buckskin, sported a few days stubble, and a lock of sun-bleached off-blond hair peeked out from under his captain's cap. His forehead was furrowed, his full mouth set in a scowl, and his expressive eyes—the eyes that I'd thought were sky blue, seemed iridescent, or just unfathomable, or...

I glanced away. "Yes...well...not right. I agree there."

"I could give you a lift to a rental agency, or," he gestured over his shoulder, "I'm sure Lottie Jane would be happy to drive you."

I tried to smile, but managed little more than a grimace as I thought of my depleted finances. "A rental agency. Uh...I'm not sure what to do yet."

"Tough to get around the island without a vehicle, or get into Brunswick for shopping."

I straightened in the chair. "Mr. Jean...Jeandeau, I really appreciate your offer, but I'll be fine."

He smiled. "Like I said, just call me Remy.

Jeandeau is tough to say. My father was Cajun."

"OK, Remy it is. Maybe you can direct me to a taxi service?"

He stiffened as he stood up. "Yes, I can do that. Magnolia Cabs. You'll find the number in the phone book."

"Thank you."

He returned to his table. I could tell by the pinched look on his face that I'd offended him by not accepting his help, but so what? What did it matter?

The darkness continued to spread through my psyche, blocking out all positive thought. I left my coffee half-finished and went over to the public phone on the wall by the washrooms.

The tattered phonebook hung by a chain from the wall. When I leafed through it, I quickly discovered that the page I wanted had been torn out. How appropriate. The book looked as if it had hung there for decades.

Lottie Jane met me at the counter. "Honey, that phone book is a relic. Doubt if the phone even works. Everyone uses cell phones now. What are you looking for, anyway?"

I handed over some cash to pay my bill. "A taxi."

"Why didn't you say so? Here." She picked up a map from the pile on the counter. "Cabs. Banks. Boutiques. Groceries. Restaurants. You name it. It's all here. Look sweetie, if you can wait half an hour I can run you home."

Tears began to form at the corners of my eyes. I nodded my thanks as I picked up the map. "You're very kind, but I need to get my groceries put away."

I walked back to my table and dropped a couple of bucks for a tip. On the way out I nodded to Remy and his friends. Although Remy looked away, the gaze of his two buddies softened as they watched me pick up my bags and go outside.

I felt like a gawky teenager again, wilting under everyone's stares. I, who had been so confident and self-reliant, had become Ashlyn, marital hypocrite, the fake therapist who helped others rescue their relationships but wrecked her own. But so what? Despair deepened as my mind wandered down one mental dark alley after another.

I called for a cab, and then paced up and down. Feeling that every eye in the restaurant was on me, I stopped pacing and concentrated on reading the posters pasted on the café window, ignoring the glances from within. Charters for deep-sea fishing. Tour of a genuine southern plantation. Waitress needed, full or part-time. Belvedere: lost chocolate lab. Jubilee Singers at First Baptist. A production of *Hamlet* at the High School. *Just what I need, a Shakespearean tragedy.*

Finally, the cab, a shiny black limo, arrived. *A hearse, how appropriate.* It looked expensive, but I could hardly refuse it now. I guess most of their clients were wealthy vacationers traveling back and forth to the airport. During the short ride to my beach house, the cabbie talked non-stop about weather, political scandals, and the fighting in Afghanistan.

*Why doesn't he shut up?*

I tried to tune him out by staring out the window and giving in to despair. At the beach house, I paid the seven-dollar fare and breathed a sigh of relief at finally being alone.

I dumped my groceries on the floor and went

out on the porch where I stood gazing at the sea. Towering clouds hid the horizon and a freshening wind whipped up frothy whitecaps. To the south a sailboat, its sails furled, motored towards anchorage. A storm was coming.

I was so tired. How had it come to this? How could God allow this to happen? Was He really up there? Maybe my faith was all a childish dream, a lie— and church, a charade.

How easy it would be to just walk into the water. Keep walking. Leave the mess behind. Let blackness engulf me. I stood up.

# 10

The sky was ablaze with streamers of scarlet, gold, and violet as I stepped into the incoming tide. It felt warm and inviting. And yet, I had to force myself through the water. Within seconds, my jeans were waterlogged, slowing me down. I lost one of my sandals but pressed on, further and further from the beach, desperate to end my misery.

*This is irrational*, I told myself. *Snap out of it, Ashlyn.*

Suddenly, a large wave knocked me over, and I gulped a mouthful of water. I came up sputtering as wave after wave from the freshening sea pummeled me.

Something brushed against me. Shark? Fish? Bit of seaweed? I stifled a scream. A shark would be good. Get it over with quickly. *Were there sharks off the Georgia coast?* I shivered.

Another incoming swell knocked me off my feet. As I went down, I swallowed a mouthful of brine, and then bobbed to the surface spitting and coughing. One side of me wanted to fight the buffeting waves. But another voice whispered, *Don't fight, Ashlyn. Swallow. Embrace the darkness.*

Fortunately, sanity prevailed. Instead of giving myself to the sea, I struggled up through the waves to find light and air. I came up gagging, my feet groping for the bottom.

I planted my feet, spit the water out and tried to catch my breath. Shocked by my suicidal impulse, salty tears poured down my cheeks as I headed back to shore.

ॐॐ

The next morning, sun streamed through the window and finally woke me from a drugged sleep. I vaguely remembered taking two sleeping pills to ensure oblivion, and then flushing the rest of the bottle down the toilet to remove temptation.

I propped up in bed and stared out the window at the ocean. *Had it been a dream? Or had I really tried to take my own life?* I shuddered. *First the idea at the lighthouse, and then the attempt. Never again. Life is too precious. Tyler and Tiffany were too important.*

Throwing off the covers, I showered, changed into fresh jeans and a T-shirt, and then put the coffee on to drip.

While I waited for the coffee, I cracked my Bible, something I hadn't done all week. My gaze ranged through a verse in Psalm 34 that I'd underlined years earlier. "The Lord is close to the brokenhearted and saves those who are crushed in spirit."

*OK, that's me, Lord, broken, crushed. Put your arms around me. Knit me back together. Save me from myself. Banish the darkness…at least a little.*

With a sigh, I got up, poured a cup of coffee and booted my laptop. Enough misery; it was time to do something.

My e-mail program had dozens of new messages. There were five or six notices about blogs I should join, people who wanted me to friend them, a message that I'd won a free cruise to the Caribbean, an offer for medication I didn't need or use, and a mysterious e-

59

mail requesting my password so my Internet server could be updated. Delete, delete, delete. My friend Julie forwarded five more of those syrupy circular e-mails designed to make you feel guilty if you didn't pass them on. I consigned them all to oblivion. I saved the latest e-mail edition of *Counseling for Impact* to read later—much later.

There was nothing from my lawyer or Tyler. Tiffany had sent an e-mail asking if I'd found out anything more about the seizure of the house or heard from her dad. She offered again to come and stay with me and told me how much she loved me. I sent her a cheery reply without burdening her with my angst.

I leaned back in the chair, took a sip of coffee, and let my thoughts go back to Tiffany's birth, her first steps, and her tear-streaked face when her dog, Skippy, died. At least Craig and I had done something right, in her and in Tyler. I missed them both. Why didn't Tyler phone or text or something? Was he injured, lost, or involved with some Aussie girl?

I sent an e-mail to my part-time secretary instructing her to postpone any scheduled appointments for at least a month. I didn't give her any concrete reason beyond a vague comment about my need for reflection on the direction of my career.

Then I turned to an earnest search for information on Craig's company. I felt a momentary twinge at realizing that this was the first time in years I'd been interested enough in his affairs to call up his website. He could have been selling pork belly futures, for all I knew. His talk about 401Ks, or mutual funds, or mining futures had always gone way over my head.

After scrolling through pages of financial gobbledygook, I concluded that Forsyth Investments specialized in uncovering value in emerging markets not normally served by the investment industry. I read, "For over ten years our team of emerging market experts has found value in a diverse range of countries including Egypt, Dubai, Mongolia, and Brazil. This dedication to finding emerging value has produced investment results which have exceeded most American indices in eight of the past ten years."

Team of experts? Besides Marlee, who were they? I'd rarely met any of his other colleagues. The company also claimed to manage over 250 million dollars of investments in domestic funds designed to balance their foreign holdings. Two hundred and fifty million!

It all looked very professional and safe. But was it too good to be true? What had he done to catch the attention of the FBI? Could he have been involved in money laundering? Something sent him into hiding.

Now that I thought of it, the whole idea of coming to St. Simons Island had been his idea—an idea that I'd embraced. To him, it must have been a way to put some distance between himself and his New York office. To me it had signaled hope for our marriage. But the whole time it must have been a ploy, the first stage in his plan to disappear.

Online, I did a search for information on money laundering and came up with a bewildering array of facts. The International Monetary Fund estimated that two to five percent of the global economy ran on laundered money. Another international group said that it was impossible to tell. The means through which illegal money earned through drugs, prostitution, and so on is introduced into the economy was mind boggling. Introducing cash into the financial system and carrying out complex financial transactions could camouflage its illegal source. Trusts and shell companies can disguise the true owner of money if the jurisdiction where they reside is lax. Money launderers or criminals can buy a controlling interest in a bank, preferably in a jurisdiction with weak money laundering controls, and then move money through the bank without scrutiny.

Where was Craig in all this? Had he been unwittingly entangled? Had the promise of easy money been too much? Is that why he'd flown to the Caribbean? Somewhere along the line he must have known what was happening.

A corrosive anger welled up like bile.

How could he do this, knowing how it would affect me—the children, my counseling credibility?

I got up and began to pace. As I thought about our whirlwind romance and the good times we had through the years, grief replaced the fury that had settled like a knot in my stomach. Then, slowly, very slowly, the grief gave way to determination.

I grabbed my purse and counted my dwindling store of cash. It came to five hundred and thirty-seven dollars.

I needed to buy a new pair of sandals. I donned sneakers and set off down Ocean Boulevard towards the village. At Island Cycle, I rented a silver ten speed and started to cycle towards the shopping area on the other side of the airport. I couldn't get the hang of the gears. Finally, the owner called me back, and gave me a couple of lessons. I wasn't ready for wheelies, but at least I was mobile again. Tyler would be proud.

At the Shoe Emporium I bought a pair of leather sandals, cheap, but comfortable. Then I headed back to the village to get breakfast.

At the Shrimpboat Café, I locked the bike to a light standard and went in.

Over two plates balanced on her outstretched arm, Lottie Jane motioned me with a jerk of her head towards a back table. I threaded my way past a couple of state police, a table occupied by four seniors wearing bright Hawaiian shirts, and another table where a father tried to persuade a toddler to eat his breakfast.

Once seated, I surveyed the diner, determined to avoid any more wallowing in misery. Most customers were either business types or seniors. Laughter rose occasionally above the drone of conversation and the clatter of plates and cutlery. Lottie glided back and forth taking orders, clearing tables, and serving.

Finally, she brought me a cup, filled it with coffee, and dumped a handful of creamers on the table. "Whew, we're busy this morning. What'll it be honey?"

I pointed to number three on the menu. "Two eggs, bacon, toast, and grits."

"Good choice. How'd you like your eggs?"

"Could I have them poached?"

Lottie Jane frowned. "Sorry honey, you can have them sunny side up, over light, or masa-kreed."

"Masa-kreed?"

"Scrambled."

"Oh, fine, scrambled."

"And will that be with light bread or cornbread?"

"Uh, light bread, please. Lottie, are you the only waitress?"

"For the morning shift. We just lost one of our waitresses. Means we're short-staffed—but that's nothing new."

I watched her buzz around while I sipped coffee.

She filled coffee cups and exchanged quips with diners, most of whom she appeared to know. In some mysterious way, she seemed to sense when an order was ready. She'd pick it up, two or three plates at a time, and deliver it to a table, never asking who had ordered what.

Some strange alchemy was at work between her and the solo cook who kept turning out plates of food as if he had a dozen men at his beck and call.

I'd never thought much about servers in the restaurants I'd frequented. High school dropouts in dead end jobs, I'd concluded. Seeing Lottie Jane in action put another spin on it. I frowned as I pondered the ad for a waitress I'd seen on the front window. Would I be able to hack it without spilling coffee and mixing orders? I certainly couldn't balance a couple of plates on my arm. But I could use a job—at least temporarily.

# 11

After breakfast at the café, I cycled aimlessly around the island for an hour or so. At the lighthouse, I stopped to wonder what it had been like a hundred years ago. Had sea captains abandoned their wives as Craig had abandoned me? From there I traveled along the Kings Way past the exclusive Island Club to the causeway. At the bridge, I paused to watch terns and gulls swoop and dive.

Five pelicans perched on the pilings of the bridge abutment, their beady eyes fixed on the water below. They reminded me of old men fishing.

The charm of the island did nothing to dispel my foreboding. I'd never faced financial hardships. My parents had lived in an upscale neighborhood and paid my way through college, even bought me a car when I turned eighteen.

Craig had made enough for us to live in luxury. To that, I'd added the quite respectable fees from my counseling practice. Now here I was with my funds rapidly dwindling—and no way to get more. The few very non-committal e-mails from my lawyer indicated that any access to my accounts wouldn't happen anytime soon—if ever.

I leaned my bike against a live oak and sat on a bench. What to do? I could return to New York and camp out with my friend, Julie. The thought of enduring the maelstrom of publicity my return would generate was too much to consider…yet.

Everyone would talk about the marriage therapist they'd all praised who had flunked out. Oh, they'd probably offer sympathy, but they'd wonder. And they'd soon find out that Craig was being investigated for money laundering.

Serve him right if I let everyone know...but what about our friends, friends who had invested with him? I'd have to get a handle on what was going on before I faced everyone.

What would I do for money? Pawn my watch or some of my jewelry? How long would the money from that last? A couple of days, a week tops.

I needed a job. But the economic crisis facing the whole nation had swollen the ranks of the unemployed here, too. Tourists seemed to be fewer and the storefronts for rent meant that there were few jobs available. I could probably find one cleaning motel rooms; they seemed always short of help. I shivered at the thought.

That left the Shrimpboat Café. Did I have the stamina to last as a waitress? How many other choices did I have?

I cycled back to the café. Only a handful of customers remained. Lottie Jane sat at a table sipping coffee with a pile of receipts. She looked up as I came in. "Back for more of our famous coffee?"

"Not exactly." I sat opposite her and hesitated.

Her eyes crinkled. "What can I do for you?"

I took a deep breath. "Lottie, I'd like to apply for that job you have advertised." I motioned towards the front window.

Before she could catch herself, she snorted, and then stifled her mirth. "You what?"

"I need a job."

She eyed me from my designer T-shirt to my dark wash straight-cut jeans. "We need a waitress, not a manager."

I looked away. "Waitress, yes, I'd like to apply for the job as a waitress."

"Have you ever been a waitress?"

"For a few months back in college, but I'm a hard worker…and I'm willing to learn…and."

"Darling." She shook her head. "I know you've got problems, but believe me, you don't want this job."

I reached across and touched her arm. "Please, Lottie Jane, give me a chance."

She turned towards the kitchen. "Hey, Claude, we've got someone wanting the job."

While she waited for Claude to join us, she speared me with her gaze. "So you want low wages and daily grief? Blisters on your feet. Being so tired at night, you fall asleep as soon as you get home. Regulars who expect you to read their minds and laugh at all their stale jokes? Customers pinching your butt? Complaints without compliments? You must love punishment—or be crazy."

Claude joined us. He was thin to the point of emaciation. An overhead light reflected from his bald head and highlighted the gray flecks in his coal-black eyes. He wore a faded tan T-shirt and khaki dungarees. In one earlobe he sported a tiny gold stud, and on the biceps of each arm, anchor tattoos. He wiped his hands on an apron while his gaze probed.

I could see him as a cook on a tramp steamer, maybe, but not attracting the clientele I'd seen at breakfast.

Lottie Jane inclined her head. "Ashlyn here, is applying for the waitress job."

Claude smiled, displaying a full set of perfect teeth. I'd expected them to be broken and stained. Here I was being judgmental again.

"You want to wait tables, huh?" he said. "Now, why would you want to do that?"

"Your coffee," I smiled in return. "I want to work at a place that makes such wonderful coffee."

He grinned.

"Seriously," I said. "I need a job and I can start immediately."

His eyes narrowed. "Waiting tables is hard work, and I'm a slave driver."

Lottie Jane snorted. "He got that right."

"I'm a hard worker," I said. "If you give me a chance, you won't be sorry."

Claude rested his elbows on the table, steepled his hands and rested his chin on them while fixing his dark gaze on mine. "Have you ever waited tables?"

"No...well, back in college."

"But what recent work experience have you had?"

"I've been a family counselor." I rushed on. "But before that I kept accounts for small businesses."

Claude raised his eyebrows and looked sideways at Lottie Jane. "Here's someone to take over your bookkeeping."

"That would be a relief," Lottie said. "But you can't afford a bookkeeper. You need a waitress. Holly and I are run off our feet."

"I'm inclined to give you a chance." Claude stated the pay, adding that I'd get tips, too. "We need someone to come in at six in the morning, starting Monday. I know the hours are horrible. Still interested?"

How could I make ends meet on a meager hourly

wage? But what choice did I have? "I'll take it. You won't be sorry."

"We'll see." Claude reached across the table to shake my hand. "Welcome aboard…Ashlyn, is it?" He drew his mouth together in a firm line. "Now, don't make me sorry for being softhearted. Lottie, take her data and show her around while things are slow." He returned to the kitchen.

Lottie Jane looked at me solemnly, shaking her head. "You don't know what you're getting yourself into."

Before Lottie left to wait on a couple of customers, she took down my social security number, cell phone number, and current address. Whenever she was free, she described how the café operated and my duties.

During this first week, I was to join her at six a.m. and work until three or four when Holly would arrive. I could take most Saturdays and Sundays off. But I had to be flexible and on call when needed.

She showed me the layout of the kitchen. She explained how to make iced tea, but skipped the coffee machine—obviously her domain.

When Lottie was busy, I sat at a corner table trying to memorize the menu.

Lottie seemed to waltz around the café. During a lull, she returned and pointed at my sandals. "Get yuh something sensible for your feet. They'll be taking a beating. As for the rest, we don't have a dress code or anything, just wear something tidy and comfortable. I'll explain everything else on Monday morning. See you at six sharp."

"Thanks, Lottie. I'll be there."

As I cycled back to the beach house, I questioned my sanity at taking the job and breathed deeply to relieve the anxiety that squeezed my chest. Anger alternated with fear.

*Could I do this?*

# 12

The weekend dragged. Beyond jogging on the beach and cycling around the island, I kept a low profile. On Sunday, instead of attending a local church, I watched television.

That afternoon, someone knocked at the door. It was Valerie, the woman who'd been so empathetic to my tale of woe.

"I was in town and wondered if you'd like to go out for a coffee."

My mouth fell open. "How did you find me?"

She wore designer jeans and a pale blue blouse that accentuated her powder blue, almost grey, eyes. "It wasn't that hard," she said. "It's a small island and I had a general idea of where you lived."

I hadn't expected to see her again. Talking to a good listener had brought some relief, but it left me a little embarrassed. I was used to being on the other end of the equation.

"Well," I stuttered. "Coffee would be nice." I pointed behind me. "I could brew some here."

"I'd like to take you out to a coffee shop I know. Introduce you to the island."

"Oh, I couldn't let you do that."

"Do you have other plans?"

I laughed. "Plans? No, I don't have any plans." Had I really laughed?

She jerked her head towards her car. "It's settled, then. Let's go."

She drove north, away from the village and past the airport to *Café sur Seine*, on Frederica Road. White lace cloths adorned the tables and in the middle of each stood a milk white creamer, sugar bowl, and jam pot. Frilly curtains draped the windows. A young brunette wearing an embroidered apron came over to take our order. She obviously knew Valerie.

Valerie turned to me. "What'll it be, coffee, tea, herbal tea, iced tea? And you must order one of their marvelous pastries."

"What are you ordering?"

"Colette knows my order by heart. Café au lait and a cheese scone."

"Then I'll have the same."

While Colette went to get our order, Valerie chattered away about places to see and things to do on the island. She seemed to instinctively realize she needed to engage me in light-hearted conversation.

I wondered if I could keep from dumping the whole load of my anger and grief on her slim shoulders. I kept glancing at the waitress, wondering if I could ever handle things as expertly as she did.

Valerie said something that I missed. "Sorry, what was that?"

She touched my hand lightly. "Here I am chattering away. I just asked if you had ever been to Fort Frederica?"

"No."

"Oh, I must take you. And there's a marvelous old plantation up '95. Are you a birdwatcher?"

"Well, not really, although I like nature."

After the waitress brought out coffee and scones, Valerie went on to tell me about Gould's Inlet on the East Beach where one could see all kinds of sea birds.

She enthused about the wild horses on Cumberland Island and the Sea Turtle Center on Jekyll Island. Her animated descriptions of the area's features almost made me forget about the tsunami I was living through. Almost.

"These scones are wonderful," I said. "And the coffee is even better than Lottie Jane's at the Shrimpboat Café."

"Oh," she said. "So, you've discovered one of the island's best kept secrets."

"I got a job there," I blurted. "Start tomorrow." I filled her in on what had happened. When I described my car being seized, she interrupted.

"Oh, no! That's terrible. I don't know how you've been able to cope with everything that's happened."

"I haven't coped…I feel like my life is a shipwreck." I finished the scone and took a gulp of coffee.

When the silence had gone on for a long minute or two, she reached across the table to give my hand a squeeze. Her gentle demeanor dismantled the last defenses and I began to pour out my despair. I told her how my sense of hopelessness and failure had led to suicidal thoughts. I didn't mention how close I'd come to ending it.

She scrawled on a napkin. "Here's my phone number. Call me any time, day or night. I'll come pick you up and we can talk. I'll be praying for you. Do you promise to call?"

"OK," I said.

Who was this woman? Was she an angel sent from God?

When we parted at my beach house, she gave me a hug and made me promise again to call her.

❧⸙

On Monday, the jangling of the alarm woke me from a troubled sleep. I lay there for a few minutes trying to recall why I'd set the alarm so early. Suddenly, I remembered and bounded out of bed, bolted to the bathroom and hurriedly prepared for the day. After a last look in the mirror, I dashed outside, grabbed the rented bicycle and took off.

As I cycled through the silent streets, euphoria began to build. Things would work out. Money would come in, enough to live until this mess was sorted out. What more could go wrong? Surely, I'd burned through my allotment of trouble.

When I arrived at the café, ten minutes late, the lights were already on. I locked the cycle and let myself in the back door.

Lottie Jane paused in her work of filling the coffee machine. "Good morning, Ashlyn. Isn't it a beautiful day?"

"Yes, yes, I guess it is. To be honest, I hadn't noticed. I was concentrating on rubbing the sleep from my eyes."

"Too early for you?"

"No, no…uh, well, I'm not used to getting to work by six…but don't worry, I'll be here on time tomorrow."

"Good. Now let me show you what has to be done. Claude will be here at quarter to seven. You need to unload the dishwasher, check all the tables to make sure there's nothing missing. We fill sugar dishes and wrap cutlery in napkins at night, but sometimes we miss a table. When you've done that, I'll get you to string beans, shell peas, that kind of stuff. Have you had breakfast?"

"No."

"Grab a bagel. I'll have coffee ready soon."

By the time Claude arrived, I had the dishwasher emptied.

He donned an apron and came over. "I see you made it."

I nodded and smiled. I wondered how many waitresses Claude had hired and lost.

Before the first customers arrived, Lottie had me stringing beans and shelling black-eyed peas in one corner of the crowded kitchen. As soon as the café got busy, Lottie had me collecting dirty plates, refilling coffee mugs, and re-setting tables. During any lull, I went back to prepping veggies and cutting wedges of lemon. She took care of all the orders.

Just when I felt like I had to sit down or collapse, Claude handed me a bag of oranges. "Cut half this sack in wedges. I need some fast, for garnish."

I looked at the oranges in bewilderment. *What did he mean?* Rinsing a couple of oranges, I took the knife he'd handed me and began to cut them like I had the lemons.

"No, no, not like that," he said. "Let me show you."

He sliced an orange into a series of thin half-moons.

I attempted to follow, but didn't measure up.

"She's destroying the oranges. Show her how to cut these things," he said to Lottie when she came into the kitchen.

My eyes were threatening a downpour. I'd never had anyone talk to me like Claude did. *And for such low wages!*

Lottie nodded towards Claude, and whispered. "Don't let him get to you. It's his way. Here, let me show you how to do it."

Carefully, she cut up half an orange and then passed the knife to me. "Here, you try."

After a couple of messed up oranges, I got the hang of it.

Claude even grunted his approval when I passed him the bowl of slices.

About eleven-thirty the café filled up again, and I was kept busy clearing tables and prepping veggies. That included a couple of bowls of sliced tomatoes that apparently met Claude's exacting standards.

When I wasn't prepping, Lottie had me go around refilling coffee mugs and clearing dishes.

At four o'clock, an African-American woman with her hair done up in tight, beaded braids entered the café.

Lottie brought her over. "Ashlyn, this is Holly, our other waitress."

I shook her hand. "Pleased to meet you, Holly."

"Ashlyn is going to work the morning shift."

Holly eyed me up and down before smiling. "Welcome. Any help's most welcome."

I could see doubt wrinkling her brow, so I responded. "I'm green as grass, but I look forward to learning from you two."

Slim and attractive in jeans and a khaki blouse, I guessed Holly to be in her late thirties or early forties. The sun seemed to break forth in the café when she finally smiled.

Lottie pointed towards the door. "Ashlyn, honey, you'd best be headin' home. You've had a long day. Be sure and soak those dogs or you'll have blisters tomorrow. We divvy up the tips at the end of the day. I'll give you your share in the mornin' when you come in. That is, if you still want to come in."

# 13

By the time I got back to the beach house, I was dead on my feet. I kicked off my shoes and collapsed on the sofa. I woke up in darkness. I dragged myself into the kitchen, threw a frozen dinner in the microwave, and headed for the bathroom. After a long shower, I changed into my pajamas, and returned to the kitchen. I soaked my feet while I ate a tasteless dinner and watched re-runs on the TV until I couldn't keep my eyes open any longer.

When I arrived on Tuesday morning, Lottie handed me sixty-two bucks, my share of the tips.

*Wow, I'm solvent again.*

About eight-thirty, Peter arrived. According to Lottie, he was one of their most eccentric customers. He came for breakfast in what I learned was his usual get-up: a corduroy checked shirt beneath a worn red crossing-guard vest and faded jeans. His ball cap was weighed down with a score of badges of every description and topped by two turkey feathers.

Lottie sent me to wait on him; my first real customer as a waitress. He ordered number two, which he explained must have eggs sunny-side up, but not too runny, bacon cooked crisp, but not over-cooked, whole-wheat toast, and grits with one pat of butter.

When I brought his order he stared at it a few minutes, stabbed one of the eggs, and flipped over the bacon. He shook his head and had me take it back.

When I returned, flustered, Claude snorted, but

Lottie smiled and explained. "He always sends it back. Gives him a sense of control, or something. But he tips real good, so we humor him."

Tuesday night I felt more tired than I'd ever been in my life. But I slept soundly and didn't have the energy to plot revenge on Craig or bemoan my state. I even began to sense more confidence oozing into my psyche.

On Wednesday Lottie made me responsible for a group of tables. I felt triumphant until I mixed up a bunch of breakfast orders. I was so flustered; Lottie Jane had to come to my aid to sort things out. It happened again during the lunch rush.

Claude commented when I picked up orders. "You sure you got the right table?"

I'd unconsciously been trying to act like Lottie, who never wrote anything down. From that point on, I wrote down every order along with the table number and position of the customer.

While I tried to smile and be cheerful with customers, I felt uneasy. Instead of relating to them from a position of competence as I'd done while a therapist, I felt unsure. I couldn't shake my own insecurity. I'd been unsuccessful in convincing myself that being single again was a good thing. Although I still wore my wedding ring, the sense that I was abandoned—damaged goods—seldom left my mind.

The way some of the men treated me didn't help. On Wednesday at lunch, two middle-aged men with prominent beer bellies leered as I took their orders. One rose in his chair to stare down my blouse while the other called across the café, "Hey, Lottie, who's the new girl? She's a looker."

I felt a flush creep up my neck.

Lottie came over with her hands on her hips. "Bud, you and Emmet here ought to treat our waitresses with respect...that is, unless you've decided you don't want to eat here anymore."

One of them threw up his hands. "Hey, we meant nothin' by it. Just bein' friendly."

By Thursday I had begun to get into the rhythm. I was still responsible for stacking and clearing the dishwasher and folding cutlery in napkins, but I now shared the other tasks including waiting tables.

At noon, Remy and his two pals came in for lunch, but they chose a table assigned to Lottie so I was saved from the embarrassment of having to wait on them. I did pause at their table to thank them again for the help they'd given.

About one o'clock, the café was empty, and work was caught up so Lottie suggested we grab a bite. We sat together at a table near the back and chatted while we ate burgers and fries.

"So you have two kids?" Lottie asked.

I nibbled on a fry. "Yes, sure do." I wiped my fingers on a napkin and fished in my wallet for a couple of pictures to show her.

"Your son looks like you," she said. "And your daughter is a doll. Bound to break a lot of hearts."

"She's a charmer, like her dad."

Lottie wiped a dab of mustard off her chin. "Craig's your husband?"

I grimaced. "Was...twenty-one years."

"Hey, don't worry. Sometimes, we're better off without them. Look at me. I've been living fancy free for ten years. Ever since my ex took off. Good riddance I say, not that your husband is a drunkard like Lee."

I remained silent, munching on my burger.

Lottie reached over and touched my arm. "Darlin', I understand…a little, anyway. Things will get better. Life will go on. And you've got two wonderful kids to live for."

Determined not to give in to tears, I swallowed, took a deep breath, and changed the subject. "So, Lottie, do you have kids?"

"Three. All grown up and married. Oldest, a girl, is in Atlanta, a boy in Memphis, and another in Kansas."

"Grandkids?"

Lottie smiled. "Five. Here take a gander." She fished in her purse and pulled out a small plastic album bulging with pictures.

I thumbed through the album. "You must be very proud."

She beamed. "You can say that. My kids have done me proud, no thanks to my no-account ex."

Wanting to keep the conversation from focusing on me, I asked. "How long have you been working here?"

Her brow furrowed. "Ten, eleven years. Claude took me on the very week Lee ran off with a barmaid from the Grotto. I helped Claude get the café back on its feet, trimmed the menu, and redecorated. 'Bout five years ago he cut me in for a quarter share of the profits."

Unusual, but it made sense. Claude's cooking attracted customers, but Lottie Jane's personality kept them coming back. She wasn't just a friendly waitress. No, she really cared about people and showed amazing competence.

A couple of customers came in, so we had to break off our conversation.

By Friday, I'd begun to really believe I could do this. The day started well with generous tips and no mixed up orders.

Claude even gave me a back-handed compliment. "I guess you'll do," he said.

Then I dropped a whole tray of dishes.

It was about nine in the morning and the place was abuzz with conversation and laughter. Silence fell.

I could feel every eye in the café on me. I was wrong. I couldn't do this.

# 14

With a lump in my throat, I knelt to clean up the mess of broken crockery. I rehearsed how I'd apologize to Lottie Jane and Claude and tell them that I'd tried, but the job just wasn't working out. I'd never quit a job before. What would I do for money? Where would I go to find another?

Just then Lottie came over and said in a loud voice, "Attention, everyone. Ashlyn has received her baptism of fire. She is officially declared an honored waitress in her own right."

Everybody clapped and cheered. No wonder everyone loved her.

I put my plans to quit on hold.

As Friday wore on, I got more and more weary. I went about my duties like a zombie, but was extremely careful not to drop dishes or forget orders. The weekend couldn't come soon enough. I planned to sleep in, read a book, and wander down the beach. That's when my plans changed—or got changed.

Valerie came in about one, and I went to take her order. "So, Ashlyn, how's it going?" she asked.

"OK, I guess, if you don't count dropped dishes and forgotten orders."

"I'm sure it's nothing to worry about. I've rarely been in a restaurant where someone doesn't drop something. Once I was in an expensive French restaurant in Atlanta where the waitress brought me an order of foie gras instead of the quiche I'd ordered. I can't stand goose liver—to be honest, liver of any kind."

I smiled. This gal was an inveterate optimist. We went on to chat a minute about the sunny weather predicted for the weekend before she ordered the shrimp platter.

When I came by later to clear her dishes and give her the check, she looked up. "How about going with me to Cumberland Island tomorrow? I haven't been there for years. We could take a picnic."

"Oh, I don't know…"

"Have you got something planned?"

"Well, no…beyond sleeping in."

"Please, you'd be doing me a favor. I lost two friends recently to cancer. I need to do something to distract my mind."

"Well."

"It's settled, then. I'll pick you up at eleven. Is that too early?"

I laughed. "No."

When she left, I paused to watch her go. How is it that some people make you feel better just by being around them?

Shortly after Valerie left, Remy came in with his two buddies.

Deep down I'd been hoping he'd appear. The sight of him awakened an unfamiliar yearning within. With his somewhat battered captain's cap and unshaven look, one wouldn't call him handsome. But there was something solid—dependable—about the way he carried himself. What in others could be viewed as a tough guy image was moderated by azure eyes that seemed to radiate warmth rather than ice and a mouth that telegraphed good humor.

When I went to take their orders, Gaston, the older man, spoke first. "How are you coping with your car seized an' all?"

"I'm doing OK. Got a bike to get around."

"We hear good things," Remy said, "about your waitressing."

"Somebody's stretching things. If you had been here earlier, you'd have caught me dropping a whole tray."

He winced. "Embarrassing."

"That's putting it mildly. What can I get you guys?"

They all ordered coffee and country-fried steaks. Gaston and Remy wanted mashed potatoes, Ches ordered fries. The place was busy, so I didn't get to chat with them anymore until Remy came up to pay their bill. Before turning away with his change, he asked if I had ever sailed.

I admitted to loving it.

"I have a small ketch that I'm thinking of sailing to Cumberland Island on Saturday. I wondered if you'd like to come. We could pack a lunch."

"That's a coincidence! I just agreed to go there with a new friend. But thanks for the invitation." I felt a flush creep up my neck.

His face fell. "Perhaps some other time."

"Yeah."

*Don't even think about it, Ashlyn. You're way too vulnerable to come within a mile of this guy.*

સ્જી

I slept in on Saturday. Waking more rested than I'd been in days, the realization dawned that the bouts of bleak despair or blazing anger were beginning to moderate.

The weekend actually looked bearable until a phone call from Tiffany rekindled feelings of longing for what our life had been.

I steeled myself to be cheerful and positive.

She told me about a call from her dad assuring her of his love and that her bills were taken care of. She described her classes and mentioned a cute guy in sociology. When she heard that my car had been seized, she got really worried. "There must be some mistake. Dad would never do anything dishonest."

"No, I don't think so, either. But from what I've researched about money-laundering, he could have invested money for an apparently legitimate company—then found out later it was connected to organized crime. That would bring the FBI down on him."

"Does that mean we'll never get our house back? Or your car?"

"I'm hoping for the best. But even if your dad is innocent, the innocent don't always win in court. And it could take years. I think we have to be ready to go through a couple of bad years. At least your tuition is paid."

"But why would Dad call from a public phone and not give me his new cell phone number?"

"I think he must be afraid that the FBI would monitor his calls."

I heard a catch in her voice. "But where is he? And why is he allowing this to happen to you? I thought you guys..." She broke off.

"I don't know, honey. I thought we came down here to work on reviving our marriage. Our relationship has been rocky for a while, but this…"

I heard Tiffany blow her nose before she replied. "What are you doing for money?"

"I've got a job. As a waitress in a local café."

"A waitress…you!"

"I know, but…" I paused as I phrased an answer that would reassure her. "It was hard at first, but I'm doing good, and the tips are great."

"I can't believe it. You, a waitress?" She rushed on. "How are you getting around without a car?"

"I've got a bicycle. Think of all the exercise I'm getting. I must have lost five or six pounds already."

"Mom, I'm bringing my car. You can use it."

"You need your car. You're in a spread-out town; I'm on a small island."

We parted with a promise to call each other every few days and arrange a visit. After the phone call, I collapsed on a sofa and stared out the window.

At first, I regretted having agreed to go on a picnic with Valerie, but the outing to Cumberland Island lightened my mood. Scattered ruins combined with maritime forests, undeveloped beaches, and wide marshes lent a certain air of mystery. We even caught a distant view of feral horses.

Valerie told me a lot about herself, perhaps to help take my mind off my own problems. Her husband had died of a heart attack three years earlier and her two closest female friends had died of cancer within three months of each other. Although her grief was still raw, a deep faith buttressed her life.

Having gone through so much loss, and with her only son living in Seattle, I wondered how she managed to be so upbeat. I sensed that her church family had something to do with it.

Listening to random comments about the people she knew and programs she helped with at church, I felt an emptiness. I missed my home church. But when, or if, I returned, how would I relate to my old friends as a newly divorced, middle-aged woman? And would people believe I wasn't implicated in the FBI investigation?

When Valerie wasn't telling me about her life and her love for the island, I blabbed on and on about my life. How could a woman I'd just met seem like a kindred spirit? I didn't even know her last name.

On Sunday, beyond jogging and collecting shells, I stayed in the beach house most of the day. I still didn't feel like showing up at any of the local churches, although Valerie had asked me to go. I did revive my habit of daily devotions.

By Sunday night I was looking forward to returning to work at the Shrimpboat Café.

The first two days of the new week passed without any catastrophic incident. I even handled Peter without getting frustrated.

With the tips multiplying, I became more optimistic—until two FBI agents showed up. It was Wednesday. I assumed they were business colleagues. The man wore a dark suit and a white shirt with a conservative tie. The only thing different about the woman's dress was her open-necked white blouse. He ordered the burger combo with coffee while she settled on a Greek salad and a diet soda.

When I cleared up their dishes and presented them with separate bills, the man smiled. "That was a really good meal." He placed a badge on the table. "We're with the FBI. We'd like to ask you a few questions about your husband."

I looked from one to the other. "Now? I have work to do."

"It'll only take a few minutes," the woman said. "Besides, you don't seem very busy."

The man smiled again. "Just routine. Nothing to worry about."

I felt my stomach contract into a tight ball. Why ask me questions? Did they think I was involved? Finally, I answered. "I'll have to ask Lottie Jane to cover. And not here. I'll meet you at one of the tables in the park across the road."

# 15

After I explained to Lottie, I went to the staff washroom. My chest was tight with anxiety as I rinsed my face and reapplied makeup. Police of any kind always made me nervous. They'd taken my car and frozen my accounts and credit cards. Since they obviously couldn't find Craig, maybe they'd put the screws on me—as if I knew anything.

By the time I crossed the road, anger began to overcome anxiety. I fanned it into a smoldering coal of resentment. I found them seated at a picnic table.

The man stood and waved to get my attention, and then pointed to the seat opposite. "Thanks for coming. I'm Larry Cutter and my colleague is Susan Tibbs."

"I didn't have much choice," I said.

The woman, Agent Tibbs, frowned. "We could have taken you to one of our facilities for interrogation."

Agent Cutter put his hand on Tibbs's arm. "Whoa. Let's keep this friendly."

So they were going to work the good cop-bad cop routine on me.

"Friendly?" I raised my voice. "Like seizing my car without any notice, and then freezing my accounts and credit cards? Is that what you call friendly?"

Agent Tibbs raised her eyebrows. "Look, we're not the ones breaking the law here."

"Oh, is that right?" I said. "So I'm guilty, am I?

Guilty of what?" I was fed up with bearing the brunt of whatever Craig had gotten himself into.

"Suspected of…" Tibbs said.

"Mrs. Forsyth," Cutter interjected, "We're not here about you. We just want your help in locating your husband."

I pointed at Agent Tibbs. "She seems to think I'm guilty of something. Whatever happened to the presumption of innocence?"

Tibbs rolled her eyes. "Playing the innocent, are we? You had no idea about your husband's racketeering? Very unlikely."

I jumped up. "Racketeering! He's not a mobster, and you know it." I wondered why I'd flown to Craig's defense. What did I really know about his business? Until the last six months, money had seemed as abundant as crickets in August.

Agent Cutter held up his hand. "Give us a moment, please."

They walked away a few paces and turned their backs.

Finally, Agent Cutter returned to the table and pointed to a seat. "Please, Mrs. Forsyth. I apologize for my colleague."

Agent Tibbs sat beside Cutter. "I was out of line. I'm sorry."

I reluctantly sat.

"My colleague learned this morning that the Russian mob killed her key informant…tortured her to death. Her emotions are a bit raw."

"Oh, that's terrible," I said, "But I don't see—"

"Let me explain," Cutter interrupted. "We are closing in on a branch of the Russian mafia that we've been shadowing for nine or ten years. In the course of our investigation, we discovered that they've been laundering money through the subsidiary of a company listed with Forsyth Investments—your husband's company. The death of the informant has set us back. Your husband could have been unaware of the source of these tainted funds, but he may have information that can help us. People he met. Contacts. E-mails. That kind of thing. The sooner we find him, the easier it will be for him to clear his name, if, as you say, he is innocent. So you'll be helping him by helping us find him."

"But that's just it. I don't know where he is."

Agent Cutter flipped opened a small notebook. "You arrived together almost three weeks ago on a Friday."

"You've been keeping track of our movements?"

"Mrs. Forsyth, it's part of our job." Cutter ran a hand through his short, black hair. "Your husband is at the center of a major investigation; he's given us good reason to keep him under surveillance. He failed to appear at depositions, he's been most uncooperative."

"With all your surveillance, as you call it, you should know then that he left me on the Sunday of the weekend we arrived. He served me divorce papers in church and drove away. I haven't seen him since."

The two agents looked at each other.

"You didn't know?" I said.

Cutter rubbed his forehead. "No, we didn't."

Agent Tibbs grimaced. "We're sorry to hear that— about your divorce, I mean."

"Yes, well, he left me almost broke. You obviously know about my financial state, if you've been spying on us."

Cutter frowned. "I'm sorry you look upon it as

spying. As I said, it's part of our job. We did wonder why a successful family counselor would take up a job as a waitress."

"I had to. All of our accounts are sealed."

Tibbs brushed a lock of hair out of her eyes. "The more you tell us about Mr. Forsyth's contacts, the sooner we'll be able to find him. What about phone calls since he left?"

One side of me wanted revenge on Craig, the other wanted to protect him. I shook my head. "No calls. I think he has a new number."

Cutter flipped through some pages in his notebook. "What about e-mails from either his personal address or business address?"

"Not a one. I'm not surprised. He told me he was dropping out of sight; that he'd be unavailable."

Tibbs began to fiddle with her sunglasses. I'd seen this kind of nervous habit often in counselees. "What about your kids?" she asked. "Didn't he call them?"

"He did call my daughter, Tiffany, but wouldn't give her any number. She thought he might have called from a public phone. She was quite agitated that he wouldn't give her a way to call him back."

"And your son, Tyler," Cutter said. "Any contact there?"

"Tyler is backpacking in the Australian outback. I haven't even heard from him. His sister hasn't, either."

Agent Cutter nodded. "You must admit his actions look highly suspicious. This is no way to act if he wants to prove innocence. And besides everything, he's dumped you. Sorry to be so blunt, but for your own good and his, we urge you to give us every bit of help you can. Can you describe for us his contacts, his friends, his relatives—anything that would help us find him? Take your time. Think about it."

I looked from one to the other.

Tibbs stuck her sunglasses back on her head. "Both you and your husband are in grave danger. The branch of the Russian mafia that has been laundering money through Forsyth Investments is extremely dangerous. They've littered the Eastern seaboard with the bodies of competitors—anyone who crosses them. They won't hesitate to squeeze you for information about your husband's whereabouts."

I stared out to sea where a pod of dolphins frolicked.

Agent Tibbs leaned across the table. "Mrs. Forsyth. We can't emphasize enough how treacherous these people are. They're called the Bratva. My colleague told you about the torture and murder of my informant. Don't think that because you're a woman they'll go easy on you. My informant was a woman. And they have a lot at stake here. Near as we can gather, they blame your husband for losing ten million or so of their investment dollars. Market downturn or not, they're not going to write-off that much money."

I threw up my hands. "OK, you've thoroughly scared me, but what can I do? As I told you, I haven't a clue where Craig might be."

"Does he have a cottage or cabin where he might hide?" Cutter asked.

"I never thought of that. He has a cabin near Lake of the Woods, Minnesota. I've never been there, but I think it is close to the Canadian border."

"We can find that fairly easily. What about his parents? Brothers? Sisters? "

"His mom and dad live in California. Vista. He's an only child."

Agent Cutter jotted down information in his notebook while Tibbs took up the interrogation. I gave her the names of his friends at church, his fishing buddies, and his business colleagues.

"What about Marlee Farber?" Tibbs said.

"Marlee? You know about her?"

Cutter looked up from his notebook. "I'm sure we're not telling you what you don't know. Your husband and Ms. Farber were seen several times staying overnight at high-end hotels."

I replied in a trembling voice, "Craig drove off with her...on the Sunday he gave me the divorce papers."

I went on to tell them all I knew about where Marlee lived, her friends, and her relatives. Then I fell silent as I tried to combat the corrosive feelings of hatred her name aroused. *What kind of a blind fool had I been? How could Craig have betrayed me so easily? OK, we'd been sniping at each other for a year or so but...if the mafia caught up with him—with both of them—it would serve them right.* Even as the thought reverberated in my brain, I cringed at how judgmental I'd become.

Agent Tibbs interrupted my thoughts of revenge. "What about anything unusual you may have noticed in your husband's schedule or in the people he met during the weeks before you came to the island?"

I traced a pair of initials carved on the table while I pondered his question. "For the last month or so, he's seemed gloomy, worried, but he wouldn't tell me what was bothering him. Other than that...oh, I remember, he did fly down to Bermuda quite suddenly."

"When was that?" Cutter said.

"About three weeks before we came here...and there was one other thing. A couple of days before we left, an expensive looking foreign sedan pulled into our driveway. Craig rushed out to meet the occupants of the car. One was short, dressed in a baggy suit, the other was stocky and wearing a T-shirt. I thought at first they were from the car dealership where Craig had been talking of buying a car. When Craig came back in he was evasive about who they were."

Agent Cutter pulled out his phone, spent a moment scrolling, and then showed me the images of six different men on the screen. "Do you recognize any of these men?"

"I don't think so. But I didn't get a good look at the men."

Cutter passed across his card. "OK, you've been very helpful. Let us know the minute your husband contacts you. Or if you remember anything else that might help us."

Agent Tibbs touched my hand. "Call us day or night. Be careful, the Russian mafia is ruthless."

I sleepwalked through the rest of my shift. My stomach churned as I tried to digest the information. Money laundering for the Russian mafia? I might become a target? How could Craig leave me so vulnerable? He had been so adamant about honesty and integrity in our finances. Had the lure of big money blinded him and set him up to break marriage vows?

My state of mind led me to get orders mixed up.

Sensing my distraction, Lottie Jane sent me home early.

After another tasteless microwave dinner, I went to bed early, hoping a new day would brighten prospects.

# 16

A creak splintered the dark silence into jagged slivers. Someone was in the room, hovering over my bed.

I stifled a scream. Could I reach the revolver under my pillow without being seen? I couldn't move. Waves of terror washed over me as I awaited the attack. I forced one eye open.

A wane beam of moonlight filtered through the curtain revealing…shadows, nothing but shadows.

I shuddered. A nightmare? I had no revolver under the pillow. Where had that idea come from? But something real had interrupted the terror. What was it? I took a deep breath, eased back the covers and padded across the room to check the window. Securely locked. The clock radio told me it was 2:48 a.m..

I prowled the bungalow, flipping on lights, checking doors and windows. All secure. I turned on an all-night classical music station to banish the oppressive silence.

The interrogation by the FBI agents had frightened me more than I'd realized. Craig always said I let my imagination run wild; that I should learn to be more rational.

*Don't go down that road.*

I put on the kettle for a cup of tea, and then paced the room trying to avoid thinking about the torture that Agent Tibbs had described in graphic detail. I could see the informant's broken nose, her bloodied cheek, the missing fingernails. I shuddered. But when I forced that from my mind, Craig's perfidy bubbled to the surface.

With the tea ready, I curled up in a lounge chair and took up a novel. But I kept glancing around at the dark windows. Dropping the book, I turned on my laptop and read e-mails. Still nothing from Tyler.

Tiffany had sent a cheerful missive telling about college, further describing the young man in her sociology class, and again urging me to borrow her car.

I tried to get interested in Facebook, but it all seemed so banal compared to my reality. The nearby barking of a dog startled me. I shivered. As I shut down the laptop, I prayed. *Lord protect me.*

I went back to bed and after tossing and turning I must have fallen asleep.

The alarm went off at six.

☙❧

I was late for work. The judicious application of makeup couldn't hide the circles under my eyes, something Lottie Jane noticed.

"Bad night?" she asked.

"I didn't sleep well, but I'll be OK as soon as I get a cup of your coffee."

"Those two agents give you trouble?"

"How did you know they were agents?"

"Plain clothes detectives. Off-duty cops. FBI. I can smell them a mile away. Comes with the territory. Among the first people they interview in a small town are waitresses and barbers. So, were they FBI?"

"Yeah."

"Thought so. Bureau types give off a certain vibe;

dress a certain way." Lottie enveloped me in a hug, and then held me at arm's length. "Listen, honey, I don't need to know your business, but if they give you any trouble, you come to me. I'd tell them where to get off. I have an uncle in the Bureau—high up."

I wiped moisture from the corner of my eyes. "Thanks, Lottie Jane."

The morning passed quickly. Both Lottie and I were run off our feet by an influx of tourists vying for space with our regulars, the tradesmen and business men who frequented the café.

Valerie came in about eleven-thirty, but it was so busy, we were only able to exchange a few words. When I cleared her table, she passed me a brochure for the Howfyl Plantation and suggested we visit it on Saturday. I promised to let her know.

All day scattered thoughts skated around my mind as I took orders, refilled coffee, and tried to put on the face of a friendly server. I was too distracted to be very successful—and the tips showed my lackluster performance. By the time I got home I realized I couldn't put off returning to New York.

I'd often found that walking helped clarify my thoughts. So after another microwave supper, I changed into shorts and a T-shirt and headed down to the beach.

Too weary to jog, I meandered on the strand. A slight breeze riffled the water and sandpipers fast-walked down the beach ahead. I caught a dolphin surfacing just as my cell phone went off.

I glanced at the caller ID. It was Martin, my lawyer. He had seemed to be out of his element, unable to get any clear information from the FBI, or to find Craig.

"Martin, I'm glad to hear from you."

"Ashlyn, how are you?"

"To be honest, barely coping. I hope you have some good news."

There was a pause on the other end. "Not exactly good news."

"Have you heard from Craig?"

"A copy of divorce papers came by courier, but he has dropped out of sight. No phone number. No e-mail. No contact information whatsoever. The FBI have even come to my office looking for him."

"What about the house, my business account?"

"That's what I wanted to talk to you about. I have some papers for you to sign, so we can get more aggressive in demanding the FBI give us access to the house and release your account. Any chance you'll be coming to New York in the next day or two?"

I scuffed the sand. "That's a problem."

"Ashlyn, I really need you here in person to go over what I want to file."

"I'll give it some serious thought and get back to you." I hung up, and continued down the beach, checking my phone for messages as I went.

Tiffany had left me another of her texts. "Love you Mom!!!!"

I'd returned her texts with similar messages. In the last week, she'd also called a couple of times, worried about me, offering to put me up in her dorm room until I could find an apartment. I'd have taken her up on it but staying in Urbana would be too far from New York—and I could not put off returning home.

What home?

A wave of loneliness swept over me. I missed Tiffany. And where was Tyler? Why hadn't he called? I also missed Julie, my friend from church, who had left a dozen messages on my cell phone. I hadn't had the courage to reply. As soon as I did, she'd pass on the news—as a prayer request. And everyone would be talking.

A diving pelican gave me an excuse just to stare out at the ocean. But even fishing pelicans couldn't distract me. Life could be good again, but not without a plan, something more than working as a waitress. And that plan started with returning to New York. According to my secretary, my clients were getting impatient. Martin's call told me I couldn't put it off any longer.

*Craig, where are you? Why have you done this to us?*

Suddenly decisive, I turned around and headed back towards the beach house. It was time to take action. Stop mewing like a wounded kitten.

Back at the cottage, I called Tiffany to ask if she had time to drive up to New York and meet me at the bus station. She was not happy about me taking the bus.

"Mom, have you ever ridden in one of those long distance buses? Can't you fly?" Tiffany rushed on. "Is it because you're short of money? I could loan you some."

"Sweetheart, I'm sure the bus will be OK. And I'm getting good tips, so I have some money."

"But where will you stay when you get here? With your friend Julie?"

"No," I said. "I'm sure she'd be happy to put me up, but she'd quiz me unmercifully. I can't face her family yet. I was thinking about staying at the Maple Motel."

I promised to text her the details. As soon as I got

off the phone, I researched bus schedules, but was shocked to learn it would take over 24 hours. Next, I looked at Amtrak schedules and found I could take a train from Jesup and get to New York in the morning. It would cost over $300, which would leave a serious dent in my funds.

I slept well that night. Making a decision eased my mind. The thought of seeing Tiffany again also helped.

On Friday, the café had so many customers I didn't have time to think how I'd handle my clients or what I'd say to Julie and my friends at church. During my lunch break, I called Valerie to tell her I couldn't go to the Hofwyl Plantation on Saturday. She insisted on driving me to the station.

Lottie Jane not only agreed to let me take Monday off, she made me sandwiches for the train.

# 17

Settled in an aisle seat on the train, I took deep breaths to relax. My nervousness wasn't just due to uncertainty about what I'd face at home, but concern about travelling with no credit card. Credit was king and cash suspect. I'd had an argument at the ticket counter about why I hadn't reserved a seat online. The window seat beside me was empty, a good place to put my overnight bag.

Across the aisle, a professor type in a Harris tweed jacket with elbow patches was absorbed in a thick book. Behind him, a grey-haired business man leafed through papers from his open briefcase. A teenage boy vibrated in his seat to some beat pumped through earphones. A few seats behind me, a couple of women were planning their assault on New York's shops and restaurants.

I took out my cell phone. What should I tell Julie? I'd have to limit what I told her until I could see her face to face. She was bubbly and emotional where I, until recently, had been calm and in control. Her enthusiasm gave her an edge in her field of real estate.

She answered on the second ring. "Ashlyn, honey, where have you been?"

"Hi to you, too."

"I've been so worried about you. Your house—"

"You know about that, huh? Look, Julie, I'm really sorry for not answering your messages, but I've been so overwhelmed. I didn't know how—"

"Ashlyn, just say the word and I'll fly down to help you. Whatever trouble you're in, it doesn't matter. That's what friends are for."

"Julie, honey, you're so sweet, but I'll be in New York in the morning and—"

"Wonderful," she bubbled. "You can stay with us. We can go to a spa. I've got a new one that is superb. I'll pick you up at the airport—"

"Julie, hang on. I'm coming by train and Tiffany is picking me up. I'll be staying with her."

"But—"

"I called to see if we could meet at Rodney's for coffee tomorrow afternoon and go to church with you on Sunday—if you want. I've got a lot to tell you, but not over the phone."

"Rodney's? Sure, no problem, but Ashlyn, can't you tell me what's going on? Your house? The FBI..."

"Craig left me. He's getting a divorce."

"Aye! Is he crazy? Doesn't he know how fortunate he is to have you? Half the young men in the church were goo-goo over you before he cut them out and popped the question."

"You're exaggerating. Besides, that was twenty years ago." I paused. "Our marriage hasn't been so great for a while now. I'll fill you in tomorrow, OK?"

"Oh, Ashlyn, honey, I'm so sorry. Are you sure you won't stay with us? The kids miss you."

"And I miss them, but I need to spend time with Tiffany."

"I understand."

"So, three o'clock at Rodney's, then? And Julie, please promise me you'll keep quiet about this until I can talk to you."

Next, I sent a text asking the pastor for a few

minutes of his time after the morning service. I'd have to explain about cancelling the marriage seminar he'd scheduled Craig and I to teach. Then, I sent a text to my lawyer asking for an appointment on Monday morning.

Now there was the matter of my clients. *Sorry, any advice I would give about your marriage would be suspect seeing as how my husband has dumped me for another woman. If you have similar problems, get back to me in a year or two and I'll tell you how to handle it.* No, I guess that wouldn't do.

Finally, I put together a generic letter that sang the praises of another professional family counselor, suggesting her as a substitute and introducing my need for an extended sabbatical to sharpen my counseling skills. I apologized for giving them such short notice and sweetened the message by cancelling their last bill. Was the letter accurate? Not exactly, but it was the best I could do. And I could truthfully say that being a waitress had sure broadened my counseling experience. Maybe all therapists should intern as servers.

I typed up the draft and, using the train's Wi-Fi, sent copies to my client e-mail list and my secretary. I'd have to talk to her in person when I got to New York.

By the time the train got to Charleston, my eyes were heavy. I blew up a pillow Lottie Jane had loaned me and attempted to find a comfortable position.

"Hard to get comfortable on a train. Better than a bus, though."

I turned towards my neighbor across the aisle. He was fiftyish with a graying goatee that failed to hide his prominent Adam's apple. I vaguely remembered him getting on in Jesup, where I'd boarded.

I nodded agreement while I tried another position.

He pointed towards my laptop, which I'd set on the window seat beside me. "Legal secretary or something?" Why was he interested in my laptop?

"No," I said, "Nothing like that. Just sending e-mails."

"Going to Washington?"

"New York," I mumbled as I stuffed the laptop into the overnight bag.

He leaned across the aisle. "Can I get you a coffee or something…a glass of wine?"

"No, thank you. It's been a long day; I just need some shut-eye." Had the FBI tasked him to follow me? Was he Russian mafia? Or was I just too paranoid?

Not deterred by my cryptic answers, he pointed to my finger where a pale ring of skin betrayed the absence of my wedding band. "Separated?"

I frowned. Could he actually be hitting on me? Part of me was flattered that anyone might consider me attractive, but mostly I was irritated and suspicious. Ignoring him, I slid into the window seat, and positioned my overnight night bag beneath my blow-up pillow.

"Sorry to annoy you," he said. "I find that conversation helps the time pass more quickly on a long trip."

I massaged my forehead as I glanced back at him. "I'm just not in the mood for conversation. OK?"

He nodded and looked away.

I scrunched up on the seat and tried to put my suspicions to rest while I labored to empty my mind of all I had to do the next day. After spending an hour or so squirming into various positions, the slight swaying of the train and the rhythmic *clickety-clack* of the wheels lulled me into a stupor that must have deepened into sleep. I vaguely remember the bustle of stations, people coming and going, but little else until sunrise found the train approaching Washington.

Fortunately, the friendly professor had moved forward a couple of seats to converse with a blonde who seemed delighted by his company. He was probably just a lonely man.

When we arrived at New York's Penn Station, I followed the crowd to the 7th Avenue exit. Tiffany caught me waving and after circling the block, outmaneuvered a couple of limos to pick me up. The dents and scratches on her ten-year-old car seemed to give her an edge.

"Mom, hop in quick!"

I threw my stuff in the back and jumped in. "Sweetheart, it's so good to see you."

She looked me up and down before shooting back into traffic. "Mom, have you lost weight? Are you eating enough?"

"It's hard to gain much weight as a waitress."

As she drove the familiar roads through the Bronx towards Yonkers, I kept up a steady stream of questions about college life. Silly, I knew, but it seemed important to pretend for a short while that life was normal and avoid the questions that were almost too scary to face. I learned she had a part-time job at the campus information center and had dated the guy in sociology a couple of times. She quizzed me about what it was like to be a waitress.

As we entered Yonkers, where we had lived for most of two decades, I fell silent.

"Mom, do you feel like getting a bite to eat? I'm starved."

"Harry's High End Burgers!"

"Just the place."

We took our Ultimate Burgers to a booth near the back where we could talk in private.

Tiffany dug in. My beautiful daughter. I felt tears form.

She looked up and her robin's egg blue eyes clouded slightly. "What?" She pointed at my plate. "Aren't you hungry?"

"I'm just so glad to see you."

She reached across the table and gripped both my hands in hers. "So am I."

To keep from bawling, I turned to my burger and began to eat in earnest.

"Why doesn't Dad keep in touch? He could send a text or an e-mail or use a throw-away phone, or something. "

"He's probably afraid of the FBI finding him, what with all their surveillance technology."

"Would that be so bad? He could turn himself in. Prove his innocence."

"That might be difficult, and there's more to it." I took another bite of burger.

"More? More than divorcing you, running off with Marlee, losing our house, and getting your accounts seized?" Tears glistened in her eyes. "Oh, Mom. I can't believe he'd actually sleep with Marlee. How could he? It just doesn't sound like Dad."

I looked away as the taste of bitter fury rose in my throat. I took a deep breath. "I had a visit this week from a couple of FBI investigators looking for your dad. They confirmed that he's been seeing Marlee—for some time—not in a professional capacity—spending the night with her in high end hotels—when I thought he was away on business."

"Oh, Mom."

I pushed my plate away, no longer hungry. "To be honest, ever since you and Tyler have been away, we've been drifting apart."

"But he read us Bible stories as children. He prays such elaborate prayers at meals. He's a deacon! How could he break his marriage vow so easily?"

"I don't know how he reconciles all this with his faith, but as you know, Christians are tempted like everyone else. They stumble, they fall into sin."

"Sin," she said. "Yeah, but what caused it? Did you and he stop—?"

I flinched. "If you're talking about making love, that had become infrequent—"

"Infrequent, as in never? Mom, you're a marriage counselor. You know sex is a necessary part of marriage. God created it, for Pete's sake!" She paused and looked away. "I'm sorry, here I am lecturing you."

"Touché. I deserved that. And here is my little daughter, such a grown up, wise woman. If I could, I'd take back the last couple of years and do it differently. But I can't. I can try to forgive your dad, take him back if he wants to come back. But he's already filed for divorce…and we have a bigger problem."

"You mean the FBI?"

"And the Russian mafia."

Her eyes widened. "The mafia?"

I pondered how much to tell her. "The two agents, who interrogated me, warned me that the Bratva—I guess that's another word for Russian mafia—were searching for Dad also. They claim he lost ten million dollars of their money."

I went on to tell Tiffany everything I'd learned

from the agents. "They warned me," I said. "We could be in danger. They could try to kidnap one of us, force us to help them find your dad. Tiffany, be very careful; be suspicious of any stranger."

"Don't worry. The residence has around-the-clock security." She frowned at her soda. "So what's next on today's agenda?"

"How about we check into the motel? I could use a shower. Then I'm meeting Julie around three at Rodney's."

She leaned back with a quizzical expression on her face.

We fell silent while I finished my burger and fries.

"We're not getting the house back anytime soon, are we?"

"No, 'fraid not."

"All my winter clothes are there," she said. "My skates. My keepsakes. They're of no help to the FBI, but I need them. Why don't we sneak into the house tonight?'

"Break in?"

"It's our house! Our stuff. Besides, I know a way in they couldn't have found."

I stared at her with my mouth open.

# 18

After freshening up at the motel, Tiffany drove to our neighborhood.

My heart leaped as we drove slowly down the street beneath the towering maples. We saw no sign of FBI surveillance vehicles, so Tiff parked across the street.

Home was a clapboard frame house built in the 1920's. We had lovingly restored it, inside and out. It didn't look attractive with the yellow police tape blocking off the steps leading up to the porch and the large notice pasted to the front door. It looked more like a house raided for a marijuana grow operation.

"Sad, isn't it?" Tiffany pointed to the unkempt yard. "Looks like they haven't cut the grass in weeks."

Images of Tiff and Tyler chasing each other around with the hose, tricycles on the sidewalk, Craig cutting the grass, and Tyler breaking his arm falling from the big maple tree filled my mind and kept me from answering.

"The way in is around the back hidden by that huge clump of rhododendrons."

"You mean the old covered steps down to the basement? I thought that was all boarded up."

"I used to sneak out that way to meet Erin when you thought I was asleep."

"What!"

"We were teenagers, Mom. What did you expect?"

I swatted her on the arm. "I guess parents are the

last to know."

"Anyway," she said. "We'll be in and out in a jiffy. All we need is a couple of flashlights. We can come after dark, park down the street."

"Let me think about it. Now let's go or I'll be late for Julie."

Tiffany dropped me off at Rodney's, an upscale coffee house that served a dozen kinds of cheesecake. Before she drove off to visit one of her friends, she promised to be back in an hour and a half. I wanted an escape plan in case Julie pressed too hard for details.

Inside the door, I scanned the room. I had the hostess seat me in a booth near the back. Choosing an obscure corner had now become second nature. I fiddled with the menu while I waited. What was I going to tell her? The whole truth? Could she handle it?

"Ashlyn!"

The conversation in Rodney's stopped as everyone turned to watch Julie march towards my booth. She wore slim black pants and a white blouse. Raven-black hair framed her flawless complexion and she wore red lipstick.

I felt dowdy.

When I jumped up to meet her, she grabbed me in a crushing hug.

"Julie, honey," I said. "So-o-o good to see you." And it was.

"Ash, I've missed you."

She broke the clinch and looked me up and down. "You've lost weight. Are you eating enough? I need to get you into one of my spas. Why don't we—"

I laughed. "Hold everything, sister. Can we just have a coffee and catch up?"

The waitress arrived before Julie could grill me anymore. She ordered a lean cappuccino and a chocolate truffle cheesecake while I settled for Brazilian bold coffee and cherry cheesecake.

Julie's eyes narrowed as she looked at me. "What's this about Craig seeking a divorce? It can't be true."

I glanced away, unable to look her in the eye. "I'm afraid it is. He told me in a letter, not in person…gave me the papers and everything at the end of a church service. Drove away with a colleague from work." I took a deep breath. "Been sleeping with her for I don't know how long."

"That's—that's horrible. I'll kill the guy next time I see him."

I looked down at her perfect nails and hid mine below the table. "That may be a problem. He's disappeared."

The waitress arrived with our order so we fell silent.

"Disappeared?" Julie leaned in.

"Gone. Vamoosed. Cancelled his cell phone. Totally dropped out of sight. Gone off with his little tramp. "

"Oh, Ashlyn, honey." She daubed at her eyes with a napkin. "I'm so sorry."

I gritted my teeth, but couldn't hold the tears at bay.

Julie came over to my side of the booth and put her arms around me.

I wept until I began to hiccup. "Oh, Julie. I don't know what to do—my marriage—my counseling ministry—the church! How could I have been so blind? Where do I go from here?"

"It's not you who's blind. Craig would have to be

blind and dumb to do this to you." Julie's voice took on a hard edge. "Some men are animals."

I fished in my purse for a tissue. Blowing my nose, I pointed to the cooling coffee. "I'm OK, now. I think I just needed a good cry. You're such a loyal friend and I haven't even called you."

Julie returned to her side of the table. "Sweetheart, we'll get through this. Why don't you move into our guest room until we can sort things out?"

"Thanks, but I can't. Let me freshen up and I'll explain." I fled to the restroom where I tried to rinse the red out of my eyes and repair the damage to my makeup.

Back in the booth, I tried to explain. "Julie, there's much more than our marriage involved here. I need to try to sort things out before I come back to New York for good."

Between sips of coffee and bites of cheesecake, I told her the whole story: the cancelling of my credit cards, the freezing of my bank accounts, the seizing of the house and car, the FBI interview, the warning about the Bratva, and my job at the Shrimpboat Café.

"You're saying that Forsyth Investments is in trouble?"

"Big trouble. I'm quite sure Craig didn't launder mob money knowingly, but that may not mean much once the FBI began an investigation. I can't see this getting sorted out any time soon."

Julie slumped in her seat. "Damian and I have quite a bit invested with Craig. So do the Gladstones. There must be others at the church."

I covered my mouth with my hand. "Oh, I didn't know."

Julie reached over and patted my hand. "Oh, well,

what is money, after all, but paper? There's always cheesecake."

"This is terrible. And he's a deacon. How can I face people at church?"

"You can sit with our family—somewhere near the back."

෩

That evening Tiffany and I parked a block away from our home. For a while, we sat and watched. There were no other cars on the street. Lights shone from windows, but there was no one about.

We wore jeans and dark T-shirts and carried flashlights.

Tiffany had a cloth carry-all.

I had a backpack.

Part way down the street to our house the fierce barking of a dog made me jump.

Tiffany rested her hand on my shoulder. "Just the Peters's German shepherd. Always barks."

Except for a porch light, our house was dark. We slipped through a gap in the hedge and went around the back where we stopped in front of an overgrown rhododendron bush.

Tiffany parted the branches and disappeared. "In here," she whispered.

I followed into her childhood bower, a space about five feet high sheltered beneath the rhododendron against the wall of the house.

Tiff heaved open the old wooden door covering the outdoor steps. A moldy smell assailed my nostrils. We froze to see if the screeching hinges had aroused interest.

Her flashlight revealed worn brick steps strewn with leaves and years of accumulated debris. At the bottom loomed the forgotten door to the basement. We gingerly descended. She gave the door a yank, but nothing happened.

"Are you sure it isn't locked or boarded shut?" I asked.

"Doubt it," she said. "Give me a hand."

We both yanked, but to no avail.

I pointed down. "It opens out but all this debris at the bottom is stopping it."

Using a couple of old boards, we worked away at clearing the leaves and dirt. We were finally able to open the door. That done, we faced a new problem; the entrance was blocked by cardboard boxes piled on an old fridge and a washer/dryer pair.

"We're going to have to push these away," Tiffany said.

It took us ten minutes of heaving before we had opened up a large enough space to squeeze through.

"Let's make this fast," I said, brushing some of the dirt and grime from my clothes.

Tiffany ran ahead and began to climb the stairs to the first floor. Before she opened the hall door, she turned. "Mom, make sure to shield your flashlight, don't shine it at any windows."

I giggled. "You've been watching too many cop shows."

I paused to gaze into the living room where the porch light filtered through the drapes. Thoughts of Christmases and birthdays and parties welled up and almost set me weeping. I bit my lip and turned towards Craig's office. Nothing but his desk. Only wires showed where his computer had been and indentations on the carpet where his filing cabinets had stood.

"Hurry, Mom." Tiffany called softly from upstairs.

I ran up the stairs and went to our bedroom. Every drawer stood open, books littered the floor, our mattress slumped against the window, pictures had been ripped off the wall, and clothes formed a disorderly trail from the closet to the bed frame. I went to the bureau and began to rifle through the drawers. I stuffed some of my good underwear and socks into my shoulder bag along with a couple pieces of costume jewelry. The drawer for our bank books, family records, and tax stuff was empty. From the closet, I picked a pair of good pumps, two of my favorite dresses, and a couple of tops. I paused to look around.

What about the emergency fund?

Craig had taped a fake envelope with a few dollars and some minor papers to the back of the bureau and another one to its bottom. I pulled the bureau out from the wall. Sure enough, they'd found the decoy, but had they found the real thing? I crouched on the floor and shone the flashlight underneath. Eureka! I reached in, tore off the thick envelope, and stuffed it in my bag.

"Mom, we've got to go. I think I heard something beep when we walked through the hall." Tiffany stood in the doorway, her backpack stuffed full.

"Beep as in—"

She cocked her head to one side. "Sirens!"

We raced down the stairs two at a time. We left the way we had entered, being sure to close the door. The sirens were louder by the time we had retraced our steps to the bower beneath the rhododendron bushes. We crouched there, uncertain whether to bolt or hide.

# 19

The sirens ended with the screech of a car pulling to the curb.

Tiffany pointed across the back yard. "There's a hole in the fence behind the cedar hedge and a way across the neighbor's backyard. Come on."

We squeezed through a gap in the cedar hedge only to come up short against the fence.

"Where's the hole?" I said.

"It was right here," she whispered. "Looks like the neighbor has repaired it."

"They have a dog?"

"No."

At the sound of raised voices we glanced back to the house.

Tiff threw her backpack over the fence, grabbed my bag, and tossed it over, too. Grasping my hand, she motioned for me to step into her cupped hands so she could boost me over. I didn't hesitate. After hoisting me over, she climbed the fence like a monkey, and joined me on the other side where we froze. No shouts, nor the sound of running feet.

Tiff grabbed her backpack and waved a hand for me to follow.

Lights shone from the second story windows of the neighbor's house.

We crept through the yard from one shadowy tree to another until we gained the corner of the house. No sound came from within, so we slipped down the side of the house to the street beyond. Then by a circuitous route, we returned to her car and quickly left the neighborhood.

"Do you think they caught us on video?" Tiffany said.

"I doubt it. Not enough light. Probably motion sensors, though."

"The FBI might have some kind of ultra-violet or infrared thingy."

I smiled as I brushed the dust from my jeans and dabbed a scratch on my arm. "If they did, all they'd see were a couple of ghosts. We're covered with dust from the basement. Besides, I don't care if they do identify us. They have no right to seize our house without letting us take personal stuff."

"That's the spirit, Mom!"

I reached over and squeezed her shoulder. "Talk about spirit; you've got it!"

As soon as we were settled into our room, Tiff put the clothes she'd stuffed in her backpack onto hangers.

I ripped open the envelope and dumped the contents on the bed. "Eureka," I cried. "We've hit the jackpot!"

"Wow, that looks like a lot of money."

"One hundred, eight hundred, one thousand, eight thousand, there's twelve thousand dollars here! Where did your dad get that kind of money without going through his accountant?"

"I don't know, but you can sure use it."

"We both can," I said, counting out a thousand and handing it to her. "You take this to help with college."

Besides the money, there were birth certificates for all the family, social security cards, our life insurance policy, and one of those little brown envelopes that banks give to hold a safe deposit box key.

I lay awake that night for some time wondering if the money was dirty and pondering the possible uses of my birth certificate and social security card. Could I get a new credit card? The money would be enough to buy a used car.

ॐॐ

The next morning we arrived at church late, hoping to avoid having to answer questions. Even so, Harry, one of the ushers, welcomed us with a twitch of his eyebrows which I knew heralded a lengthy conversation. We slipped through the vestibule door, leaving him with his mouth open, his questions unasked.

Julie had saved us seats on the last row. She gave me a hug. Her husband, Damian, waved at us from the other end. Between them, her two girls leaned forward and grinned at us.

I smiled back.

Pastor Ray's gaze ranged over the congregation as he went through the announcements. When he spied Tiff and me, he stumbled over what he was saying. He caught himself, but it was enough to cause a ripple of curiosity to travel through the congregation.

I looked down, but not before Moira Reycroft, three rows ahead, caught my eye and gave me a tiny wave. Beside her, Elizabeth Cunningham smiled. Others glanced over their shoulders and spied us. Some smiled, most frowned, or kept their faces expressionless.

How much did they know? Did many have money

invested with Forsyth?

I scanned the bulletin. There was the announcement of our coming marriage seminar. That had to be cancelled, and fast.

"Can we leave on the last hymn, or do you want to talk to people?" Tiff whispered.

"Let's leave during the last hymn."

But the more I thought about it, the more I realized I couldn't avoid people forever. I remained distracted through most of the service. I knew I needed to be honest. My worries didn't keep me from being uplifted by the service. I'd always appreciated the mix of modern choruses and grand old hymns. During the singing of *Blessed Assurance* I fought to keep from blubbering.

Pastor Ray's sermon on the parable of the unmerciful servant gave me hope that Craig's unfaithfulness could be forgiven. Did that mean our marriage might be restored? I had to believe in the possibility, even though reason told me otherwise.

Julie squeezed my hand, reminding me how good it felt to be among friends and back in a service again. I'd missed the comfort and encouragement of the church family. I passed Tiff a note explaining that instead of leaving right away, I needed to linger to talk to people, and then to the pastor. She nodded.

At the close of the service, I whispered to Julie. "Would you mind staying with me for a few minutes?"

"Wouldn't think of leaving you for the wolves," she said with a smile. "Don't worry. It'll be OK."

We threaded our way through the crowd to the foyer. On the way, several people hugged me. Others murmured. "Welcome back Ashlyn...good to see you. Hope you had a great time down south. Didn't see

Craig, is he off on another business trip?"

I didn't do more than nod, return hugs, and give non-committal answers. In the foyer we were surrounded by Moira, Elizabeth, and others from our small group Bible study.

"Excited to see you back, Ash."

"When can we start up again?"

"I'm so looking forward to the marriage seminar."

"Hold on. The marriage seminar will have to be cancelled." I plunged on. "Craig isn't on a business trip. Some criminal group has targeted his company, and the FBI has gotten involved. I'm sure he will be exonerated, but in the meantime, as many of you know, our house has been seized."

"Oh, Ashlyn," Elizabeth said. "That's terrible. How—"

"Craig and I are going through a rough patch right now." I gulped. "To be honest, he's left me—started divorce proceedings. I'll be staying down south for a while."

Shocked expressions registered on almost every face.

Megan, a slim thirtyish blonde, didn't look surprised. Had she already suspected?

I felt anger begin to rise. Had he made a pass at her? Before I could follow that line of reasoning, Julie broke in.

"Ashlyn is going to need our understanding. This is very difficult for her to talk about. Let's not press her for details, just love her, and pray for her."

Megan stalked off, throwing words back over her shoulder. "Fine example you are, Ashlyn!"

"Hey," Julie said, "Don't mind her. This is not a time for accusations, but for love. Let's gather around and pray for Ashlyn, right now." She signaled for everyone to close in. "Father, you know how much Ashlyn is hurting. You hurt with her. Draw very close to her. Assure her of your love. Comfort her. Strengthen her. Show us how we can support her. And if it be possible, restore their marriage. In Jesus's name. Amen."

After hugs all around, accompanied by whispered assurances of prayer and offers for help, I wiped the moisture from my eyes, smiled, and left the group. Then I went to join the pastor in his study.

As I walked through the church hallways, I smiled at people I passed, but my mind was on Julie. She was a much better friend than I'd expected, and I'd been so slow to call her. I'd even worried that her effervescent personality signaled a tendency to share confidences. I wondered how many other people I'd judged wrongly while donning my 'marriage counselor' persona.

Pastor Ray was waiting when I arrived at his office. He waved me to a chair. "Can I get you a coffee, a cold drink?"

"No, thanks. I'm sorry to bother you after a service, but this will only take a few minutes. The marriage seminar will have to be cancelled. You see— Craig has left me, filed for divorce."

"I'm really sorry to hear about this Ashlyn, but I can't say I'm surprised. I knew something was wrong. A few weeks ago I got a letter from Craig, resigning from the deacons' board. No reason given and no return address."

My mouth fell open. I seemed to be the last one to find out about everything. "But the announcement in the bulletin?"

"I didn't want to pull that until I heard from you.

The main thing is; how are you doing?"

"Not good, but I'm coping—no delete that. Pastor, I'm miserable, angry, depressed, and furious."

He reached across the desk to touch my hand. "I can't begin to understand how you're feeling, but Kim and I will try. We'll be praying for you daily. And whatever you need, just say the word and we'll be there for you. Kim and I look upon you not just as a member of Riverview Community, but as a friend. We're not here as a church to blame you or Craig, just to love you and help you in any way we can."

"Thanks, pastor."

"I'm serious, let me know if there is anything we can do."

"I will."

Before I could exit the church, Bill Pasterchuk accosted me. "Ashlyn, where is Craig? I really need to talk to him. I've received no statements from his company for a couple of months. He doesn't answer e-mails, or phone calls, or anything. What's going on?'

"Bill, I'm sorry, I'm as much in the dark as you. I wish I could help you."

"But—you're his wife—"

"You may as well know." I looked around the almost empty foyer. "He's left me and I have no way of contacting him."

"But we've got a lot of money invested with him. Please, can't you just—"

"I wish I could help you, but I can't."

As I left the church, I glanced back over my shoulder.

Bill stood there with his shoulders drooping and his tie askew.

# 20

Monday, Tiffany and I both slept in.

I yawned, stretched, and padded over to part the curtains. A grey drizzly scene greeted me.

Careful not to wake Tiff, I settled into the only comfortable chair in the room and opened the Gideon Bible. I began to read from Psalm 146. I hadn't felt much like praising God since going to St. Simons. But that morning, in spite of the weather, I felt more upbeat than I had for months. Was it being with Tiffany? Julie's support? Being in my home church? Finding the money?

As I thought back over the past few weeks, I realized events had really rocked my faith. I'd begun to question God's love. Why was my faith suddenly resurgent when a couple of good things happened? Was it so dependent on circumstances? In the last year or two, had I become so complacent and self-confident that it took a personal earthquake for God to get my attention?

I closed the Bible and began to silently pour out my heart to the Lord.

❧❦

After a leisurely breakfast, Tiffany drove me to Martin Reitman's office.

Martin's secretary, Rita, nodded as I entered, but failed to exude her usual warmth. "Martin said to go right in."

"Thanks Rita."

Martin grasped both my hands in his and scanned my face. "Ashlyn, this is a terrible business. How are you holding up?"

"Honestly—most days I feel like I'm in the midst of a nightmare and I'll never wake up."

He waved me to a chair. "Come in. Come in. Let's see what we can do to help you."

Martin had been our family lawyer for over two decades. With his impeccable tailored black suits, expensive shirts, college ties, and wingtip shoes he cut a distinguished figure. Silver hair crowned his head. The perpetual twinkle in his blue eyes gave one the impression of a kindly old gentleman rather than a no-holds-barred lawyer. I'd only seen those eyes frost over twice, both times while dealing with abusive men; cases that I'd sent his way.

"Ashlyn, this whole business is bizarre. I'm not making any headway with the FBI. They're unwilling even to explain how you could be implicated. They just say that the case is ongoing."

"Implicated—they claim that?"

"It's just a smokescreen to give them broad powers. I'm sure you'll be exonerated, but in the meantime, I don't know how you're coping. Look, if you need a loan or anything—just say the word. You're a friend more than a client."

"That's very kind Martin, but I'm doing OK. In fact..." I reached into my purse and took out an envelope which I passed to him across the desk.

"What's this?" He opened the envelope and whistled. Then he tried to pass it back to me.

"No, no, keep it. It's only five hundred, but it's a

start on paying my bill."

"I haven't given you a bill! In fact, I've been meaning to talk to you about that. The way the FBI people have jerked you around has got my dander up. I've been planning to do this pro bono. Besides you've given me a lot of work over the years."

"That's very thoughtful of you Martin, but please, at least keep this."

He knit his hands together and rested his chin as he stared at me. After a moment, he nodded. "OK. Let's get down to business, then. Have you got your account print-outs?"

I reached in my purse again, took out a thumb drive and passed it to him. "It's all in there. My business accounts for the last five years."

He plugged it into his computer. After a few minutes of scanning my spreadsheets, he turned back to me. "It looks good, but I'm no accountant. You didn't receive any payments from Forsyth Investments? No connection whatever?"

"Beyond being married to the CEO, none at all."

"They shouldn't hold that against you. I'll get a forensic accountant to use your data to prove you had no connection with Craig's investment firm. It may work, but you never know with the FBI. They might argue that your marital connection to the CEO is enough to cast doubt on your innocence. Now what about this divorce business?"

"You've received papers from Craig?"

He nodded. "Do you want to proceed with the divorce—or?"

I stared out the window for a few moments before answering. "No. I don't want to give up on two decades of marriage without at least sitting down and talking to Craig."

"That may be difficult. He seems to have gone off the grid."

"I told you about the two agents who interviewed me. It's clear that the FBI can't even find him. But let's hold off on doing anything about the divorce. Give him a chance to make contact."

Martin leaned back in his chair. "At least he's been fair in dividing up the assets. He leaves you the house and its furnishings, half the outstanding shares in Forsyth Investments, plus half of his investment portfolio."

My voice rose an octave. "Half of nothing! He can hardly give me what the FBI has seized. When I see him, I'll wring his neck."

"I hear you. Leave it with me. I'll prepare a writ for reinstatement of your credit cards, access to your personal possessions in the house, and return of your car."

"Realistically, what are our chances?"

He fiddled with a pen, moving it from finger to finger. "There's always hope—but I'm afraid, to be honest, this is going to be a long fight."

"I know you'll do the best you can."

After I'd signed some papers authorizing Martin to act on my behalf, he walked me to the door. "Now, Ashlyn, remember you're not just a client, but a friend. Let me know if there is anything else I can do."

❧◌

Tiffany and I spent a couple of hours shopping at the mall.

I almost felt giddy, having the money to replenish

my limited wardrobe. I called my secretary to explain what was happening and promised her three months' severance. When the call went to voice mail, I felt a sense of relief at not having to talk to her in person.

Tiffany and I met Julie for lunch at Chez Pierre where we laughed and told stories, avoiding any mention of Craig. I felt more relaxed than I had for weeks.

After lunch, Tiff drove me to the Penn Station where I caught the 3:15 Silver Meteor. Once settled on the train I booted my laptop and began to check for e-mail. Many clients expressed thinly concealed annoyance or astonishment. Each client required a carefully worded reply. That kept me busy until it began to get dark, when I fell into a stupor. I dimly sensed the sway of the coach and the slowing and acceleration of the train as it entered and left stations: Richmond, Rocky Mount, Fayetteville. Then nothing until I awoke with a stiff neck as the train came to a stop in Savannah. By the time we arrived in Jesup, Georgia I had awakened enough to brush my teeth and freshen up.

Lottie Jane had promised to pick me up, even though it meant getting Holly to come in early to open up the café. But on the platform in Jesup, there were only a few people waiting. Lottie Jane was not among them. I grabbed my briefcase and overnight bag and headed to the parking lot to look for a taxi.

"Here, let me grab those."

Remy strode towards me from the end of the platform.

"What are you doing here?"

"Lottie Jane couldn't get off. She sent me to pick you up. I thought you'd be at the other end of the train."

"But it's so early. I could have gotten a taxi."

He took my laptop and overnight bag, and motioned towards the parking lot. "I'm up at all times of the day or night. Besides, I've got nothing better to do." He grimaced. "That didn't come out right. Let me rephrase it. I enjoy playing the knight in not very shiny armor to the beautiful damsel in distress."

The heat of a blush climbed up the back of my neck. I patted a couple of errant hairs back into place. If only I'd taken time to put on make-up. Why was I attracted to this man, especially in the midst of the turmoil that was now my life?

"I'm not in very much distress at the moment," I said, "But thank you very much, kind sir."

Remy's pickup seemed to be an older model, but it was in surprisingly good shape. There were no discarded coffee cups or beer bottles on the floor—no debris of any kind. Instead of butts, the ashtray held a couple of pencils and a pen. On the seat lay a clipboard with some kind of tally sheet. A faint fishy odor pervaded the cab. This was the second time Remy had come to my aid. Really, three times, if I counted how he had kept me from falling off the dock on that terrible Sunday.

Without moving my head, I glanced sideways at him as we sped down the highway towards Brunswick. A couple of day's stubble couldn't hide the sculpted lines of his craggy, weathered face. Locks of sun-bleached blond hair peeked out from under his cap. Wrinkles radiated from his astonishing blue eyes as if he could barely control some hidden fount of laughter. How old was he? Fifty? No, more like forty.

He radiated strength and dependability, but with

an underlying civility and gentleness. In another lifetime I could have easily fallen for him even though we had nothing in common. To keep my mind from wandering down that dead-end alley, I looked out the window.

"Good trip to New York?" he asked.

"Yes, and no."

He glanced my way.

"It was wonderful to see my daughter and friends again."

He nodded.

"As far as my main problems are concerned, nothing is resolved. No car. No house. No credit cards. No husband." Why was I telling him all this?

"I'm sorry to hear that," he said. "Look, you don't have to explain anything to me. I was just making conversation—there I go again—saying the wrong thing. It's not that I'm not concerned—I just don't want to come across as nosey."

"Remy, you've come to my aid twice...plus picking me up today. I really appreciate it. I don't think you're nosey, just very helpful."

"Like I said, rescuing damsels in distress is the specialty of us southern men."

He turned and our gazes met.

I glanced away, but not before I felt something flash between us that quickened my pulse.

# 21

Most of the trip passed in a slightly uncomfortable silence.

I broke the silence by asking him about shrimping, or making comments about the scenery. And my lack of a car. "Remy, do you know where one can buy a dependable used car?"

"How much are you looking to spend?"

"Between five and seven thousand. Too little?"

"Not a lot, but it should be possible in this poor economy. People are hurting. Losing their houses. Selling their second and third car. Are you looking for any particular brand?"

"No, just a dependable car that is good on gas. I did enjoy my import, but I think that will be out of my league. "

"Why don't you leave it to me? I'll ask around, see what's available."

"If you could just give me some suggestions where to go—"

"Hey, I love doing this kind of thing. I know all the scams. Besides, my middle name is *mechanic*. Working on a boat, you have to know engines."

"I'd really appreciate your help," I said.

When Remy dropped me off, I thought about offering to pay him for the gas, but I sensed such a suggestion would offend him. Instead, I just thanked him and waved as he drove away.

After a shower, I made myself a peanut butter

sandwich and turned on my laptop. Munching on the food, I scanned the inbox, deleting spam as I went. I was about to delete one from an unfamiliar address when I saw it was from Tyler. Excited, I read the contents.

He went on for paragraphs about aborigines, kangaroos, lizards, fairy penguins, and trekking in the outback. Nothing about receiving any of my e-mails or calls.

*I'm having a fabulous time. What a country! I may try for a job in Melbourne. The father of one of the Aussies I'm trekking with has a construction company there. Then if I make enough money, I could spend a few weeks in New Zealand on my way home. Don't worry, I'll be home for Christmas.*

*Mom, I know you're probably worried that you haven't heard from me, but everything is cool…just haven't been near many phones or computers—and I've got to save my money for food and travel. Someone stole my cell phone at a hostel where I slept. DON'T WORRY!!! Sending this from a cattle station. Isn't that cool? Love ya tons. My love to Tiff and Dad. Tyler.*

Relief that Tyler was OK flooded my soul. I reread the message, forwarded a copy to Tiffany, and then sat there staring out at the ocean.

Christmas. What would Christmas be like this year? A bleak, wintry feeling of sadness threatened to overwhelm all the relief I felt at hearing from Tyler.

I jumped up and tidied up the kitchen, hung up my new clothes, and prepared for my afternoon and evening shift. But before long weariness overwhelmed me and I fell asleep on the sofa.

I woke with a start from a terrible nightmare. I'd been asleep in our bed back in Yonkers, Craig spooned against me. But then I seemed to be looking at Craig standing at the bedroom door, dressed in a suit and tie while I wore my favorite negligee. He marched over to the bed and said, "I never loved you. It was all a sham. I'm leaving."

"No," I cried. "You do love me." I ran after him down a roadway lined with laughing neighbors, but he disappeared in the distance while I collapsed in a heap.

With a shudder, I sat up. Light streamed in the window. Almost two o'clock in the afternoon. I paced around the living room trying to counter the terrible feeling of loneliness and despair that gnawed at the corners of my consciousness.

*You are not alone. Tiffany and Tyler love you. Julie loves you. God loves you. Craig did love you and he will love you again. Oh, get a grip, Ashlyn. Stop moping.*

❧

Lottie Jane welcomed me back with a hug. "Sorry I couldn't meet you in Jesup. Holly had to do something about her youngest. Besides, Remy seemed happy to go."

"No problem. It gave me a chance to learn about shrimping."

Lottie raised her eyebrows. "Shrimping, huh? So, how was New York?"

Before I could do more than describe how good it had been to see Tiffany, a couple of customers entered.

"Welcome to the Shrimpboat Café," I said as I handed a menu to a balding, fiftyish man wearing a bright blue Hawaiian shirt open half way down his chest. "May I bring you coffee or tea?"

"Darlin', what I need is a bourbon, straight up."

"Sorry, how about an iced tea, instead?"

"Brandy? Vodka? Tequila?"

I shook my head.

"A lager? Red wine?"

I eyed the mermaid tattooed on his chest as I continued to shake my head. "I'm sorry, we don't carry alcohol." I pointed up the street. "Can I direct you to the bar up—"

"No, I want to eat here! I've heard the grub is real good. Make it an iced tea, then."

"You've got it."

I was so busy with new customers and fending off Mr. Hawaiian shirt's clumsy attempts at flirting that I forgot all about my angst. It was good to be back.

The rest of Tuesday went off without a hitch. Wednesday started well, but ended with a crisis. The big walk-in cooler broke down and Claude had to pay a refrigeration technician overtime to fix it. For the rest of the week he kept mumbling about technicians stealing him blind whenever Lottie Jane or I got within earshot. He even began to talk seriously about raising prices. Fortunately, Lottie Jane talked him out of it.

On Thursday, Remy and his two crewmen came in just before my shift was over. I'd been looking forward to seeing him again—wondering if he'd found a car that would suit my budget. After they finished their dinners, Remy suggested I pull up a chair.

"I've found a couple of cars that might work," he said passing over three printouts. "All private sales."

I leafed through the sheets. They listed the vitals of a 2001 German car, a 2002 Japanese compact, and a 2001 American SUV.

"The compact," he said, "Is the best on gas, but highest mileage. We can probably get that for six thou'. The sedan is also good, but a later model and more money."

"What about the SUV?" I said.

Ches, Remy's young crewman piped up. "It's in tip-top shape. It's some couple's third car. Rarely left their garage. You could offer them five thou'. It's sporty, not as good on gas as the other two, but has four-wheel drive, though not as if you're going to need that, are you?"

"No," I said.

Gaston fondled his mustache. "The cars would be safer choices than the SUV."

"What about their condition?" I asked. "I don't know anything about cars."

Remy pointed to the printouts. "We picked these three out of fifteen or twenty listed. Ches gave the SUV a spin, Gaston checked the compact, and I checked out the German car. All three are in good shape, and reasonable. The choice is yours. If you decide, or want to look at all three, give me a call. We can arrange for you to see them after work on Saturday."

❦

On Friday FBI Agent Tibbs came in.

"How's it going?"

"Fine," I said, pouring her a cup of coffee and passing a menu.

She poured cream into her coffee, and then made eye contact. "I didn't see you over the weekend."

I looked away. "I don't work on weekends."

"Or Mondays? Have a good time in New York?"

So they'd been keeping me under surveillance.

"Can I take your order?" I said.

She handed back the menu. "I'll have the shrimp salad with house dressing."

Beyond delivering her order, I ignored her. *Who did the FBI think they were? Seizing property. Hassling ordinary folk. If she knew I'd been to New York, did she suspect Tiffany and I had broken into our house? They couldn't have an infra-red image, could they? Were they even now interrogating Tiff?*

Her presence in the café made me so nervous that I went into the washroom for ten minutes hoping she'd pay for her meal and go. But when I returned she was still there. She waved the bill. Reluctantly, I took the twenty she offered and made to turn away.

"Why don't you sit down for a moment? Someone broke into your house. Quite a coincidence, you being in Yonkers, and all."

"I'm busy with other customers."

She looked around. "You don't look busy to me."

I felt anger begin to rise as I sat down. "Are you following me?"

She kept her voice low. "We're doing our job: keeping you safe. But what were you doing?"

"It's none of your business!" I said, my voice rising.

Lottie Jane and the only other customer in the café glanced our way.

I lowered my voice and using the tip money I carried, began to count out change from her twenty. "Anyway, what right do you have to seize my personal property and that of my daughter and son?"

She leaned forward. "Your house has been seized as part of an ongoing investigation into a very serious case of money-laundering. That includes everything in it. I'm sure you don't want to be charged with impeding an investigation."

"You're the big investigators. If you had done your job, you'd know that my counseling business had no connection whatever to my husband's business. Do you think my daughter's winter clothes might be evidence to use against Forsyth Investments, or perhaps my son's music collection? This whole business is ridiculous and I'm tired of you snooping."

I made to get up but she motioned me to stay seated.

"Please." She rubbed her eyes, which looked bloodshot. "Look, I'm not unsympathetic to your situation. We'll try to do something about freeing up your personal stuff. But I don't think you realize the danger you are in. One of the investment counselors employed by your husband's firm has disappeared. We have no doubt that the Bratva have seized him. You could be next. You need to be very careful. Let us know immediately if you see anyone suspicious."

She passed me a card, and left without picking up her change.

# 22

On Saturday after work, I met Remy outside the café. Together we walked around the SUV he had driven over. It looked good: a dark blue with grey leather seats.

"What about the engine, the tires, that kind of thing?" I said.

"It's in amazing condition. Low mileage and relatively new tires. Engine ticks over like a Swiss watch. Air conditioning works well. I think it was a hobby car that the owner rarely used." He threw me the keys. "Do you want to take it for a spin?"

I hopped in and drove down Ocean Boulevard to the East Beach Causeway and back. Before I'd gone a block, I was sold.

Remy's evaluation clinched it.

Back at the café, I jumped out of the car feeling more jaunty than I had in years. I was independent again! "I love it already!"

"Then it's yours—for sixty-two hundred dollars. I couldn't get the owner to come down any more. But if you give him half the money down, he'll let you drive it over the weekend. I'll take care of the paperwork for you on Monday."

"Oh, Remy, you've done so much already. I can't expect you to do that."

"No problem. I have a knight-in-blue jeans complex, remember?"

"OK." I laughed. I rummaged in my purse and

pulled out an envelope with the money in it. "I don't mind giving him the whole amount as long as I get a receipt."

And so it was that I had wheels again. I felt so free after feeling that people were hovering too much, feeling sorry for me, wanting to help but not quite knowing what to do.

Now, Remy didn't hover, he just stepped in with practical help, not that Lottie Jane or Holly, or my new friend, Valerie, weren't practical, but...well, Remy was different.

I felt comfortable with him. And I could trust him. He didn't hit on me. Was it only comfort I felt? *Ashlyn, don't go there.*

I immediately phoned my insurance company to transfer the policy to the SUV. The FBI had not contacted them when they seized my other car, so they had no problem with my request.

To celebrate my new mobility, I drove to Savannah early Sunday morning. On the way my conscience began to trouble me about using the money I'd found. If it was dirty money, I should have turned it over to the FBI. But I'd already spent a lot on the car. But if I did that, I'd have to admit to breaking into the house. What to do? As I thought back through the years to the day Craig and I had hidden the envelope, I realized that it could only have been cash we earned and paid taxes on.

In Savannah, I slipped into the back of a lively church I'd attended as a teenager and enjoyed the service immensely. All the way to the beach house, I sang at the top of my lungs. It was good to have hope again.

God was on His throne. I was His child. He would

take care of me. God could even bring Craig back.

I christened my new wheels Lemonade after my mother's frequent reminder that if life hands one a lemon, one made lemonade.

Things were looking up. Even though I'd continue to use the bicycle a lot, I could drive to work now if I wanted.

The next couple of weeks went off without a hitch; no dropped dishes, no rebukes from Claude, and no visits from the FBI. I'd begun to enjoy waiting tables with Lottie Jane. Doing something that kept me busy probably kept me from outright depression.

The regulars seemed to accept me and the tips increased. Every couple of days I'd have a long chat with Tiffany or Julie over the phone.

One Saturday Valerie took me to visit a local plantation which had been designated a historic site.

Most Sundays I drove to a church I found in Brunswick where I'd sit at the back and leave right after the benediction. It was good to be anonymous. I didn't feel comfortable going to a church on the island.

My feelings for Remy were an enigma. After the Monday when he brought me the car papers to sign, he didn't appear in the café again until the middle of the next week. I'd found myself hoping he'd appear. When my mind wandered in his direction, I'd give myself a lecture. *Hadn't I promised to love Craig until death do us part?*

It was as if two voices battled within me. One argued; *It's your Christian duty to forgive Craig. Haven't you told your clients that for years? Even if he's become callous and hurtful, aren't you supposed to love your enemies?* The other countered; *that's a laugh. As if he cares what you do or say. Right now, he and Marlee are probably in some Caribbean resort engaged in an orgy of love-making. I'm better off without the pig. Surely, I deserve some happiness.*

The battle within continued, especially in the evenings when I went home to an empty cottage. I'd argue with myself as I prepared supper. *Ashlyn, Ashlyn, you know that marriage was created by God as a beautiful life-long union of a man and a woman...and...and for years yours was wonderful. Isn't it worth recovering? Hah! As if that's going to happen. Your marriage is in more pieces than the mirror you smashed the day he left!*

Most nights I slept better than I had during the first few weeks of Craig's desertion, but I'd often wake disoriented. Some nights I resorted to over-the-counter sleeping pills I'd bought to replace the ones I'd flushed down the toilet.

About a week and a half after buying Lemonade I took a break and was finishing the last of my plate of shrimp when Remy and his crewmates walked in. A flush began to climb up my neck. I looked towards Lottie.

With a slight motion of her head she indicated I was to wait on them. I shook my head. She frowned at my response. I took my dishes to the kitchen and walked over to their table.

"I just had some of your shrimp," I said. "Marvelous."

Remy smiled up at me. "We can't take any credit for what the ocean produces, nor for Claude's culinary skill."

"Maybe a little," Gaston said. "The captain knows where to drag."

"Amen to that," Ches said.

Remy took off his cap, laid it on the table.

"Enjoying your SUV?"

"It's so wonderful to have wheels again. I really appreciate your help."

"No, problem."

"Been busy shrimping?"

"Actually, I never left the harbor. Got caught up doing repairs. With boats you're never done painting, fixing, repairing nets."

A tiny smile creased Gaston's lined face as he seemed to sense some chemistry between us. "The captain's a slave driver."

Although I could tell Remy and his crew would have continued to chat, I cut it short by asking, "So gents, what'll it be?"

I took their order, returned to the kitchen to inform Claude, and then filled the dishwasher. When I returned with their orders, I overheard snatches of conversation about the weather. I was nervous about the feelings Remy conjured up. I even failed to ask the universal question of waitresses everywhere; "How is everything?"

When I brought their bill and cleared their table, Remy passed me a picture of his sailboat. "Isn't she a beauty? You'll have to give me another chance to show you how smoothly she sails."

Scrambled thoughts rocketed through my mind. Would that be wise? I searched for an excuse but couldn't find one. "That would be fun. Would a Saturday or Sunday work?"

"Great, I'll get back to you after our next sweep."

At the end of my shift, Lottie Jane beckoned me to join her. The café was empty and Holly hadn't yet come in to take over my duties. I could tell by the moisture welling up in her eyes that something was seriously wrong.

"What is it, Lottie Jane? Claude wants you to let me go?"

She shook her head. "Nothing like that darlin'. Claude even told me you were doing good—for a Yankee. That's high praise coming from him."

"I'm not a Yankee!"

"I know that, so does he. No, it's nothing about you." Her eyes took on a hunted look. "I've got cancer."

I sucked in a breath. "Oh, Lottie, I'm so sorry. Are you sure?"

"No doubt at all. Remember last week when I took off? I went to the doctor about a pain that has been building over the last few months. She immediately sent me in for a scan. I have a fibroid that is growing in the uterus. Tests of tissue came back yesterday. Positive for cancer."

I reached across the table and squeezed her hands. "They can get it out, right?"

"I go in for surgery in about ten days. I'll be off for a couple of weeks, at least. There will also be chemo after the surgery. That's going to make it difficult to run the café, which is why I wanted to talk to you."

"Getting better is the most important thing. Surely, you can close up the café for a few weeks, or a month."

Lottie Jane swiped at a tear that trickled down her cheek. "Claude says no. So, what we're going to do is hire a couple of waitresses to work part-time and ask you and Holly if you can extend your hours. Holly will organize the schedule in my absence, generally run the front of the restaurant, that kind of thing. Will you be OK with that?"

"I can do that. And I'll be praying for you every

day that you'll have a full recovery."

Lottie Jane shrugged. "Prayer. Yeah, can't hurt. I sort of drifted away from that stuff when my drunken ex left. But your willingness to take on extra hours? Now that will really help."

And so it was that the rhythm of work at the café changed. The next day, Lottie introduced me to two high schools kids who would be working part-time. Elise was a buxom, red-haired, teen who seemed to have her head in the clouds, but proved to be a hard worker.

Peggy Ann was a slim pixie-faced girl who always seemed to wear a frown. During the next two weeks until Lottie's surgery was scheduled, they came in for a few hours every other day to get used to the work.

I could see that Peggy Ann might cause some problems. When she had a minute free and she wasn't texting, she curled up with one of the current fantasy books. On her first day at work, Claude chewed her out for spoiling half a dozen oranges she was cutting up.

Elise mixed up a few orders.

Lottie Jane began to be absent more. Most days, Holly would do split shifts, helping me in the morning, going home for the afternoon, and returning for the evening.

But sometimes, I'd be the only waitress until one of the high school kids came in at two or three. By the time I went home at night, I was so exhausted I'd often fall asleep on the couch without supper. I'd wake up in the darkness, fix myself a cup of tea and an omelet or cheese sandwich and check my e-mails.

One evening during that period, a message from an unidentified sender appeared. The subject line of the e-mail read, *Lonesome Pine,* a name loaded with meaning.

It must be Craig. Surely, he would be apologizing, asking for forgiveness by harking back to that romantic setting where we first met.

I paused before opening the message, afraid of what I might find.

# 23

I opened the e-mail.

*Ashlyn,*

*I'm truly sorry for the way this has played out. I never intended to hurt you. One of my reasons for dropping out of sight has been to insulate you from my problems. I can't go into details, but a couple of years ago a very reputable company invested a considerable amount of money. Only recently have I learned what that company didn't know. Hidden under four or five layers of respectability, the money came from the Russian mafia.*

*Somehow the FBI got wind of it and is investigating me for money laundering. What I did was in good faith. I hope to be vindicated in the end.*

*The problem is that the money took a big hit in the recent downturn and the mafia is demanding the full amount be repaid—with interest. They've threatened my life. I had to disappear. But I've been dropping them hints to draw them away from you and the kids.*

*I've also been trying to establish contact with the FBI so I can cooperate in their investigation without losing my freedom to act in recovering some of the lost money. When I do, I'll make sure they know that you haven't been involved.*

*In the meantime, I've deposited a considerable amount under your name at the Gallagher Bank and Trust in Philadelphia. Your pin number is the date (year + month) we met at Lonesome Pine.*

*As for our marriage, it's been a hollow shell for a couple of years. I couldn't go on that way. I'm sure I've been responsible for many of our problems. You're better off without me. You're now free to get on with your life and career without being dragged down by my financial mess.*

*I'll leave you the house and half our assets as soon as this is cleared up.*

*I'm sending this from an Internet café but by the time you get it, I'll be gone.*

*Give my love to the kids.*

*Craig*

I ground my teeth, feeling my face harden.

*Insulated me from his problems, had he? Yeah, real insulation, dumping me on St. Simons with no car and no cards! Endangering the kids. Losing our house. So, he thought he could buy me off with money? As if love and commitment were a commodity like his blasted stocks that could be bought and sold.*

I sucked in my breath to try to control the rage. I began to pace back and forth. Before I knew it, I was throwing whatever I could find. It felt good. Soon there were books and magazines strewn over the floor along with pillows and shattered coffee mugs. One pillow hit a lamp knocking it over.

Good. Broken like our marriage vows. With that, I burst into tears.

Leaving the mess behind, I slipped out onto the porch where I stood gazing on the ocean. The darkness was relieved by a million twinkling stars. During the past couple of months, I'd often retreated to the porch to let the sound of the surf soothe my soul. It was as if it's very regularity spoke of God's faithfulness and grace in a world marred by pain and evil. But that evening the surf did nothing to soothe my feelings of rage or dispel thoughts of revenge.

❧

Before I knew it, we were into the third week of October. After receiving Craig's e-mail, I kept telling myself that fantasizing about reconciliation was useless. I poured myself into work at the café, which helped a lot. While most days I was successful in projecting a cheerful front, underneath I'd often be fighting off dark thoughts of despair. Or I'd have to extinguish the anger that flared into flame from the burning coals deep within.

Often these moods were triggered by thoughts of our home. I'd missed the flaming colors of the maples along our street. I wondered how long my rage at Craig's desertion would last. I knew the bitter anger was harmful, but I seemed powerless to banish it. I called Tiffany almost every day and fired off e-mails to Tyler without even knowing if he received them. I also talked to Julie regularly. I went out with Valerie for coffee a couple of times, but with the new schedule couldn't accept any of her invitations to concerts.

A week or so after first asking me, Remy repeated his invitation to go sailing.

*Why not?* We set out on a Sunday afternoon, the only time I could find free. A brisk wind blew cotton candy clouds across an azure sky, ruffling the water. The day was unseasonably warm for the end of October.

After we'd motored out of the harbor, Remy had me steer the boat while he unfurled the jib and mainsail. Then we traded places. Soon we were flying across the water with spray in our faces. It was exhilarating.

I settled down on a cushion behind the mainsail facing Remy at the tiller. I felt quite self-conscious in the close quarters of his tiny sailboat where our knees almost touched. If I had thought about it, I'd have worn blue jeans and a jacket instead of Bermuda shorts and a sleeveless shirt. But it was too warm, anyway.

"Not feeling queasy, are you?" he said.

"Not at all."

When I reached up to catch some of the spray coming over the bow, I touched one of his hands that had been fiddling with the boom. "Sorry," I said.

"No problem, but you'd better duck; the boom is coming around."

The touch had sent a tiny frisson of energy pulsing through me. Remy was not just any man, but someone who, in another life, I could have easily fallen for. Was that already happening?

Not handsome by most standards, his lined, sun-burned face reflected strength and rugged dependability. Not arrogant or crude like many men I'd met as a counselor, he seemed almost like a throwback to an earlier age when chivalry ruled. I smiled as I thought of how foolish I was to romanticize about this tough fishing captain.

"Something amusing?" he said.

My mind raced as I tried to think of a fib to cover the real direction of my thoughts. "Not really," I stammered. "Just thinking of how wonderful and free I feel out here. No wonder you love the sea."

Remy flicked a lock of sun-bleached hair out of his eyes. "Free, yes. Out here we're beyond bankers and telemarketers, all the greed and competition, and all the ranting of the politicians."

"The bankers giving you trouble?"

He sighed. "Afraid so. Bank's squeezing me for payments."

"So you don't own your boat outright?"

"Oh, I own the boat. But every year I have to take out a loan for new equipment, docking fees, engine overhaul, salaries, that kind of thing. And much of the year we catch next to nothing, so there's no money coming in. Paying off the bank is just one of our problems. The multinationals want to take over all the offshore fishing, while the fishery department keeps imposing new restrictions. Big industrial plants are pouring poison into the sea, killing off the shrimp stocks."

"I didn't know fishing was so complicated. Not that I know anything about it."

"Sorry, Ashlyn. Here I am blabbing about my troubles. It's what fishermen do when they get together. I'm just not used to conversing with a beautiful lady. "

My mouth fell open and I felt my face heat up. "Beautiful? You must have come face to face with too many flounders if you consider me beautiful."

He chuckled. "That's a good one. No, seriously, you're very fetching when you smile. Too often I've seen your face troubled and creased with worry."

So he had been noticing me? To hide my embarrassment, I turned towards the spray. "Are you flirting with me?"

"I'm just saying what is obvious. You're a very attractive woman. Sadly, you're dealing with more problems than anyone has a right to endure. But this is such a beautiful day. Let's let the sun and sea wash our troubles away—for a day, anyway."

"Let the sun and sea wash them away! You're very poetic."

"Deal?"

"Deal," I said with a sigh of contentment.

He skillfully maneuvered us out of the bay into the open sea where he set a course south. From time to time, he pointed out features on the shore or places where he'd trawled for shrimp. We soon left Jekyll Island behind.

After a few minutes, he pointed ahead. "See that cove? We'll anchor near the shore."

"I don't see any cottages. Is that the mainland or an island?"

"Cumberland Island."

"Maybe we'll see some of those wild horses the brochures talk about."

"Quite possible. They love to gallop along the beach."

When the sails were furled and we were anchored, he pointed to a locker. "Can you grab the picnic basket?"

He placed a piece of plywood between us, resting on the gunwales. From the picnic basket, he brought out a flowered cloth which he spread over the board, and we had a floating picnic table.

Soon we were sipping from sodas and munching on pastrami sandwiches and potato chips.

"Too bad about Lottie Jane," he said.

"Really sad."

"When is the surgery?"

"Within a week, I believe. But they're giving her real hope for a complete recovery."

Remy scowled. "That's what they said to Carol Ann."

"Was she a friend?"

"My wife. Died six years ago. Same kind of cancer."

"Oh, Remy, I'm so sorry."

His voice took on a dark intensity. "Cancer is from the pit. No one should have to suffer so." He sighed. "I thought I'd gotten over it, but every time someone else is diagnosed it brings back terrible memories."

I touched his arm.

"I'm getting all gloomy again," he said, "after suggesting we leave our troubles behind. Look—"

Just then, a pod of frolicking dolphins arrived off the port side. They lightened our mood with their antics.

For the rest of the sail, we both avoided serious conversation, choosing instead to let the magic of the day throw a deceptive blanket of optimism over our problems.

# 24

The day after my sail with Remy, I felt more cheerful than I had in months. But the schedule at the Shrimpboat Café was so tight that I didn't have time to ponder my change in mood. It was the first week that Lottie Jane didn't come in at all.

Holly joined me for the morning shift then left after lunch and returned for the supper crowd. I had to extend my hours to five in the afternoon to overlap with Holly an hour or so.

The two teen girls, Elise and Peggy Ann, came in on alternate afternoons and all day Saturday, so with their help, I was able to take some time off over the weekend.

In the middle of that week, I drove to Brunswick to buy groceries and look for a more serviceable pair of shoes. I'd bought my groceries and was putting them away in the back seat when someone came up behind me.

"Mrs.Forsyth, can I have a word?"

I jumped, banging my head on the door jamb.

"Sorry, I didn't mean to startle you," Agent Tibbs said.

I rubbed my head. "What are you doing here?" My voice rose. "Are you still following me?"

"Never mind that. Can we talk?"

"Do I have a choice?"

"We're not your enemies. We're trying to keep you safe." She pointed across the parking lot to a bench.

"Please."

Reluctantly, I joined her on a bench.

"Ashlyn, have you heard anything from your husband? We really need to find him. He's in grave danger."

"From that mafia bunch?"

"Exactly. So have you heard from him?"

I massaged my forehead. I wanted to go home, take a long shower, and get to bed early. "He sent me an e-mail last week, but it was from an Internet café."

She grimaced. "You should have called us immediately."

"It wouldn't have been any use. He wrote that he'd be gone by the time I got the e-mail."

Her voice rose. "You don't know that. We could have had a man there almost immediately. Followed the trail he left. Can you get me the e-mail? We still might be able to salvage something."

The e-mail's content had contained information on money deposited for me in a Philadelphia bank. They'd seize that, too. "It was personal—and private."

We fell silent as a lady walked by gripping a shopping bag with one arm and holding the hand of a little boy with the other.

When they were gone, Susan reached into her blue blazer and pulled out a sheaf of pictures. "I wanted to spare you this, but you must understand how dangerous the Bratva is. Concerns for privacy sometimes have to be put aside to ensure safety. If you and your husband are to be spared their brutality you need to level with us."

She passed me a photo. "You remember me telling you about the financial advisor they kidnapped? This is what happened to him."

I stared at the picture of a man tied to a chair. His face was so bruised and bloody it was almost unrecognizable. His chest was bare and crisscrossed with lacerations. It was Ed, one of Craig's colleagues Six of his fingers were bloody stubs, missing the fingernails. I pushed them away.

"Look at them all," Susan said roughly as she passed me the rest of the photos. "Notice the car battery on the floor. They love to use electricity in their torture."

I shuddered as I leafed through them. Then I suddenly jumped up, threw them back into her lap, and ran to the curb where I retched. When I returned, she passed me a couple of tissues.

"I'm sorry to have to do that. But they're sure to be looking for you. You need to be on the watch."

"I'll send you the e-mail." I cradled my head in my hands.

"If you're really worried about the e-mail being overly personal, you could delete the personal bits before you send it on. We mainly need the IP address." She passed me a card. "Here's our contact information. Put the number on speed dial and contact us at any time, day or night."

I drove back to the beach house in a state of terror imagining mafia gangsters behind every tree and in every car that passed me. Inside, I locked the door, checked all the windows, drew all the shades, and turned on a classical music station—loud. Then I booted my laptop and sent Susan Craig's e-mail with the banking instructions deleted.

After another microwave dinner that I gulped but didn't taste, I searched the TV for something to distract me. I finally gave up and went to bed. I must have lain awake for an hour, tossing and turning before I fell into a nightmare-filled sleep.

I awoke the next morning with a splitting headache. Several heavy applications of makeup repaired my ravaged face.

The week that began on such a cheery note after my sail with Remy, became dark and filled with dread. I tried to be cheerful with customers, but I was suspicious of everyone, even some of the regulars. I could hardly wait to leave every night, go home and lock myself in the beach house with all the shades drawn.

Noting my mood, Holly took me aside one day. "Ashlyn, you seem very worried. Is there anything I can do to help?'

"Sorry. I guess I haven't been very successful at putting on a cheerful face. I'll try harder."

"It might help to talk about it," she said. "I don't want to pry, but it's no secret about your husband's desertion, nor your car and credit cards being seized. We women have to stick together. Are you short of money? I could loan you some."

I felt my eyes moisten. "You're very sweet to ask, but this is not about money, except—." I looked down. "Well, I guess it is, in some way; not that I need money, but Craig—"

"Ashlyn, sweetheart, both Lottie Jane and I have grown to love you. But you don't have to tell me anymore if you don't want to. I'm just concerned."

I wiped a tear away with the sleeve of my blouse. "Did Lottie Jane tell you about those FBI agents?"

"Are they bothering you again?"

"One of them really scared me. The FBI warned me that people are searching for me—to find out if I know where Craig is. I don't." I paused. "Susan, the female agent, showed me some horrific pictures of what they do to people. I can't get the images out of my mind."

"That's terrible. Do you think the FBI's concerns are well founded?"

"Probably."

"Oh, Ashlyn, no wonder, you're worried." She reached over and touched my face. "Why don't you stay at my house for a while? I'm sure we can make room."

I gripped her hand tightly. "Holly, you're so thoughtful. But no, I'll be OK. I already feel better just telling you about it."

"Think about my offer."

"I will. There is one thing you can do."

"Anything."

"Let me know if anyone comes around asking for me. And keep an eye open for anyone who looks Russian."

"I will—and I'll be praying night and day for your protection; praying that God will send his angels to guard you. He does that, you know."

"I haven't thought of angels for ages. I guess I've been wallowing in my problems too much." I stood up. "Thanks, Holly."

She gave me a long hug.

# 25

Talking with Holly and knowing she was praying for me made everything seem more bearable.

A number of the regulars had begun sharing their problems and asking me for advice. There was nothing like hearing another's problems to take one's mind off one's own.

On Sunday afternoon, Valerie persuaded me to visit Fort Frederica. We had a happy time wandering the grounds, imagining what life must have been like in 1742 when the British defeated the Spanish. Valerie had prepared a sumptuous picnic that we enjoyed while scanning the marsh for cranes.

The next week, thoughts of Lottie Jane and her cancer also distracted me. After her surgery on Thursday morning, Holly and I took turns visiting her whenever we could. Lottie didn't look good. Her face seemed grey, drained of color.

But the thing that most lifted my spirits was a call from Tyler that I received one evening.

"Hi, Mom. I'm calling from Melbourne."

My heart skipped a beat. "Oh, Tyler, honey, it's so good to hear from you. I've been really worried."

"I've finally got Internet access again, so all your e-mails have caught up with me along with some from Tiff. What's going on? You and Dad? FBI? You're kidding me, right?"

"I'm afraid not, honey."

"But a divorce—the house seized? That's crazy."

"There's more. I haven't told you everything."

Tyler's voice rose. "What could be worse?"

"The FBI has been searching for your dad, but he's disappeared. It's been almost three months, now."

"I knew something was wrong. I just picked up a money order here in Melbourne with a note from Dad saying something about 'loving me whatever happens.' Wild."

I went on to tell him everything about the FBI, the seizure of our house, the freezing of our accounts, and the involvement of the Russian mafia. I waited to the end to mention the gory details surrounding Craig's filing for a divorce.

"I'm getting on the next plane..."

"No, Tyler, honey, don't do that! I couldn't sleep at night if you did. I know you want to be with me, but it's too dangerous. The Bratva, that's the Russian mafia, would grab you and use you to try and find your dad. They're looking for me, too, but the FBI have me under surveillance. Besides, they'll never find me on St. Simons Island. Tiffany is safe in her college dorm. And you're safe there."

"I'm coming. I can't let a bunch of scumbags threaten you and Tiff."

Tears began to roll down my cheeks. "Please, Tyler. Stay there. Please. For my sake. You have no idea how they torture their victims."

Tyler's voice softened. "Mom, I want to help you."

"You will, if you stay there. I'll send you e-mails every few days. Let you know when the coast is clear. And we'll talk more on the phone. I want to hear about your trekking in the outback. At least, promise to wait a couple of weeks."

"OK, if you say so."

 ৯৩৫

November began with a glorious sunrise promising a beautiful day ahead. Or was that a warning of storms to come? I forget the sailor's jingle. I'd have to ask Remy.

I was prepping veggies when Holly motioned to me.

"Two men just came in and ordered coffee and pie. Before I even had a chance to serve their order, they quizzed me about a woman they were looking for. They are looking for you."

"What kind of men?"

"Not police. Weird dudes, one skinny and one built like a prize fighter. Said they represented a relative looking for you to settle an estate. Even gave your name."

My stomach fluttered. "I don't have any relatives who are settling estates."

"I knew it was a blast of swamp gas. I told them I hadn't seen you."

I slumped against the wall. "Could they be another team of FBI agents?"

"Nah, looked foreign to me. From Eastern Europe or someplace like that. Could be Russian."

"What am I going to do?" I whispered as I pressed my hands to my chest trying to stifle the thumping of my heart.

"Head out the back door, now. Go home. I'll cover for you."

"But it's not fair to you. Besides, you shouldn't get mixed up in my troubles."

"Darlin', don't you worry. Just skedaddle. I'll call

Elise to come in early. The men haven't seen you and it's Friday. You have Saturday off and we're going to close Sunday because of Lottie Jane's surgery. Go home; lie low until Monday. If there's a problem, I'll call you."

I hugged her, slipped out the back door, and cycled home on back streets. Taking the cycle inside, I locked the door and pulled the blinds on all the windows. This was becoming a habit, living inside, afraid to go out except to work.

After trying again to get into the book I'd started, I gave it up and wandered around the beach house tidying up. But I was tired of letting a bunch of mobsters dictate my movements. I needed to work off some of my anguish. So I changed into shorts and a T-shirt, adding a ball cap and dark sunglasses.

I set off down the beach. A slight offshore breeze riffled the water. A flock of sandpipers fast-walked down the beach ahead of me.

It looked like the divorce was final, only waiting for my signature. Nothing could be done to restore our marriage. I needed to get on with my life.

A couple of dolphins gave me an excuse to stop and just stare at the ocean. But nothing could allay my anxiety. When an image of the pictures Susan had shown me popped into my mind, I fought the terror by racing down the beach until I was out of breath.

Martin, my lawyer, still seemed to be out of his element, unable to persuade the FBI to give me access to my accounts or the house. I'd have to stop being passive, confront the FBI and demand some action on my frozen accounts.

Back at the beach house, I sprawled onto a lounge chair on the veranda.

Suddenly, two men appeared around the side of the cottage. I jumped and started to get up. The shorter of the two motioned with his hand that I remain seated.

The man on the left looked like a scarecrow in a suit. His companion, at least six inches taller and fifty pounds heavier, wore khaki pants and a tank top, exposing tattoos on his chest and shoulders.

I gripped the arms of the chair. "What do you want?" I squeaked.

Scarecrow smiled. "Just a little help, Mrs. Forsyth. I'm Pavel, and my partner is Gorya. We're sorry to bother you like this, but we need your help."

"How do you know my name?"

"We're business associates of your husband. He spoke of you often."

I tried to still my raging pulse, loosening my grip on the arms of the chair. "How can I possibly help you?"

Pavel mounted the steps to the veranda and came to stand in front of me. "A simple thing, really. We represent a Russian conglomerate, one of your husband's financial investors."

I looked from one to the other. Russian? No!

Gorya, the big guy, smiled, exposing teeth that appeared to have stainless steel caps.

"All we want to know is his whereabouts," Pavel said.

I shook my head. "I have no idea where my husband is."

"He's your husband, and you have no idea?"

I tried to get up again, but Pavel motioned for me to remain seated. "Please."

I strained to make my voice sound normal. "Like I

said, I haven't a clue. The scumbag left with some bimbo."

Pavel frowned. "Left? When?"

"Almost two months ago," I said. "If you find him tell him to contact me."

Pavel gestured towards the cell phone clipped to my shorts. "Let me see your cell phone."

My voice rose. "That's private. You can't have it."

Gorya extracted a knife and fondled its edge. A drop of blood appeared on his middle finger. He gave no indication that he felt the cut.

Pavel's eyes narrowed as he held out his hand.

Without a word, I relinquished the phone.

Pavel scrolled through the phone's history and address list, made a few notes, and then dialed a number. He listened and then shut it off. "Your husband's number has been disconnected."

"Like I told you, I've no clue where he is."

Pavel smiled as he broke the phone into two pieces and tossed it into my lap. One of his eyes had a slightly milky cast, as if in the first stages of a cataract. "Think. Who were his customers? Did he have any outside of New York?"

I tried to think of an avenue of escape. Maybe I should scream. With most of the beach houses empty, were there neighbors near enough to hear?

Pavel's voice rose. "Mrs. Forsyth, tell me."

"He doesn't tell me about his business…sometimes, he'll fly to the Bahamas, or maybe Bermuda. Sometimes, he'll visit clients upstate."

"We know about Bermuda, and we know about upstate New York. Where else?"

Beads of perspiration formed on my forehead.

Terror coursed through me.

In an instant, Pavel's countenance darkened. He reached out, gripped my face, and squeezed.

Blood pounded in my neck and I tried to scream, but all that came out was a muffled squeak.

He let go and slapped me hard. "You scream and we'll cut your pretty face. Would you like that?"

My heart hammered as I touched my stinging cheek. The salty taste of blood filled my mouth.

"Do you understand?"

"Y…yes."

"Your husband owes us a great deal of money. Now, tell us about anyone he might visit, any place he might go."

"Ch…Chicago," I whimpered. "He had a client in Chicago, I think, and, and Boston, no, Baltimore." I couldn't tell them about his sister in Seattle, or his parents in Arizona.

"Go on."

I tried to slow my thudding heart. "Please, I really don't know. I have my own business and he doesn't bring his work home. His office…"

"Yes, we know about his office. He's closed it up. Let his secretary go. Did you know that?"

So that's why I couldn't reach her.

Pavel began to pace up and down the veranda. Finally, he came to stop. "You're coming with us. We'll see what you're worth to your husband. If nothing—well." He turned to Gorya. "Bring her to the car and put her in the trunk."

The thought of being thrown into the trunk of a car turned my insides to water. I jumped up, knocking the chair over. "No-o-o!" I screamed.

Gorya clamped one hand over my mouth and

squeezed my face until my eyes watered. He dragged me, kicking and scratching, off the porch. I grabbed onto a railing to try to wrench myself free, but Pavel punched my arm, leaving it numb.

My terror intensified as I realized that once they closed the trunk lid I would be as good as dead. They'd never find Craig. Even if they did, he'd probably be glad to be rid of me.

I bit into Gorya's arm. When he cursed and loosened his grip for a moment, I screamed again. In response, he punched me in the stomach and squeezed my nose until tears began to pour down my face.

"Quiet, or you'll be sorry!" Gorya dragged me to their car.

Pavel stood by the open trunk.

I caught the glimpse of a pickup truck approaching. I heard the screech of brakes and the slamming of a door.

# 26

Remy stood by the door of his truck pointing a shotgun. "Let her go!"

Pavel snarled. "Mister, this is none of your concern!"

"I'm making it my concern," Remy said.

I struggled to get free, but Gorya squeezed my nose again, leaving me gasping for breath and sobbing from the pain.

"Hey, scarecrow, keep your hands where I can see them," Remy said, addressing Pavel.

Gorya barked something in Russian and advanced towards the voice, holding me in front of him as a shield.

"Stop where you are, or you'll never walk again."

My captor continued towards Remy. A gun blast rang out and Gorya screamed as he collapsed, flinging me to one side.

Ears ringing, I shook my head and looked around.

Smoke drifted from the shotgun Remy held.

Gorya lay crumpled on the ground, cursing as he stared at the blood oozing from the tattered remnants of his left shoe.

Remy waved the shotgun back and forth. "Ashlyn, run to the truck!"

I struggled to my feet, ran towards his truck and pulled myself into the cab.

Through the open window I saw Pavel pointing his finger at Remy. "You don't know who you're messing with."

"I'd say the same to you," Remy said, waving the shotgun. "But I don't have time to chat. Now, very carefully take out the gun you have slung under your left arm and throw it in the bushes. Very slowly, muzzle down…that's right."

"You're dead!" Gorya yelled.

"Shut up!" Remy said. "Do you want the same treatment for your other foot?" He took a step towards him.

Without warning, he pumped a series of shots into the rear tires of their black sedan, barely missing both men. Then, still covering them with his gun, he backed up, and jumped in the truck. Aiming the shotgun at them with his left hand, he started the truck with his right and shouted, "If you come after her again, it won't be just me on your case. I'll set the Klan on you." With that, he hit the accelerator and roared away.

Before we'd driven a hundred yards, I heard a series of gunshots followed by a couple of metallic *thunks*. Hunched in the seat, I glanced over my shoulder.

Pavel stood in the middle of the road firing some kind of automatic pistol. The rear window cracked and I ducked down in the seat.

Remy swerved the truck from side to side, as he continued to accelerate down the road. "We've got to get you off the island," Remy said, as he raced down Ocean Boulevard.

Some of the drivers he passed on the narrow road were so riled they broke island protocol by blasting him with their horns.

At the traffic light in the village, he accelerated into oncoming traffic with his horn blaring and his hand out the window waving them onto the shoulder.

I shook as if in the grip of a high fever—not from his driving, but from the evil that radiated from the Russian kidnappers. Even my legs twitched.

Remy motioned towards a jacket on the seat between us. "Shock. You'd better put the jacket over your shoulders."

I shrugged into his jacket and pulled it tight around my neck as I tried to control the shudders. Although the jacket had a few mysterious stains and smelled a bit rank, I took it gratefully. "Th…thanks. I…I don't know where you came from…but if you hadn't c…come along, I'd…I'd be..."

"No problem," he said. "I thought I'd check to see if you'd like another sail in my skiff. Not luck, but providence, as my ma would say."

I turned to stare out the back window. Beyond a couple of drivers waving their fists at us, no one seemed to be in pursuit.

"You can relax. Those gang bangers aren't going anywhere."

"They could steal a car…come after me."

Remy set his captain's cap more firmly in place. "Don't worry, we've got a big head start."

I took a deep breath and tried to slow the thudding of my heart. Just being in Remy's truck had begun to dispel my terror. Dressed in a skimpy T-shirt and jogging shorts, I wasn't comfortable, however. I shrugged out of his jacket and draped it over my bare legs.

How many times had Remy come to my aid? He radiated strength. A couple days' stubble couldn't hide the lines on Remy's craggy, weathered face. Locks of sun-bleached blond hair peeked out from under his cap. His brow was furrowed in a frown.

With the Sea Island Golf Club behind us and the Causeway to the mainland ahead, he began to slow down. "Don't want any cops to pull us over...unless you'd feel safer in their hands. If you want, I can drive to the station."

My mind was in a state of confusion. In spite of their apparent surveillance, the FBI had not been able to protect me from the Bratva. I doubted if local police would do any better.

"I don't know what to do...but I don't think the local police will be able to protect me from those guys."

"We've got to find you some safe place...fast." Remy fell silent as he scratched the stubble on his chin. He glanced in my direction. "Who were those guys, anyway?"

"Not sure. Said they were from a Russian investment firm. The FBI talked about the Bratva. I understand it's a name for the Russian mafia."

"What could they want with you? Not that it's any of my business."

I fingered the bruises I knew were forming on my face. "I guess you deserve some kind of explanation, although I'm not quite sure myself. I do know it has something to do with money my husband owes them. They wanted to use me to get to him."

The sound of approaching sirens interrupted my explanation. Two patrol cars headed for the island, roared by us on the causeway; lights pulsing, sirens wailing.

Remy watched them in the rearview mirror. "Someone must have called it in."

"The shots?"

"Yeah. The sight of that black sedan with shot-out

rear wheels is going to make the cops almighty curious. Sure you don't want to just go to the nearest station?"

I slumped in the seat. After a long pause, I said, "Remy, I don't think you should get involved in this. Just…just drop me off at the bus station in Brunswick."

"Bus station? I doubt if you have much money on you. How will you buy a ticket? Where will you go?"

"I've got a few bucks." I ran a hand through my hair. "Remy, why are you doing this?

"I have a knight-in-blue jeans complex, remember? Seein' as how you're from the New York area you may not be used to neighbors jumping in to help each other." His eyes twinkled. "But that's what we do down here. Of course, it's not every day I get to rescue damsels in distress."

"Do modern knights carry shotguns?"

"What can I say? Us rednecks like our guns." Laugh lines radiated from his eyes. "Besides, with all the trouble you've had, you deserve a break, and I kind of like you."

To cover my confusion, I smiled. "I'm grateful, very grateful. Where you're concerned, I can believe the age of chivalry has returned."

"Just doing what comes naturally. I've read about those attacks on the subway when no one comes to the aid of the victim. Unbelievable. When someone is attacked down here, especially a woman, any man worth his salt won't stand by without doing something. It's not fitting."

"Fortunate for me." I paused, not sure how to ask, except outright. "Are you really in the Klan?"

"Nah. Just bluffing. All I could think of on the spot."

I thought about what to do. My clothes and laptop were all back at the beach house. So was my wallet with its useless credit cards and the cache of money. Fortunately, I had twenty or thirty dollars in my hip pack. My cell phone was busted. If I could borrow one, I could call Julie of Tiffany and they could wire me money. Or I could sneak back, get Lemonade, and drive north.

Remy broke into my thoughts. "When we get you to a safe place, you can call your husband. Surely, even though you're separated, he'll help you."

"My husband...yeah...I'm afraid that's not an option." Tears began to leak from my eyes. "He's put through divorce papers—taken off with another woman—disappeared. I can't reach him. Changed his cell phone."

"I knew you were separated, but not the rest."

I poured out more of the sordid story. What was there about this man that made me feel safe enough to allow my anguish to spill over?

Remy listened without comment. "I hate to say it, Ashlyn, but it sounds like he's a nasty piece of work. Maybe you're better off without him."

"I can't understand what happened," I said. "It's unlike him. He's always been a good father—good husband. Oh, our marriage..." I stopped in mid-sentence.

"Were those gang-bangers after your husband, then?"

"Yes. They must have trapped him, somehow. I can't see him knowingly investing money for criminals."

"So, no help from your husband. Parents?"

"Both passed away," I said.

"Friend in the area?"

"Holly at the café would help, but they'd suspect her immediately."

"Let's get you safe first, and then we'll think about options." Remy flipped open a pouch on his belt, took out his cell phone, and hit a speed dial number. Putting it to his ear, he waited. After a lengthy interval he said, "Gaston, hightail it to *The Esperance*. Get her ready to go in five minutes...no, I'm not crazy...I know all about the weather...just do it! And we'll have a passenger."

# 27

Remy left the causeway behind and drove through a maze of streets in Brunswick until the river came into view. Along a branch of the South Brunswick River, a dozen or so shrimp boats were tied up to pilings, which supported a weathered stretch of plank docks. Remy drove the truck behind an old shed and stopped. "OK, let's go."

"Me? You're thinking of me going with you on your boat?"

"Ashlyn, it's all I could think of on the spur of the moment."

"But..."

"I can't just let you off on the street! Besides, those gang bangers will never think of looking for you on a shrimp boat. And we're due to sail, anyway. We need to be in place when the sun sets."

I looked down at my bare arms and legs. "I can't. I just can't. I'm grateful for your rescue. I'm sure you saved my life. But..."

"You said you enjoyed sailing."

"It's not that," I said, as I pondered the problem of having no clothes to change into, no cosmetics. It was silly to be worried about appearance after trauma, but I was. And I would be endangering Remy.

"You're worried about clothes. That's a bit of a problem, you being so slim and all. But I'm sure we can find you some jeans and a shirt. We always have changes of clothing onboard. We get soaked a lot."

With my hand on the door handle, I hesitated. Back on the island somewhere, two members of the Russian mafia would be relentless in their search for me. When they found me, I could expect nothing but torture and death. And I had no information to give them. I shivered, as I thought of their rough treatment. I touched my swollen cheek and nose, and then nodded. "OK."

*Had he really called me slim?*

He gestured towards *The Esperance*, where Gaston and Ches stood waving. "There she is. Let's get on board."

About 40 feet long, *The Esperance* was painted white and grey with burgundy trim. A bewildering array of lines and nets hung from two towering booms and a shorter, stubby boom angled abaft. A white, one story cabin forward of the boat's centerline took up maybe a third of the deck space. On its roof perched a rubber dingy and electronic gear of some kind. The rumble of a diesel engine told me she was already under power.

Remy climbed aboard, and then reached down to help me over the gunwales.

Gaston nodded to me, but I noticed him raising his eyebrows as he turned towards Remy.

Remy barked, "Get ready to cast off. I'll explain later."

Ches ran towards the bow and Gaston went to the stern to throw off the dock lines.

Remy motioned me to follow him into the wheelhouse, which was quite spacious, but crammed with lockers. Windows all the way around let in abundant light. On the starboard side, he pointed to a padded bench built over a couple of the lockers. "Have a seat while we get underway, and then I'll see what we can find for you to wear."

He strode over to the wheel, settled into a swivel captain's chair, and began flipping switches and checking gauges. After a few minutes, he waved out the window to Gaston.

The timbre of the engine increased as the ship eased away from the dock into the current of the South Brunswick River. When he turned downriver, the engine took on a deep rumble, and the deck tilted slightly as *The Esperance* picked up speed. An occasional burst of spray hit the windows.

Gaston came into the cabin, stuck his hands in the pockets of his worn jeans and slouched against the port side of the boat. He avoided looking at me.

Ches, the younger of Remy's hands, followed Gaston in, collapsed on a seat opposite me, and ran both hands through his black hair in an attempt to tame it. "Good to have you aboard, Ashlyn."

"Thanks, Ches. I'm sorry to impose on you like this."

"Hey," he said. "No problemo."

Remy motioned for Gaston to join him, and then pointed to the captain's chair. "Take her out."

With Gaston in control, Remy stood up. "Ya'll are wondering why Ms. Ashlyn is aboard. Well, if she wasn't she'd be stuffed in the trunk of a car driven by a couple of gang bangers."

Gaston glanced over his shoulder with his mouth open. "What?"

"Yeah," Remy said. "I liberated her from a couple of nasty characters. No telling what they would have done to her."

Ches frowned. "But why? You're not..."

Thankful for Remy's leather jacket, I wrapped it more firmly over my legs. "No, Ches, I'm not a prostitute. Nor am I involved with drugs. I…"

A blush spread over Ches's face accentuating a couple of his pimples. "I didn't mean—I'm sorry."

"Get that out of your mind," Remy said. "You've seen Ms. Ashlyn at work in the café and you can tell the kind of woman she is. You were there when her car was seized, so you know she's going through a bad patch. The nature of Ms. Ashlyn's troubles are none of our business, except to offer her help."

"That's OK, Remy," I said. "They have a right to know something." I paused. "My ex-husband is being investigated by the FBI. And somehow, he's got involved with the Russian mafia. I don't understand what's happened myself." I looked around at the three men. "If your captain hadn't come by, I'd probably be…well, it'd be horrible. I'm sorry about this, but…grateful. And please call me Ashlyn."

Gaston cleared his throat. "Ms.…uh, Ashlyn, we have no truck with the FBI or any kind of law enforcement, for that matter. I, for one, am happy to do anything I can to help you, but isn't there someplace safer than on a shrimp boat? There's a bad blow coming."

Remy fingered the stubble on his chin. "The pigs who grabbed Ashlyn are vicious." He pointed towards me. "See what they did to her face? If I know anything about the Russian mafia, they have a long reach. So that makes us targets. You can imagine what they do to people who get in their way. So, let me put it to you this way. If you're not comfortable about getting involved by having Ashlyn onboard, we can put in to the Jekyll Island pier and I'll get off with her. Gaston, you and Ches can take over, drag for shrimp and I'll meet you back in Brunswick."

Ches jumped up. "Hey, I'm in."

Gaston ran a hand over his bald head. "Captain, it's hard enough handling the work with three men, let alone two. I was just concerned about her comfort. This is no yacht."

"I don't expect comfort," I said. "But there could be another solution. You could let me off on Jekyll Island. They'd never think of looking for me there."

Remy shook his head. "Where would you stay? No, it wouldn't work. Besides we're just passing the island now." He looked from Gaston to Ches. "I take it you agree?" Without waiting for a verbal answer, he strode over to one of the lockers, leaned down and began rummaging through a pile of clothes. Picking out a pair of jeans and a shirt, he motioned for me to follow him below.

We descended a steep set of stairs where he pointed out the head, the galley, and a couple of bunks bolted to the starboard and port sides of the vessel.

"You take that berth. We'll rig up a blanket later to give you some privacy. About Gaston, don't pay him no mind. He's superstitious, but he'll get over it."

"Superstitious?"

"He's an old salt. Has the notion that having a woman on a fishing boat brings bad luck. Crazy, really, since boats are considered female and often are named after women. Most used to have female figureheads. Don't you worry, he's got a warm heart."

"Is there no other alternative? No other place you could let me off?"

"No. You're stuck with us for a couple of days."

"I'm grateful, and I won't get in your way." I

shook my head. "If you hadn't come when you did…"

He paused at the base of the steps and looked back. "Forget it." He traced a knot on the wooden paneling. "Have you ever been on a trawler before?"

"No."

"This will be a lot harder on you than us. You may stink of fish for days. I take it you don't get seasick?"

"Never have."

"Well, if you feel like you're going to be sick, don't use the head. Come up top and throw up over the side."

I nodded.

"I'll leave you to change, then. No one will come down until we get to our station."

I went into the head. The face that stared back from the scratched mirror shocked me. The brown eyes were red-rimmed; the mole high up on the left cheek prominent, the brown hair mousy, and the bruises on my face and nose had begun to darken. I had no makeup to disguise the damage. I washed my face gingerly and tried to comb my hair with my fingers before donning the heavy work shirt and faded blue jeans Remy had left. Both were clean, but well worn. I felt strange putting them on, sort of embarrassed. Were they Remy's?

The shirt felt like a tent and the pants were many sizes too big for me. I could roll up the shirtsleeves and the pant legs, but the waist was another matter. I'd have to find something to use as a belt. I left the head and wandered around the cabin, but found nothing that would suffice.

# 28

Gripping the faded jeans, I climbed the stairs and peered into the cabin.

Remy was back in his captain's chair.

Ches had his head buried in a magazine.

Gaston was out on deck.

The radio squawked something unintelligible.

I cleared my throat.

Ches grinned, "Hey, we've got another crew member."

Remy smiled and said, "You look a lot better than any sailor I've ever seen in jeans. Welcome to the crew."

"I've got a problem," I said. "Do you have any kind of a belt that I can use to hold these up?"

"We'll have to improvise. Ches, take the wheel."

Ches jumped up and ran to take the wheel.

Remy strode over to a locker where he took out a coil of line. Extracting a knife from a sheath I hadn't noticed, he squinted at me, unrolled a length, and severed it with one slice. "Here try this."

"Thanks, that should work." I threaded the rope through the belt loops, pulled it tight, and knotted it. My jogging shoes were substantial enough to grip the deck, which had begun to pitch and yaw as the trawler left the shelter of the barrier islands behind, and headed into the open ocean.

"Should serve, until we can get you something better. We've got a few hours before we get to our shrimping ground, so why don't you get some rest. You may have some delayed shock. If you don't, I'll be surprised."

I crawled into the port bunk and tried to let the motion of the ship ease me into sleep. Finally, I gave up and lay there staring at the ceiling. What if Remy had not come by? I pulled the blanket tighter as a spasm of shudders shook me. A feeling of utter desolation crept over me. I fought against giving voice to wails of fear and grief.

*I have nothing left. No husband, no friends, no career, no church—nothing. The home I'd spent so much time decorating, the garden I'd planted, gone, all gone. My credit cards, the money I'd been saving, gone. What have I done to deserve this?*

I wallowed in self-pity for a long time. It was as if I derived some perverse sense of gratification from stoking the fires of my misery. The voice of my mother broke in on my melancholy.

*Count your blessings. There's always someone worse off than you.*

*Yeah, mom, sure. But right now, I can't think of anyone.* I wiped my tears on the rough blanket. *Ashlyn, you're forgetting Tiffany and Tyler. And what about Remy, who has been so wonderful? And Lottie Jane, at the café? And there's Valerie. And Holly and...*

A slowing in the rhythm of the engine woke me. On the deck I could hear a flurry of activity and yelling back and forth, and then nothing but the throbbing of the engine and the sound of the sea hissing beneath the boat. I climbed the stairs.

On the aft deck, both Ches and Gaston were busy clipping nets to cables. Off the starboard bow the ocean reflected a fiery sunset slashed with streamers of crimson fading into fuchsia and amber.

Remy was talking into the radio, apparently describing his position. I caught the word, Cumberland. Turning to me, he said, "Feel better?"

"Some," I answered, joining him. "Where are we?"

"Off the Altamaha estuary, about ten miles north of Sea Island."

"Oh, I thought I heard you say Cumberland Island."

He grinned. "Disinformation. We don't want any more shrimpers horning in on what promises to be a good catch." He gestured left and right. "Already four or five boats here."

Silhouetted by the setting sun I caught sight of two shrimpers to starboard and three off the port side. A mile or two separated each boat.

"The try net promises a good catch, so we're readying the main nets for a run."

"Gorgeous sunset."

Remy grimaced. "Yeah, there's that. Going to be a blow. We'll probably have to cut short our run."

"What can I do? I think it would help if I could do something."

"Why don't you rustle us up some coffee in the galley? It's going to be a long night. And if you can fry some of that sausage, so much the better. There's biscuits, too. Just heat them up in the pan. We're not fussy."

જ્જ

Ches held up his mug. "Much better coffee than Gaston makes. His is like crankcase oil!"

Gaston swatted him on the side of the head. "You

couldn't tell good coffee from bad. Although, I've got to compliment Ms. Ashlyn on her cookin'. The sausage is not burnt like yours, an' the biscuits is warm."

We were sitting around in the cabin, drinking coffee and eating. It had taken me a couple of tries to figure out the temperamental stove. It made me feel better just to be doing something.

The last sliver of golden sunlight was fading when Remy stood. "OK, let's get to it."

Powerful lights illuminated the aft deck as I seated myself on a bench to watch the crew spring into action. The great sock-shaped nets splashed into the sea and the winches whined as they let off hundreds of feet of steel cable. Out of nowhere, a screaming flock of seabirds began to wheel and dive behind the ship.

Remy gave me a running commentary as I watched. "The narrower part of the nets have weights called doors that drag them down towards the bottom. The nets themselves spread out like wings behind the boat, oh, 200 feet or so down. These wings have lead weights at the bottom and floats at the top to spread the net vertically through the sea so they catch and drag everything towards the tail bag. Ahead of it, we have ticklers that encourage the shrimp settled on the bottom to leap up and get caught in the net. We've got to keep just the right forward motion or the net sucks up mud from the bottom. Or if we go too fast the net doesn't get close enough to the bottom to catch the shrimp."

"It must be quite a skill to learn all this."

"Oh yeah. Almost got to be born with it. I went out with my daddy when I was seven or eight."

"What about imported, farmed shrimp? Isn't that hurting you?"

"That and the environmentalists. They value turtles over fishermen. But you're right about imported shrimp, they've decimated the industry. Some ports have three quarters of their boats rusting at anchor. But the white shrimp off Georgia and the Carolinas are the sweetest of all. Still a big demand for them up and down the coast."

After trawling for about an hour, Remy slowed the boat while Ches and Gaston threw the winches into gear. In a few moments, hundreds of feet of cable were wound around the winch drums, and the otter doors rose from the sea.

Remy hit the throttle and *The Esperance* raced ahead, rinsing the sand and mud out of the catch, and pushing it to the end of the net.

Gaston grabbed a line and hauled the end of one of the two nets, called the tail bag, onto the deck.

Ches pulled on another line and the bloated bag disgorged a pile of marine life.

My mouth fell open as I watched the wiggling starfish, scuttling crabs, and flopping fish. A stingray beat its wings in an attempt to escape to the sea. Throughout the mass, hundreds of fiery, orange eyes glowed in the overhead lights.

"Looks like a good haul," Remy said. "See all those eyes. They're shrimp. And we've got a flounder or two, plus a few mackerel we can sell. But we got a lot of trash, too."

Ches and Gaston began throwing the inedible sea life through the scuppers back into the sea, where they were snatched up by diving seagulls or drifted to the ocean floor. The shrimp and saleable fish they scooped into baskets where they were cooled with ice, and then stored in the hold. They repeated the whole process with the second net.

Again and again throughout that memorable night the nets went back into the sea, were towed, lifted, and emptied of their burden of sea creatures.

I kept the coffee coming and even took a turn at filling baskets with the spiky shrimp.

As the night wore on the spirits of the crew became more and more ebullient. Instead of being a curse, Gaston said my presence on the boat was ensuring an unusual bounty of shrimp that would earn them hefty bonuses.

"It's God, not me," I said to him.

As the hours ticked away the seas became rougher and the stars disappeared. Several of the other shrimp boats had hauled up their nets and made for shore.

Creases lined Remy's forehead as he listened to weather reports indicating an approaching front.

Around three in the morning, Ches and Gaston came into the wheelhouse after clearing the deck of another haul.

Gaston took a handkerchief from his pocket and wiped the moisture off his bald head. "Best catch we've had in years. One more run, Cap'n?"

Remy shook his head as he pointed off to the starboard quarter. "Secure the nets. Jump to it. We're going to have to run for it. Just hope and pray that we find shelter before that hits us."

# 29

I looked off to the south-east where forks of lightning lit up a bank of ominous clouds.

Gaston and Ches ran back outside and began to secure the nets.

"Ashlyn," Remy said. "Can you go below and make sure the stove is off? Put anything that is loose in the lockers. See that they're well secured. We're in for some rough weather."

I could feel the motion of the boat begin to subtly change as I went below. We had gone in a wide arc, at one point the deck sloped to the port before righting itself. The vibration increased as the diesel engine took on a throatier rumble. The sound of water against the hull increased in pitch. By the time I'd finished, I was feeling queasy.

Remy had turned the ship around and was beating towards a harbor.

On the aft deck, Ches and Gaston were methodically unfastening the nets from the outrigger lines, or whatever they were called, and hoisting them out of the water. Their progress seemed agonizingly slow. Before they were half-finished, gusts of rain began to pelt the boat, drenching them both. They came in, donned oilskins and returned to their task with renewed urgency.

I went to stand near Remy, bracing myself as the action of the rising sea caused the ship to pitch and yaw.

The glow of the radar scope illuminated the lines on Remy's weathered face as he glanced over his shoulder at the progress of his two crew members.

Every few minutes there were squawks from the wireless as other ships radioed their positions and, in some fisherman's code, described conditions.

Remy answered them calmly, giving his co-ordinates.

"Is it going to be bad?" I said.

"Bad enough. Don't you wish you'd stayed on land?"

"No way. In spite of everything, I feel better than I have in weeks…I love the ocean. Mind you, it's been a long night, but I'm glad to be beyond the reach of those men."

He rubbed his eyes, which were red with fatigue. "Ever been in a storm at sea?"

"No."

"Well, you'll soon be able to cross that off your bucket list…that is, if we make it to port."

"You're kidding, right?"

"I hope I'm kidding, that it's just a squall that will blow itself out, but I have a feeling that it's going to be bad. We'll try and make it to shelter in the lee of one of the islands before the worst of it hits. These shrimp boats are not meant for heavy seas. I should have headed for port an hour ago. It's the fisherman's curse."

"Fisherman's curse—having me on board?"

"No, not that. We've had the most successful shrimping run I can remember. It's the lure of white gold. Shrimpers, like all fishermen, think that if they make one more run, let down their nets one more time they'll hit the big time. Make a ton of money. So we take chances with weather. It's a temptation as old as Adam. I should know better."

Just as conversation became impossible, a squall line hit us.

Remy guided the ship through a sea that was becoming increasingly turbulent.

The noise was deafening: rain pelting the roof of the wheelhouse in torrents, the squeak of the ineffectual wipers, the howl of the wind, the roar of the engine, the crash of waves on the stern of the ship.

Gaston and Ches were still wrestling to secure all the nets and lines. Ten minutes later, they were clinging to the gunwales while a huge wave swamped the rear deck. When the wind eased slightly, they flung open the door to the wheelhouse, and plunged inside, letting in buckets of water.

I had to bite my lip to keep from throwing up all over the deck.

Ches doffed his oilskin, adding to the wash of water on the deck. "Secured, Cap'n." His voice had taken on a higher pitch. He ran hands through his hair, now no longer spikey, but plastered to his head.

Gaston swore as he discarded his oilskin and mopped his face with a stained bandana. Then, seeing me, he frowned. "Sorry ma'am."

"I've heard worse," I said.

"I don't guess you've seen worse, though," he said. "I've got a bad feelin' about this."

Ches's voice squeaked. "Bad feelin'? You've always got a bad feeling."

Gaston came forward to stand on the other side of Remy. "How're we doin' cap'n? How far to shelter?"

"Too far," Remy said. "We're going to have to ride it out until the worst is over."

Gaston joined Ches on a bench bolted to the floor.

During a brief lull in the gale, Remy shouted for everyone to brace themselves.

I crab-walked to a bench opposite Gaston and Ches.

Remy turned broadside to the sea.

I gripped the bench with one hand and the bulkhead with another as the boat began to pitch wildly. For a moment I thought the towering booms were going to dip below the surface and cause the ship to capsize, but in a heartbeat the valiant *Esperance* righted itself and turned its bow into the teeth of the gale. Not to be thwarted, the wind, like some primeval beast, began to shriek in earnest.

Horizontal torrents of rain lashed the cabin. Above the wailing of the wind, I could hear a pinging as the guy wires that held the booms erect vibrated. I expected them to crash through the roof at any moment.

Occasional flashes of lightning lit up the sky, giving glimpses of the wild sea.

I watched, mesmerized, as the ship plunged down the back of one wave after another. Would the ship make it up the other side or bury itself in the watery cliff and flounder? What if the wind on the booms blew us over? No one would ever find us. I prayed, thankful to be in God's hands and not enduring what Pavel and Gorya had intended.

Time ceased to matter. There was a sudden shriek of rending metal followed by a loud ping as something hit one of the guywires.

Ches shouted above the roar of the storm, "Just lost the life-raft, cap'n. It bounced off the starboard gunwale and is gone."

Remy tapped the flickering radar scope a couple of times. "It must have hit the radar antenna when it blew off. Gaston, you and Ches check the guywires. Make sure it hasn't done any more damage."

Gaston and Ches donned lifejackets and oilskins before slipping out into the maelstrom where they tethered themselves to a secure line.

"Isn't that dangerous?" I cried. "Them going out there?"

Remy set his cap more firmly on his head. "Has to be done. They know to take precautions. Besides, they're a bit sheltered in the lee of the cabin."

# 30

Gaston and Ches came back inside the cabin. Gaston's bald head glistened in the dim light.

"Guywires look OK," Gaston said. "One of the nets is shredding, but we'll have to wait to see how badly."

For the remainder of the night, time was measured in the intervals between wave crests and valleys. Every time we dived into a valley I was sure we'd never make it up the other side—but we did. I gripped a stanchion and clutched the plastic bag Remy had given me in case my determination proved too weak to stave off a spasm of retching. My arms ached and my stomach heaved.

Finally, I sensed a diminishing of the wind and rain, an easing of wave action. A faint grey light spread across the eastern horizon.

When the wind lessened even further, Remy took the ship in a wide curve and steered shoreward. An hour later, we left the open sea and gained the relative shelter of some island.

I went below, collapsed on a bunk, and tried to snatch some sleep. I woke to the sounds of activity on the deck. I washed my face and ran fingers through tangled hair. I found a lipstick in the pocket of my hip pack and that lent a little color to my chapped and swollen lips. I still looked a mess, but it would have to do.

Remy and his crew were manhandling crates of

shrimp from the aft hold to the dock, where a couple of other men loaded them on a truck.

Remy yelled from the top of the stairs. "Ms. Ashlyn, you awake?"

"Sure am."

"If you're ready to go, I'm going to take you to my mother's house. You'll be safe there."

In spite of the storm, I'd felt safe on Remy's boat, but I couldn't presume any longer on his kindness.

Could Gaston or Remy fetch my car? No, the Bratva would be watching the beach house.

I could call Tiffany to come and pick me up.

Remy would let me use his cell phone.

Holly would help me. But that would be the first place the Bratva would look. I couldn't endanger her. I had no clothes to wear and only a few dollars in my hip pack.

Ches, who had been hosing down the deck, paused as I jumped down to the dock. "Ms. Ashlyn, you brought us luck! Keep safe."

"Not me, God."

Gaston nodded his head in acknowledgement.

I waved at them and joined Remy in his truck.

Remy left the docks behind and headed through Brunswick.

"Did the storm damage your boat much?" I said.

"Ruined a good net and the radar needs repairs, but the catch of shrimp we got will offset any costs." He smiled in my direction. "So much for Gaston's superstitions. Best catch I can remember."

"Great. Remy, I know we've talked about this before and I'm eternally grateful for your help, but if you drop me at the bus station, I'm sure I'll be OK."

"Won't do."

"I've got a few dollars."

"But not enough to get anywhere. And no clothes. No cell phone." He shook his head. "I know you don't like to be beholden…but think of it as me beholden to you for such a good catch of shrimp. Besides, I've already called Holly to have someone pick up your things from the beach house and bring them to my mother's." He smiled at me again. "Called my mother, too. She's powerful curious to meet you. And she can fix you up in some duds."

"I don't know what to say, except thank you for all you've done."

"No need to say anything. Don't worry about my mom. She loves company. Working as I do, I don't get to visit her as much as she'd like. She's real lonely since Pop died."

Remy beeped the horn as he came to a stop before a weathered clapboard bungalow beneath towering live oaks and pines.

I caught a glimpse of water through the beards of Spanish moss that hung from the oaks. The door opened and a white-haired woman came down the flagstone path towards us.

Remy got out of the truck to greet his mother while I stayed seated, uncomfortable about the whole situation.

She limped slightly as she came forward. The pair of sensible, brown brogues on her feet might have classified her as old-fashioned if it hadn't been for stylish jeans and a blue T-shirt emblazoned with a picture of a shrimp boat at sea. Her snowy-white hair was cut in a pageboy style. Although she must be in her seventies, the care with which she had coifed her hair and applied makeup marked her as a classic southern lady.

"Land sakes, son, it's good to see you," she said, as she embraced Remy. "I was worried about you in that storm. Is the boat OK?"

"A little damage," Remy said, "but nothing we can't fix easy enough. And we netted the best catch of shrimp I can ever remember."

Remy's mother peered at me over her son's shoulder. "Is this the gal you were mentioning? Are you finally dating again?"

Remy snorted. "Ma, don't you start that again. No, this is Ashlyn." He beckoned me to come forward.

Hitching up my borrowed pants, I got out of the truck and walked towards them.

"Ashlyn, this is my mother, Elizabeth."

"Betty," she said. "Call me Betty."

"I'm real sorry for this intrusion ma'am."

Placing both hands on my shoulders, she studied the bruises on my face, studiously avoiding mention of the pants that were a dozen sizes too big for me. "You poor child. What happened to you?"

"A couple of men tried to kidnap her," Remy said.

"Two men started to carry me off...if your son hadn't come along... rescued me...taken me to his ship...."

"Rem, what happened?"

Remy shrugged his shoulders as if this kind of thing happened every day. "Long story. Can we go inside?"

"Of course. Come along." She looked at the truck. "Rem, what'd you tangle with? That don't look like 'gator bites."

"Russian riffraff. Really messed up my truck."

"Russian!"

"Looks like we were right lucky," he said.

She snorted. "Lucky? That's not luck. That's providence. The good Lord has been watching over you. Has been ever since you were a boy. But this is stretching his care a mite far. Well, don't just stand there. Come in. Come in."

A mossy flagstone path meandered past a profusion of azalea, rhododendron, and oleander bushes towards the bungalow.

We climbed the steps to the encircling veranda and Remy held open the screen door for us. The door led into a spacious living room evocative of the sea. The replica of a shrimp boat on the mantle over the brick fireplace dominated one wall, a stuffed tarpon on another, and a series of sepia pictures of boats and marine life on a third wall. The woodwork gleamed and I caught the scent of lemon furniture polish.

His mother motioned me towards an armchair. "I'll bring us some tea, and then you can tell us your story."

Remy followed his mother.

I heard murmured conversation and the sound of glasses clinking. On two crowded end tables beneath Tiffany lamps stood a profusion of framed photographs: a sea captain in a very formal pose, the yellowed picture of a bride and groom, several poses of Remy playing football, one of Remy and a young woman, a family group of two parents with a boy and a girl, plus five or six pictures of children.

Who was the woman with Remy? His wife or his sister?

Betty entered with a tray holding three glasses of iced tea and a plate of cookies. "Child, you must be cold." She put the tray on a coffee table and picked up an afghan. "Here throw this over you."

"Thank you. I'm sure you're wondering about my getup. On Friday, I'd just been for a jog when two men confronted me. I didn't have time to change from shorts and a T-shirt. Remy kindly loaned the clothes." I pressed my lips together to keep my emotions in check.

Remy took up the story.

I pulled the afghan up, leaned back, and pondered the enigma that was Remy. A tough man's man with stubble on his face and a missing finger, who kept coming to my aid. In appearance, a beer-drinking brawler. In action, thoughtful and sensitive. What I knew about him seemed to belie the tough-guy persona, or...was he laying the groundwork for a roll in the hay? No, he wouldn't bring me to his mother's if that was his aim. Still, he seemed too good to be true. And why did his nearness create the strange flutter in my stomach?

I smothered those thoughts and picked up a cookie. When I tuned back into the conversation, Remy was saying, "...and they were about to stuff her in the trunk."

"I'm pretty sure they were Russian mafia," I said.

"But why were they after you?" Betty frowned.

"She doesn't look like a criminal, does she?" Laugh lines radiated from Remy's blue eyes, but the hint of a smile faded. "Sorry, this is hardly a time for humor."

"I could use a little humor." I shivered. "They were looking for my husband. They wanted to use me as a hostage." Part way through the story, I stopped to stare at what was left of a second cookie. "These are amazing. Who makes these?"

"Best cookies in Georgia, made in Ma's kitchen.

Chocolate chip-pecan delights."

I finished the cookie, took a long sip of tea and continued.

Betty's eyes were moist. "You poor soul. Well, you just make yourself at home. We've got a spare bedroom that is seldom, if ever, used."

Remy stood up. "You'll be safe here, but don't go into town until we see if those goons give up looking for you. I have to get back to the boat, but I'll check back tomorrow. And don't worry about your stuff at the beach house. Holly will see to it."

"Won't they be watching the place?"

"Holly will be careful. Don't you worry."

I stood up, feeling awkward, as if I should at least hug him, but wanting to kiss him. I did neither. "Thank you, Remy. I'm very grateful. And I enjoyed learning about shrimping, in spite of the storm. I'm just sorry you and your mom got involved in my problems."

"Hey, that's what problems are for—to be shared."

I watched him leave, my eyes moist, my mind struggling with conflicting emotions.

# 31

Betty took my hand and led me to her bedroom. "Sit there while I get some aloe for those bruises on your face." She broke off a fat spike from a plant on her windowsill. Her face crinkled into a smile as she tilted my chin up. She applied the gooey juice to my bruises. "Worried? Thinking I must be a quack applying some voodoo juice?"

"I just never saw anyone use the real stuff...always thought it was just another ingredient in lotion and the like."

"Nothing like fresh aloe to soothe bruises and heal cuts. I always keep a plant or two. Always have, what with the men-folk getting banged up so much."

"Is your husband a fisherman, too?"

"Was, God rest his soul. Lost in the storm of '03."

"I'm sorry."

"Don't be. He's harmonizin' with the heavenly choir...something he couldn't do down here."

"I guess fishermen deal with storms a lot."

"They do. I was worried about Remy out in that gale. Should-a known better. Was it bad?"

"I've never seen anything like it. I love the sea and never get seasick, but..."

"Remy shouldn't have gone out with that kind of a weather report. The shrimp are not worth it."

"Do you think he did it to get me away from port? His crewman, Gaston, feels women on a ship bring bad luck."

"Gaston! Who does he think gave him birth? He believes black cats and blackbirds and black shirts bring bad luck. Phah. No, I'm sure Remy was sincere in keeping you safe, but I'd have to say, the lure of the shrimp is more powerful than anything. The main thing is, you're safe…and *The Esperance* is in port."

I touched my face. It felt cool and a bit sticky.

"Just let the skin absorb the aloe. I'll give you some lotion later. A day or two, and no one will notice the bruises. Now, you need some clothes and stuff like that. What size are you?"

"Twelve. But…"

After rooting in her closet, Betty backed out with an armload of clothes. "Here, try these jeans on. They're brand new. I must have bought them a decade ago when I started one of those crazy diets. And here's a couple of blouses, T-shirts, and such like. We'll soon get you fixed up."

"Mrs. Jeandeau—uh, Betty—you're very kind. I'll just borrow them for today."

"Phah. They're yours. My daughter keeps sending me stuff from them high-end shops in Atlanta. Stuff that would have hardly fit me ten years ago." She sighed. "Wish she'd visit more; send fewer gifts."

I felt a twinge of regret. Her wish sounded like something my mom would have said.

"You can stay in here as long you want. I keep the bed made up in case Yvette visits. She's my daughter. Make yourself at home and try on those clothes. I'll fix some lunch."

I sat down on the bed. The escape, and then the storm, had me frazzled. Tears began to course down my cheeks. Where would this end? I worried about Tiffany and Tyler. *Keep safe sweethearts. Don't do*

*anything foolish and fly here looking for me. Lord, keep both
of them safe.*

Betty tapped on the door. "Ashlyn, are you OK?"

"Sure, no problem."

"When you're ready we'll have a bite of lunch on
the back porch."

"OK, be right there."

I changed into the jeans—they fit perfectly—and
slipped a fresh T-shirt over my sports bra. I'd have to
wash it and my underwear when I got a chance. In the
bathroom, I tried to smooth my hair. I joined Betty on
the screened-in back porch where she had laid out a
plate of pimento-cheese sandwiches, a bowl of shrimp
salad, and a jug of iced tea.

"We'll give thanks, and then you can dig in."
Betty's face tightened with intensity as she bowed her
head. "Lord, once again we thank you for the bounty
of land and sea, for your love which reaches to our
deepest need and lifts us into the safety of your
presence. Now, Lord, you know all about Ashlyn's
troubles. You love her. Protect her and comfort her. In
Jesus's name. Amen."

"Amen," I whispered. This was what I needed. A
woman to talk to. A woman to pray with. Someone to
understand. Except for Lottie and Valerie, I'd felt so
alone.

Betty passed me a plate. "Help yourself while I
pour you some tea."

I took a sandwich and some shrimp salad.

Fifty feet away an aluminum boat tied up to a
plank dock bobbed in the gentle current of a slow
moving stream. Live oaks, mangroves, and the
occasional spiky palmetto lined the banks. Overhead,
streamers of Spanish moss fluttered in the breeze off

the water.

"Is that the Brunswick River?"

"No, it's called the Turtle River, though it's not much of a river. It peters out in the swamplands north of here. Great fishing, though."

"It's so peaceful here," I said. "Have you lived here long?"

"Over thirty years. Ever since Andre—Remy's father—moved us here from Louisiana. He knew how to pick a spot. Thought ahead to when the island would be swarming with tourists. Not that there's anything wrong with tourists, mind you."

I helped myself to another sandwich. "So, Remy grew up here?"

"Sure did, along with Yvette, his sister."

"Is that his sister he's standing with in the living room picture?"

"No, no, that's Carol Ann, his wife. Carol Ann's been gone nigh onto six years now. Cancer. Uterine."

"That's so sad. I'm sorry."

"Yeah, it was terrible, the way she suffered. They both did." She shook her head. "So much in love. Remy hasn't looked at a woman since…until now, that is."

To change the subject, I pointed at my plate. "I haven't had pimento-cheese sandwiches since I was a kid in Atlanta. They're delicious. And this salad. It's wonderful. It has a special flavor…"

"Cajun. We Louisiana folk always spice things up a bit. Not too hot for you?"

"No. I love Cajun."

"That Claude down at the café makes a decent jambalaya. Not too many get it right."

"Has your family always been in the fishing

industry?"

"Three generations. Maybe more."

"What made you leave the Gulf and come to Georgia?"

"It was getting too crowded down there. Andre answered an ad for a boat. And here we are."

The ringing of a phone in the kitchen interrupted our conversation. Betty went to answer it.

I relaxed a little. It seemed so quiet and peaceful and Betty was so motherly. I thought about my own mother and wished I'd been more thoughtful.

Betty returned with another jug of iced tea. "That was Sister Louisa at the church, wanting me to bring some of my jambalaya to the supper next week. Lan' sakes, that church has more suppers than you can shake a stick at. More tea?"

I waved away more tea. "Churches are like that."

"You had a church back home?" she asked.

"Yes, a large community church." I looked away. "Craig is…was a deacon."

Her eyebrows rose. "A deacon?"

"Yeah. He was on the membership and finance committees. A pillar. We interviewed people for membership and he helped audit the books. How could he do that and now…?"

"People stumble. None of us are perfect."

"I know but…the FBI is accusing him of money-laundering!"

"Maybe it's a mistake. Is that possible?"

"Possible, I guess. But he still left me."

"Oh, child, that must be so hard."

I changed the subject. "Has Remy always been a shrimper?"

"Lan' sakes, no. He was wild as a teenager.

Wouldn't pay us no mind. Looked down his nose at his dad. Said he wanted to be an engineer. Got his degree and everything, and then Andre broke his arm right at the start of shrimping season. Remy pitched in to help and has been there ever since. He loves it now."

"Did he ever work as an engineer?"

"He worked about six months for a firm in Atlanta. They stuck him behind a desk. He hated it…hey, eat up, these sandwiches won't keep. "

I helped myself to another. "Isn't shrimping a hard life?"

"You betcha. But, it's a good life. Out on the sea. Feeling the wind. Living by the tides. No clocks to punch, no boss to order you around. Not much money in it, mind you."

I stared at my empty plate in amazement. I'd eaten two whole sandwiches, a pile of shrimp salad, and downed two glasses of iced tea. Maybe the return of my appetite was a good sign.

"What about dessert?" Betty asked. "Raspberry tarts? Ice cream? What'll it be?"

I raised my hands in protest. "I thought the cookies were dessert! I couldn't eat another thing."

"Well, just so you've had enough. People always feel better on a full stomach. You must find that at the café. Remy was saying that you were hired on there as a waitress. Is that what you were in New York?"

I laughed. "Hardly." My hand flew to my face to finger the bruises the laugh had set to stinging again. "I had a counseling practice. Marriage counseling, that kind of thing."

"Oh."

"It doesn't sound good, does it? Husband of a marriage counselor divorces her for irreconcilable differences."

"I didn't mean..."

"I may as well face the facts. I made the very mistakes I tell others to avoid." I paused to glance towards the river bank where an egret had touched down. "We were trying to revive our marriage. That's why we were down here; at least, that's what I thought. I didn't expect him to run off with one of his colleagues. My life has become a cliché, a soap opera."

"You poor soul." Betty leaned down and put her arms around me. "That aloe has soaked in. Let's fix your face. You'll feel better."

She led me to her bedroom, where she applied makeup to cover the bruises on my face and nose. She was just finishing when we heard a vehicle drive up.

Betty parted the curtains to look outside. "Lan' sakes, it's Holly from the café. What's she doing here?"

# 32

Holly came striding up the flagstone walk with a laptop.

Betty waved her inside. "Holly, it's good to see you. Come in and have some tea and a raspberry tart."

"You know I can't resist your baking, but I've got to get back. I just came by to bring Ashlyn's stuff."

"Holly, how thoughtful of you!"

She set down the laptop and embraced me. "Ashlyn, honey, I'm so sorry." She held me at arm's length to stare at my face. "Those rats!"

"You've brought my stuff? How?"

"One of Remy's friends packed it all up and brought it to the back of the café. The cottage door was unlocked.

Remy said that one of those men who attacked you has been nosing around the village. He suggests you keep a very low profile. No shopping."

"Shopping is the farthest thing from my mind." I said.

"Well, I've got to go. And don't worry, if those men come nosing around, we'll send them on a wild goose chase."

My cache of money was still zipped into one of the pockets of the suitcase. My wallet seemed intact. Even my toothbrush was there. I put cosmetics on the dresser, but left my clothes in the suitcase. Then, taking the laptop, I walked through the kitchen to the back veranda where Betty was reading a book.

"Do you mind if I join you?"

"Please. Honey, I want you to feel right at home."

While I waited for the laptop to power up, I stared at the ripples where the river's current nudged the dock. The computer beeped.

I scrolled down the e-mail inbox until I came to one from Tyler. Excited, I scanned the contents. He repeated his desire to be with me, and then wrote about his friends in Melbourne and work on construction. I fired off a reply pleading with him to stay put for now without telling him about what had happened.

A measure of relief that Tyler was still safe flooded my soul. I reread the message, and then sat staring at the river. Christmas. What would Christmas be like this year? Would all this be sorted out by then, or would I be running for the rest of my life?

"Good news?"

"Yes, good news. A message from my son, Tyler."

"Does he know about...about all this?"

"Yes, he knows and wants to come and help. He's been trekking in the outback of Australia, but a few days ago he called. So far, he's heeded my plea to stay in Melbourne where he's working on construction. I just want him safe."

"Boys," Betty said. "Going wild, but loving their mothers. I remember when Remy took off hiking through Europe. Didn't hear from him for a month. Then when I really needed help he was right there."

"At least Tyler's safe in Australia."

"And you're safe, too. Nobody's gonna' find you here."

"I hope you're right."

Betty returned to her book and I turned to my

laptop.

I needed to send Tiff an e-mail. These men could just as easily go after her as me. I sat there staring at the computer for ages until I finally wrote:

*Dear Tiffany,*

*I'm staying for a few days with a wonderful southern lady on a country property by a meandering river. You'd love it. I'll explain how this happened when I get a new cell phone. The one I had is busted, so we'll have to communicate by e-mail for a while.*

*Something bad happened today that I need to warn you about. You know how the FBI has been warning me about the danger of the Russian mafia trying to find me?*

*On Friday after work, two men suddenly appeared at the beach house and tried to force me to help them find your dad. They claim he owes them a lot of money. Since I didn't know where he was, I couldn't tell them, but they didn't believe me.*

*Fortunately, someone came along and got me away from there. So, I'm going to disappear for a while until this gets sorted out.*

*In the meantime, I want you to be extra careful. These are very dangerous men. They look Slavic or Russian. Watch out for anyone suspicious around the campus. Repeat your warning to campus security to keep their eyes and ears open for strangers looking for you. In fact, why don't you go and stay with your friend at the University of Iowa? I'd feel a lot better.*

*Let me know you got this.*
*Sweetheart, I love you very, very much.*
*Keep safe and don't worry. I'll be praying for you.*
*Mom*

I sent it off. I felt the anger building as I called up a search engine on the computer and searched for *Bratva*. What I found wasn't encouraging. They were a crime syndicate involved in all manner of criminal activities, drugs, money laundering, smuggling weapons and oil.

A chill ran up my spine, replacing the anger that had begun to build. How long could I impose on Betty's hospitality? A day? Two days? A week? No longer.

I'd have to ask the FBI for protection sooner or later. I turned back to my laptop and began to delete spam and clean up my inbox.

Another message from Lonesome Pine popped up.

# 33

I read through Craig's new e-mail. He made no progress in sorting out his business problems and thus would be leaving the country. He expressed regret at the way things had turned out and urged me to get on with my life. Then he pled with me to sign the divorce papers that he had sent and said that I wouldn't hear from him again.

I sucked in my breath to control the anger that his callous missive had aroused. The coward! Why couldn't he at least face me in person?

Betty reached over to touch my arm. "Bad news?"

"Yes, you could call it that." I spit out the words. "My husband says he wants me to sign divorce papers without even talking things over."

"You poor child. You don't deserve that."

"He said it was all for the best," I snorted. "Can you believe that? Forced to work in a diner to make ends meet, and now running from a couple of kidnappers. The dumb ape!"

"Why don't we pray about it?" Betty said. "The Lord knows what to do."

"I don't feel like praying right now." My voice rose. "I feel like killing him."

Betty was silent.

"I'm sorry, Betty. My mind's just in a whirl. I need to go for a walk… try and figure out what to do.But I would appreciate you praying for me."

"I understand. Go ahead, but don't go far."

෯෧

As I walked, I tried to come to grips with the finality of Craig's e-mail. Divorce. With that, I could hardly take up my counseling practice again. My blindness to the fissures in my own marriage had dealt a serious blow to my confidence.

I wandered along the road listening to the chorus of birdsong and sniffing for the faint scent of honeysuckle.

Had it really been a good marriage, or had I been blinded to chaos beneath the surface?

We used to sit snuggled up on the living room sofa chatting about our day, the kids, our hopes, and dreams. And from that love two children had been born; two children who had grown into exceptional young adults.

But somewhere, a couple of years back, the busyness and apparent success of our professional lives had blighted the original chemistry. The powerful memory of an earlier family Christmas popped into my mind. So much laughter. Such depth of feeling as we read the Christmas story together.

I scuffed the dirt of the path.

Should I return to New York and find an apartment? The money Craig had deposited under my name in Philadelphia should be enough to rent a decent place. If I went back to the same area, wouldn't Scarecrow and his sidekick find me? I shivered at the thought.

I could rent something near Tiffany's college. It would be good to be near her. Start up a counseling practice where they didn't know me. *Not very honest,*

*Ashlyn…*

I needed to get away from this area as fast as possible. I was bringing too much danger down on Remy and his mom.

Leaving St. Simons…I'd miss Lottie Jane and Holly, and yes, even prickly Claude, the cook. They were good people—the salt of the earth. There was something authentic about them.

Thinking back over my life in New York, I wondered if I had been, at root, a snob. I couldn't think of many, if any, friends who were not professionals: lawyers, doctors, financial analysts, company CEOs, teachers. Had we all been posers?

And the job as a waitress. Every day after my shift I felt exhausted, but somehow fulfilled. As if my hard work in the public eye exposed the shallowness of the words that I spun in my counseling practice.

I picked up a stick and began to idly snap it into pieces. No, it wasn't that listening and giving people clarity about their lives was empty, but that I'd somehow become dismissive of the labor of people who worked with their hands: plumbers, carpenters, farmers, cooks, waitresses. I wondered if politicians fell into this trap.

I continued on down the path. I'd have to leave St. Simons. And that would mean never seeing Remy again. What did I feel about him? Feel? I had no right to feel anything but gratitude…but what was that sensation that gripped me when he was near? I hadn't felt anything like that for ages.

*This is ridiculous, Ashlyn. Wake up. One minute you want to save your marriage, the next start a new relationship. Are you already in boomerang mode? How many lonely women have you warned about the irrationality that follows a breakup?*

I turned back towards Betty's house as confused as when I set out, but with a determination to be more sensitive to others with marital problems. The rest of the day passed uneventfully.

Remy wouldn't be back until the morning. The most noteworthy event of the day was the Cajun gumbo Betty served for supper. It was wonderful. After helping with the dishes, I turned in early and slept better than I had in days. I felt safe.

In the morning I went for a run. When I returned there was a strange truck in the driveway. I slid behind a bush and watched the house. After a few minutes, I slipped around to the back of the house and eased into one of the lounge chairs on the porch. Hearing nothing but low conversation, I assumed Betty was visiting with a friend.

The faint gurgle of the slow-moving river eddying around the posts of the jetty cast a spell of tranquility conducive to prayer.

I was pouring out my heart to God when the door swung open with a bang and Remy burst onto the veranda. "Ashlyn, grab your stuff. We've got to get you out of here."

# 34

"Leave? I know I can't stay here, but now, right now?"

"Hurry," he said. "They firebombed my truck."

"What?"

"I left the truck at the pier last night. I didn't want to provoke interest from the police, so I had Gaston drop me at my house. In the morning, he picked me up and drove me back to the pier. My truck was just a blackened shell in the parking lot."

"That's horrible!"

As he turned away, I noticed the butt of a pistol protruding from under his shirt at the back. "Nobody saw anything, but it had to be those gang-bangers who tried to grab you."

"Oh, Remy, I'm sorry I dragged you into this."

"Hardly your fault. My choice. Only right thing to do."

"I know, but…"

"Best hurry. If they found me, they'll find my mother and you. We've got to get you both out of here. Ma put an extra suitcase in your room. Garbage bags aren't gonna hold up much longer."

As I ran down the hall to the bedroom, I saw that Betty already had a suitcase packed and ready at the front door.

Remy must have come shortly after I began my run.

In the bathroom, I brushed my teeth, freshened up

as fast as I could, and changed out of my jogging suit into jeans and a clean T-shirt. It didn't take me long to pack up both suitcases and lug them into the hall.

Betty came down the hall towards me pulling a wheeled suitcase. Her face looked flushed and her hair a bit askew. "Oh, child, this is a terrible business."

"Mrs. Jeandeau, I'm really sorry. I shouldn't have come here."

"Nonsense."

"Where will you go?"

"To my elderly aunt's place, upstate. You and I will be safe there."

"I've caused you enough trouble. I should have insisted that your son drop me at the bus station. Well that's where I'll go now. Head north."

Remy came in from packing his mother's car. "That's not wise. It'd be the first place they'll look."

"I'll rent a car, then," I said. "Or sneak back and get my car." I held up the keys.

"They'll be watching your car," Remy said. "And you told me your credit cards were frozen, so how can you rent another?"

"OK, how about an airport? Is there an airport around here? I've enough money to get a ticket to Philadelphia or New York."

"They'll check there, too. And planes don't leave from Brunswick very often. You may have to wait half a day."

Betty touched my shoulder. "Listen child, you come with me. Lay low for a few days."

I sat down on one of the suitcases with my head in my hands. "I'm not going to put you in any more danger. I'll think of something."

"You forget I shot one of them in the foot—shot up

their car," Remy said. "They're not going to leave me be—or Ma."

"The police, they're the only choice," I said.

"All in good time. First we've got to get you both somewhere safe, and then we'll bring in the police."

"What about you?"

"Have you seen some of the men Remy works with?" Betty asked. "Tough bunch. The whole shrimp fleet is like a fraternity. All for one, and one for all. Oh, they're competitive, but when one of them is threatened, they all get riled. I'd hate to see what they'll do if they catch whoever burned his truck."

"You got that right. Don't worry about me."

"Well," I said. "Drop me at a motel, then. Somewhere away from here. There are lots of motels on '95."

"I can see you're determined not to endanger Ma, and I appreciate that. But motels, bus stations, airports—that's where they'll look."

"There's always the fishing cabin," Betty said.

"Good idea." Remy's eyes lit up. "I'll drop Ashlyn there while you drive upstate."

"OK, just for a day or two," I murmured.

"She'll need some grub," Betty said.

Remy looked at his watch. "Ma, you fill that ice cooler with some basics and get a bag of groceries while I finish packing your car. And hurry."

∂∘∽

Remy trailed his mother's car until we were twenty or thirty miles out of town. Then he tooted his horn and turned down a country road through vast pine forests. A couple of times, logging trucks passed us on their way to some pulp mill.

I was preoccupied with trying to figure out what to talk about.

Remy seemed comfortable with long stretches of silence.

Without talking to each other, people remained strangers who passed each other like ships in the night. At least, that's what I often counseled in my marriage classes. Talk to each other. Listen to each other. Looking back, I admitted it was a rather limited view. People are different. Some are chatty. Some aren't. Is that what Craig thought of my attempts to converse: idle chatter? I broke the silence. "Is your truck totaled?"

"A pile of blackened junk."

"Any insurance?"

"Got insurance, but I doubt if it'll cover something like this."

"When I get all this sorted out, I'll do all I can to help you get a new truck. It's the least I can do."

A smile wrinkled his craggy face. "You don't worry about that, Ashlyn. Let's think about keeping you safe."

"If you hadn't come along…" I shivered. "I owe you a great debt of gratitude."

A scowl replaced the smile and something flashed in his blue eyes. "You don't owe me nothing. What I did was what any right-thinking person would do. What my buddies would've done for me. What we'd do to anyone mistreating even…even a dog."

"Oh…" I felt a flush spread up my neck. I'd obviously said something that challenged his southern code of chivalry. "I know you'd do it for anyone…anything. I'm just grateful."

He set his mouth in a firm line and stared ahead. "I know you're grateful. And I didn't mean to compare you with a dog. A camellia would be more fittin'."

I looked out the window to stifle the flutter that kept making me feel something I hadn't felt in a long time. This was dangerous territory. I needed to change the subject. "Does this truck belong to one of your buddies?"

"Gaston's."

"Will your boat be safe? If those men burnt your truck, might they come after the *Esperance*, too?"

"Might. If they did, they'd get a hot reception. All the other shrimpers are on the lookout. Gaston and Ches are taking turns watching the boat."

"But what about your mother's place?"

"You sure worry a lot. Mind you, I guess you have reason. To answer your question, Ma has good neighbors who'll keep an eye on the place. And when Gaston and Ches are not at the boat, they'll be watching the house."

I lost track of the number of roads Remy turned down. We passed a gas station at a crossroads, a stand selling peaches, and one small village. Here and there, I spotted a few farms, usually with a grove of pecan trees. Most of the highway cut through vast stands of reforested loblolly and longleaf pine, intersected by logging roads and firebreaks.

Remy's cell phone chimed. He listened and finally spoke. "Really appreciate that Mr. Roberts. You did the right thing. I'm much obliged. Bye." He turned to me. "That was our neighbor, reporting in. We left just in time. A couple of men in a foreign-looking black sedan came by asking for Ma. Said they represented an insurance policy taken out by her husband that had never been claimed."

"What did the neighbor do?"

"While Mr. Roberts covered them with a shotgun from inside the house, Mrs. Roberts told them Ma had gone to Orlando for a holiday, but they could leave the paperwork with her and she'd see Ma got it. Mighty inventive."

"You were right about leaving quickly."

What would have happened if they had arrived before we left? Would Remy have used the revolver in his waistband or the shotgun stashed behind the seat? He made a woman feel safe. Why hadn't he married again? Did he have a girlfriend? *Why are you even thinking about these things?*

I turned to stare out the window. The pine forests had given way to lower, swampier land where sweet gum, sassafras, and live oak predominated.

Remy pulled off the gravel logging road and turned onto a rutted causeway through a swamp. The spongy roadway ended at a weathered clapboard cabin on an acre or so of higher ground.

"Here we are, then," Remy said. "The family's fishing cabin."

# 35

The cabin looked like it had been there for a hundred years. Constructed on posts to lift it off the ground, it had a veranda across the front and a shake roof green with moss. Some of the clapboards looked warped or split.

It nestled on a hummock of dry ground in a grove of oaks with its veranda facing a murky and motionless river. Swampy ground studded with mangroves, ferns, and an occasional palmetto surrounded it on three sides. The only access was along the spongy causeway across which we'd driven or by using the red and silver aluminum boat tied up to a tilting dock that jutted out into the river.

"Well this is it. Not much to look at, but it's isolated and comfy. Come on, let's get you settled. I need to get back to the boat." Remy hauled out my two suitcases and the cooler.

Thoughts of being alone in this cabin surrounded by a swamp crawling with snakes and a river full of alligators made me shudder. However, it was much better than being stuffed in a car trunk. I opened the door, gingerly stepped down, and looked around. At least the ground around the cabin was dry and clear of brush.

"Ashlyn, are you OK?" Remy frowned as he looked my way.

"Fine. Just getting my bearings. Taking it all in."

I grabbed a bag of groceries, chattering to cover

my nervousness. "This is incredible. Like something from *The Yearling*. It could be a movie set. So isolated. How did your dad find this place? Did your family build it or get it from someone else? Or—"

"Whoa, one question at a time." His eyes twinkled as he held the screen door open. "Our family has always loved fishin', and not just ocean fishin'. Soon after we moved from Louisiana, Pop looked for a cabin near a good fishing ground. He found this property."

I paused inside the door to check for critters, careful not to react to the musty odor. To the left of the door hung a dozen or so fishing rods. Beyond them, the head of an impressive buck stared at me with one glassy eye.

Along the left wall were kitchen counters, a sink with a hand pump, a stove, and wall cabinets—no fridge.

Two doors on the far wall led into bedrooms.

On the right, a grouping of old sofas and chairs surrounded a blackened stone fireplace. Firewood and kindling overflowed a bin beside it. A coffee table held an array of dog-eared magazines and a couple of paperbacks. Old-fashioned coal-oil lamps stood on rickety side tables around the room and on the mantle of the fireplace.

Overhead the open rafters held an array of nets, paddles, and other fishing paraphernalia. Worn and faded rugs were scattered on the plank floor.

The only sign of a woman's touch was a beautiful quilt with an intricate pattern of stylized magnolias that hung on the far wall between the doors to the bedrooms.

Remy emerged from one of the bedrooms. "Well, what do you think?"

"It's…"

"Primitive?"

"Well, I wouldn't say primitive. More like, uh, rustic."

"It is that. It was really rundown when we bought it from an estate years ago. Our family has been coming here for thirty years. It's a wonderful escape from the rat race. And the fishing is good."

Rat race on St. Simons Island? My mind pictured New York traffic. My face must have reflected something of my thoughts.

"This is not the Ritz, but I couldn't think of any other place that would be safe. Just give it a few days and…"

I held up my hands. "It's wonderful. I just feel as if I'm intruding on your family's special place." I looked around. "And this is obviously an extraordinary retreat."

"You're not intruding. Here, let me show you around."

I deposited the bag of groceries on the kitchen counter.

He took out a jug of water from under the sink and poured some into the hand pump. "Need to prime it. Like this." He pumped the handle up and down a few times until brackish water began to flow. "You only use this water for washing, and for the bathroom. In that far cabinet we keep a couple of cases of water for cooking, drinking, coffee, that kind of thing."

He went on to show me around the cabin: the stock of canned goods, how to light the lamps, and how to use the propane stove. "Let me make you a cup of coffee, and then I've got to get back to the boat, see that it's repaired after that gale." He scooped grounds and water into an old-fashioned percolator on the stove.

"Do cell phones work out here?"

"No reception. Too far from the nearest tower."

Well, I didn't have one, anyway.

While the coffee perked, I wandered into the bedroom. A scarred bureau with four drawers. A window looked out onto the swamp. A door led into a bathroom. A mirror hung on a wall with dog-eared photos stuck around the edges. A rifle rested on brackets behind the built-in double bed.

Remy had piled fresh sheets, pillowcases, and towels on the bed. His mother had taught him well.

I peered at the photos. They were mainly of Remy, his teenaged sister, and an older man, all grinning as they held up fish. "How old was your sister in this picture?" I asked, as I heard him come to the door.

"Sixteen or seventeen, I'd guess," he said. "Come and get some coffee. It's ready."

He'd set two mugs, a can of condensed milk, and a bowl of sugar cubes on the coffee table. "Help yourself to cream and sugar."

I poured some milk into a mug and collapsed into one of the old armchairs before the fireplace. He took another. An awkward silence followed.

I took a sip of coffee. "This is good, strong."

"Only way I know how to make it. As you saw, we need strong coffee to keep us alert on the boat."

"So, do you fish all year?"

"No, just when the shrimp are in season. It's all regulated. Quotas. Allotted areas. That kind of thing."

"It must be a hard life."

"I suppose you could call it hard. But it's what I chose." His face tightened as he looked up at the rafters. "Not many people get to do what they love, regulate their lives by the tides, see the sun rise over the horizon, and make their living from the sea. People pay top dollar to buy a house on the shore, just to be within sight and sound of the ocean for a few weeks of the year. I get to see it every day. Watch the pelicans fish. See the dolphins cavort. Smell the fresh salty air— far from the smog of the city." This was a side of Remy that I'd caught glimpses of, sensitive, almost poetic.

"Sounds like a very dangerous occupation, though. Friday night, I thought your ship was a goner with all of us."

"That was a bad one, all right. I should'a known better. Oh, it's a dangerous business, all right. Lines getting tangled. He wiggled the stump of his ring finger. But…" Suddenly, his face split into a craggy grin. "But I haven't had to shoot anyone before, or rescue damsels in distress."

I smiled. "There's that."

"I haven't had so much excitement since a shark got tangled in one of our lines. I can make shrimping sound romantic, but can you imagine how mundane it gets day after day, hauling in smelly shrimp? Or searching for them? Which reminds me, I've got to get back to the boat; we need to prepare for the next run." He went to the door and looked back. "Will you be OK here by yourself?"

I stuffed down the feeling of panic that engulfed me at the thought of being alone. "Sure, no problem. I'll catch up on my reading."

"There's one more thing." He turned and walked towards the bedroom. "Did you see the rifle behind the bed?"

"Yeah, but…"

"We keep it there for gators and coyotes and the like."

"Gators, and the like?"

"Don't worry; they're attracted by the smell of the fish we catch. Since you haven't caught any fish, they won't bother you. But just in case...do you know how to shoot a rifle?"

"It's been a long time. But yeah, Dad taught me."

"If you need it, for any reason, the shells are in that coffee tin on the shelf with the gun."

He put his hands on my shoulders. He must have sensed my anxiety. His piercing blue gaze appeared softened by some deep feeling as he looked into my eyes. "Ashlyn, you'll be all right. You've been amazingly strong in the face of traumas that would leave most people in a mess. It's OK to be afraid. Just know that you're safe here. No one can find you. Try to relax. My mom will be praying for you and I'll be back as soon as I can."

I longed to collapse into those sun-burned arms. What would it be like to stop being strong, allow Remy to be strong for me? Instead, I took a deep breath and nodded.

# 36

Remy's truck bounced over the causeway until steely-green foliage hid his taillights from view.

I returned to the kitchen, poured another mug of coffee, and took it to the screened-in veranda where I collapsed into a lounge chair.

What had almost happened—no, what had I almost done? Fallen into the arms of another man. Not only had I wanted to feel his arms around me, I longed for much more: his kisses, the comfort of his body close to mine, intimacy. I could tell he wanted it, too. Wake up Ashlyn. This is not Camelot. This is rebound country. This is what you've warned your own clients about. Temporary insanity. Hormone heaven leading to a life of hellish regrets.

My confidence was shaken. Finally, I knew by experience what I had told others—someone in my situation would have an overwhelming need for affirmation.

And Remy was a very unusual man: handsome in a rugged way, courageous to have come to my aid, sensitive, mysterious, and thoughtful. How often did one find that combination in a single, fortyish male?

I plopped back on the lounge chair and took a sip of coffee.

Well one thing was clear, the past was gone—just a painful memory.

It was all too much to think about, so I got busy. I hauled water into the bathroom and tried to plan a meal with what Betty packed in the cooler.

In the bedroom, I laid out my cosmetics on top of the bureau. I left the other stuff in the two suitcases.

That done, I swept the floor from one side of the living room to the other. I cleaned out the fireplace and filled up the wood box. I even took the rugs outside to shake.

Finally, I collapsed on a faded couch and began to leaf through the magazines on the coffee table: magazines on golfing, hunting, fishing, baseball, racing, and auto mechanics. The bookcase held a dog-eared collection of action-adventure paperbacks by popular male authors. Leaving them to gather further dust, I rummaged in my suitcase for the book I'd been trying to read for weeks.

I snuggled into one of the overstuffed armchairs. Ten or twelve pages on, I was re-reading whole paragraphs. Closing the book, I fetched my laptop, but could detect no wireless signal.

Time passed. The light faded. I lit the lamps and began to think of supper, not that I felt hungry. Along with a plastic tub of coleslaw, a couple of tubes of biscuits, and a jar of strawberry preserves, Betty included a selection of her own frozen entrees. Chicken gumbo seemed the most promising. I rummaged in the cupboard and found some rice to go with it.

While I waited for the rice to cook and the gumbo to thaw, I paced around the cabin a couple of times. I stared out at the darkening swamp and listened to the cacophony of mysterious sounds.

On the shelf of a corner table I found a radio with a box of batteries. I inserted a couple of batteries, punched the on button and got static. Fiddling with the dial, I found an FM station from Savannah and suddenly the lilting sound of a Strauss waltz filled the cabin. Ah, music to eat by. I ate the gumbo and rice with gusto. With my plate scrapped clean, I leaned back in the chair, closed my eyes, and let the music wash over me.

Music kept the demons away until darkness fell and I switched off the radio. I took a couple of lamps into the bedroom, climbed into bed, pulled up the covers, and tried to ignore all the night sounds. I opened the novel again but kept glancing up at the crack in the window where the shade didn't quite keep out the darkness. Inevitably, I'd lose my place in the story.

I gave up and lay there debating whether to snuff out the lamps. Reluctantly, I extinguished them and lay back on the pillows. I prayed for safety for myself, for protection for Remy—and for the Lord to smother the feelings I'd begun to have for him. I pled with God to protect Tyler and Tiff. I even prayed for Craig to be exonerated by the FBI. I tried to think of all the things I had to be thankful for, but kept getting hung up by thoughts of the events that had bludgeoned me in the last few months. *Sorry, Lord, I know I need to be thankful, but it's hard.*

Every night sound was magnified. A plop out on the river became a bevy of alligators crawling towards the cabin. A vague sound beneath the floorboards became a snake slithering, searching for a way in. The snap of a twig heralded a prowling wildcat.

I tried to recite the Twenty-Third Psalm. A series of howling screams slashed fear wide open. I sat bolt upright. I gripped the flashlight, clicked it on, and turned the beam towards the rifle hanging on the rack over my head. I took it down, along with the coffee tin.

Trembling, fumbling, I dropped bullets before I figured out how to load the thing. The howls faded in the distance. Coyotes. I propped the rifle against the wall, and dived back under the covers.

&#x223D;&#x2E05;

A beam of sunshine wakened me in a tangle of sheets and blankets clutching a pillow. I stretched and sat up. All I heard was the croak of a frog, the caw of a distant crow, and a buzz of insects—no threat.

I settled into a lounge chair on the veranda with coffee. Dragonflies flitted among the reeds on the shore. A fish jumped. The drumming of a woodpecker echoed from somewhere upstream. Even the swamp looked harmless. *But there would be no jogging today.*

After a breakfast of scrambled eggs and biscuits, I returned to the porch with a second cup of coffee and my Bible. Opening to Psalm 73, I began to read. *"My feet had almost slipped; I had nearly lost my foothold. For I envied the arrogant when I saw the prosperity of the wicked...always carefree, they increase in wealth. Surely in vain have I kept my heart pure."*

Tears began to stream down my face as I echoed Asaph's complaint to God. *Why, Lord, am I being hounded? I've always been true to our marriage covenant. I've never had an affair—never even thought of one. I've tried to be a good wife and mother. I've served You in the church. Why, then, have I lost everything? And why am I on the run while men like Pavel and Gorya are free to rob and murder? Why me? How do You expect me to praise You when Craig abandoned me?*

I read on. *"When I tried to understand all this, it was oppressive to me till I entered the sanctuary of God; then I understood their final destiny. Surely You place them on slippery ground…Yet I am always with You; You hold me by my right hand. You guide me with your counsel…"*

I swiped at my tears. *OK, Lord, I know You're seated upon the throne of the universe. In spite of what I see around me…I believe it, and, Lord, I know You're grieved by injustice and evil. That's why You sent your Son. I even know that Your love for stumbling men and women leads You to be longsuffering. But how long do we wait for justice?*

*Are You always with me? Are You here? Do You hold me in Your hand? Help me to feel Your presence and please, Heavenly Father, show me what to do.*

The distant sound of a car broke into my prayer. It was early for Remy to be returning. Between the boles of two mangroves, I caught sight of a black car with a chrome grill.

# 37

How could they have found me?

I raced back inside, slipped into my jacket, and grabbed the rifle. I looked around for what I might need. I stuffed my wallet in a pocket along with some rifle shells, and then knelt to lace up my sneakers.

I jumped out the bedroom window, tearing the screen. I hit the ground with a thud, almost losing my balance. Leaping up, I took off running, keeping the cabin between the lane and me. I dashed from tree to tree until I came to the edge of the swamp, all dark water and tangled weeds.

The sound of breaking glass stiffened my resolve. I plunged in, wading knee-deep in water from one cypress to another. The muck sucked at my shoes. The stench of rotting vegetation made me gag. My left foot settled on something soft and spongy—something that moved. I stifled a scream as I shuddered. Lunging for the knobby knee of a bald cypress, I almost lost the rifle, but succeeded in dragging myself out of the water to cling to the bole of a tree. I shivered with panic. *I can't do this.*

I clung there for an eternity and tried to still my pounding heart. Should I sneak up on them in ambush; shoot them dead? I looked at the rifle in my hands. I didn't even remember how to cock it. Steal their car? How could I circle around the cabin without being seen or heard? Take the boat and head down-river? But did it have gas? And the boat could be clearly seen from the cabin.

Angry shouts shattered the silence. I looked towards the cabin but couldn't see it for foliage. Unfortunately, my path through the swamp was clearly marked by the muck I'd stirred up.

A triumphant yell set my heart pounding again. They'd found the window. I stared at the fetid water. Finally, I waded into the water up to my waist. Roots clutched at my feet. I pressed forward, trying to disturb the muck as little as possible. Here and there, I came to a rotted tree trunk that I could straddle, or a raised hillock of swamp plants that enabled me to climb out of the swamp.

"Ve know you're out there," one of the Russians yelled. "Give yourself up. Just help find us your husband. We won't hurt you."

Shortly, snatches of angry conversation ended in a loud bellow. "We can see your trail. Nowhere to hide. Give yourself up or we're coming to get you." A pause. "Last chance. Don't want to make us angry."

I gritted my teeth and stepped back into the putrid water. A plop to my left made me jerk in that direction. A "v" of ripples in the water marked the path of some creature. A gator? With a shudder, I adjusted my direction deeper into the swamp, and plowed through the water faster than before.

Which was worse, Russians or alligators?

The sound of a splash was followed by a shouted curse. "You're really starting to get us mad. Do you want to die out here? We can arrange that! And your shrimping boyfriend will be next."

Two shots rang out.

One was to my right and another found a mark in a trunk a hundred yards or so from me. Three more shots rang out.

They were just shooting to scare me. Nothing would compel me to show myself.

"Just a warning. Better give yourself up." The shout was fainter.

I pushed ahead and came out of the mangroves into a thicket of sweet gum where I collapsed on the spongy ground.

The snarl of a motor broke into a whine that I recognized as an outboard.

I tried to find a place to hide. The grove of sweet gum rose from a raised island barely a hundred feet across. It was surrounded by black water dotted with cypress. Beyond them were clumps of swamp grass and a thicket of brush crowned by pines.

Pines meant solid ground. I stared at the water, trying to probe its inky depths for movement. To the left bubbles broke the surface. I collapsed on a stump. No way.

Two more shots rang out to my right. They were going to corral me by using the boat to my left and one of them wading through the swamp to my right.

With a whispered prayer asking God to protect me and send alligators to stop them, I slipped into the water and waded towards the swamp grass.

I whispered a psalm and tried to still the shudders that shook my body. *The Lord is my shepherd...Even though I walk through the valley of the shadow of death I will fear no evil, for You are with me...what were the next verses?*

I forced my way into another sweet gum thicket which opened up into an extensive stand of pines. I ran away from the sound of the boat and the other Russian. I dodged trees and leapt windfalls. My renewed interest in jogging had increased my stamina, but even so, slogging through the swamp had used up a lot of energy. In minutes I was gasping for breath and gnawing my lips from the stitch in my side. Adrenaline kept me going until I collapsed and crawled into a tangled pile of deadfalls.

Spasms racked my body as I lay still, recovering. I listened for my pursuers. The whine of the outboard sounded distant. No other sounds broke the quiet except the faint hum of insects, the warble of a bird, and the drumming of a woodpecker on a hollow tree. Then a single shot rang out—far away.

I was safe. I lay back on the pine straw and stared up through the foliage at the sky. Pure robin's egg blue. Somewhere out there normalcy reigned: children played, teachers taught, a mother made lasagna, a subway disgorged passengers, fingers tapped on dozens of keyboards. And here I was running; my life in turmoil.

I'd escaped, through a swamp, no less. If I could do that, in spite of my fear of snakes and swamps, I could do anything with God's help. No way were they going to destroy my life. I glanced at the rifle; miraculously I still had it. I picked it up.

The nest of windfalls was near the edge of a large stand of loblolly pines. The pines, on a gently rising slope, stretched as far as I could see. Somewhere ahead would be a logging road.

Would Pavel and his henchmen use the network of logging roads to continue their search—or be leery of running into a logging crew?

The lack of underbrush meant that I could be seen from a great distance. The occasional patch of scrawny bushes might provide some cover...but...? Should I stay hidden or put as much distance as possible between the cabin and me?

The faint sound of a truck to my right answered my unspoken question. Best to stay hidden. Taking some pine straw, I wiped the mud off my sneakers before taking them off and tipping out the fetid water. I wrung my socks dry and draped them over a branch. Then, standing, I scraped the mud off my jeans with more pine straw. I emptied the sodden wallet and laid the bills out to dry. I extracted a couple of sodden tissues, a handful of change, a dripping pack of gum, and a lipstick from my pockets.

I scanned the surroundings. The whine of mosquitoes, the caw of a couple of crows, the croak of frogs, and the rustle of leaves marked the explorations of a chipmunk. The snap when I broke off a branch to wave away the mosquitoes caused the chipmunk to give a startled chirp. He decided I was no threat because he continued to search for seeds.

I made a mattress of pine straw, laid back, and tried to relax. Horrific scenarios kept reeling through my mind. Would Pavel and Gorya target Tiffany?

What about Remy? He'd be returning to the cabin soon. Would he assume I'd left? No, he'd find the torn screen, the broken lock, and know something terrible had happened. But what if Pavel waited at the cabin, shot him? Or what if they hired dogs to track me?

I was so jittery I jumped up every few minutes to stare around. I imagined a menace hiding behind every tree.

To stay calm, I started reciting all the Bible verses I could remember until a faint sound to the right set my pulse racing.

Heart in mouth, I peered through the tangle.

A hundred yards off, a doe and its fawn ambled through the pines.

After they disappeared, I gathered up my belongings, pulled on my half-dry socks, laced up my sneakers, and crawled out of my hiding place. I set off at a fast pace towards a logging road and help.

# 38

Making use of cover, I zigzagged through the pines.

When a couple of crows began a dreadful cawing, I crouched down behind a clump of holly. Nothing stirred. Deer flies circled my head.

I pulled up the hood of my jacket. The scant foliage of the pines did little to shield me from the blistering rays of the noonday sun. I moistened my lips to combat the agony of thirst.

I took one more look around before jogging through the woods. I heard the faint whine of a chainsaw. Loggers.

Correcting my line of flight, I headed towards the sound. The chainsaw fell silent, but I continued in that direction. Finally, I topped a rise and began a slow descent through a mixed forest where the underbrush became thicker, hindering my progress.

A shot rang out. With a *thunk* it hit a tree near my head. I dove for cover and lay there trembling. How could they have found me? I fumbled with the rifle I carried, trying to lever a shell into the chamber.

"Drop that gun and stand up or the next shot won't miss."

Dropping the rifle, I stood up with my hands raised.

A man stepped from behind a tree. Like a falcon, his dark eyes peered from a lined face almost covered by a grizzled rat's nest of a beard. He sported a greasy cap and a camouflage shirt. "What're yuh doin' on my property?"

"I meant no harm…I'm running away from some men." I swiped at a tear that oozed from one eye.

"Why…you're a woman."

"Please, I didn't know it was your property. Just show me the road out of here and I'll be gone."

He lowered his gun as he eyed me, taking in the mud splattered on my clothes and the scratches on my face. "How'd you get here?"

I pointed back the way I had come.

"Through the swamp?"

"Yeah."

"Nothing that a'way but the old Jeandeau place."

"That's where I was…when…when." I shuddered. "Remy Jeandeau left me there to be safe."

"Remy's a good man."

"Please, do you have a phone?"

He bent down and picked up my…Remy's…rifle.

"Fool thing for a woman to be carrying a gun. Dangerous."

He handed me the weapon and motioned me to follow.

We came to a tumbledown shack on the edge of another swampy area. Old tires, rusty cans, pieces of darkened and splintered lumber, three ancient cars and a crippled truck gave the yard the appearance of a village dump. A hound chained to a tree bayed as we approached.

He stopped at the edge of the clearing and pointed towards a lane that wound through the trees. "Follow that and you'll come to the highway. Four or five miles. There's a store there with a phone. Someone'll hep yuh." He held out the shells he'd retrieved from the gun.

I dumped them in my jacket pocket. "Could I just have a drink of water?"

He nodded and went into the shack. He returned with a chipped mug.

I hesitated, repelled by the marshy odor. Thirst trumped discretion, so I drank it down in one gulp. "Thank you." I handed back the mug. "I'm Ashlyn Forsyth and you...?"

Shaking his head, he pointed down the lane. "Don't tell anyone yuh met me, hear? Don't want no one nosin' 'round."

"Don't worry, I won't tell a soul."

I jogged down the lane. When I looked back, he was still standing there, his rifle held in the crook of his arm.

The lane ended at a gravel road. From behind a pine draped in kudzu, I listened for traffic. Nothing. Which way to the main road? Had to be right.

Keeping to the shoulder to avoid the gravel, I headed down the road at a brisk pace. What would I do when I found the store? When the owner saw me, wouldn't he call the police? Where was Remy? How could I call him without a number? What if he'd run into the Russians? What if they were patrolling the roads, looking for me?

I heard the approach of a powerful engine. Hiding in the underbrush, I watched as an empty logging truck went by. A few minutes later, a battered pickup rattled past.

I continued down the road. The faint sound of a slowly approaching car breached my consciousness just in time for me to dive behind a thicket of holly. Peering through the branches, I watched as a dark car crept by with two men scanning the woods through the windows.

I flattened to the ground.

Keeping out of sight by walking in the woods parallel to the road would slow me down. There was little cover beneath the canopy of pines. I could hike deeper into the woods, but how could I get help if I did that? *Ashlyn, this is no time to be indecisive. They'll be back soon.*

I raced down the road until I heard a truck engine. A fully loaded logging truck approached. I dropped Remy's rifle behind a clump of brush, and then jumped out and waved my hands. The driver downshifted, applied the brakes, and came to a stop a hundred yards beyond me.

"Help!" I ran to the driver's side window.

"Ma'am, what happened to you?"

"Some men are trying to kidnap me. I need a lift."

"It's against company policy but…" He scratched his head. "How do I know you're telling the truth?"

"Did you pass a black foreign sedan with two men in it?"

"Yeah."

"They're the ones who attacked me. Look at me. I had to escape through the swamp. Please, believe me."

"OK, get in."

I climbed into the cab.

He reached over and swept a couple of fast food containers onto the floor. "Sorry about the junk. Not used to having a lady in the cab."

I leaned back. "No problem. I'm not used to wading through a swamp, either. I'm just thankful you stopped."

The driver concentrated on getting the truck up to

speed. "I'm Quincy."

"Ashlyn."

"I'm taking this load to the mill in Brunswick. There's a strip mall near the mill entrance, where I can let you out...or anywhere along the way."

"The strip mall will be fine."

Quincy picked up his cell phone. "So, shall I call the sheriff? Have him meet you there?"

"Uh...no. No, I'll call the police when you let me out. Save you getting involved."

"Don't mind, now."

"It's OK. You're wondering why someone would kidnap me."

"None of my business. Just concerned is all."

"I guess you deserve some explanation. My husband (*was he still my husband?*) got tricked into investing dirty money for some mobsters. (*Did he really get tricked?*) He lost a lot during the recent financial crisis. Now, he's disappeared. The mobsters are trying to kidnap me to put pressure on him."

"You've got to be kidding."

"I wish I was."

After ten minutes or so, Quincy broke the silence that had fallen. "Look, if you're hungry or thirsty, I can stop and get you something."

"Thanks. I'll be OK...but could I use your cell phone?" I realized I could call Holly at the Shrimpboat Café.

He handed it over. "No problem."

I dialed.

# 39

"Good afternoon. Shrimpboat Café."

"Holly, it's Ashlyn. I..."

"Ashlyn, are you OK? We've been so worried."

"I've been better..."

"What's going on? Remy's called twice in the last half-hour. Said you'd disappeared from his cabin."

"That's just it. Those Russian mobsters showed up. I had to escape through the swamp."

"Oh, Ashlyn, honey! Where are you now?"

I glanced over at Quincy who was staring straight ahead, as if to give me privacy. "A gentleman in a logging truck picked me up. I'm on my way into Brunswick. I need someone to meet me there. Do you know where Remy is?"

"He was just leaving the cabin fifteen minutes ago. I can call him on his cell. Where will you be in Brunswick?"

"Let me ask."

I turned to Quincy. "Is there a fast-food place in that strip mall—or someplace where I can wait?"

"Yeah, there's a Burger Barn at the corner of the road where I turn off for the pulp mill."

"Holly, there's a Burger Barn at the corner of the highway and the turnoff for the pulp and paper mill. I'll wait there."

"I know the one. I'll call you back."

Holly called back with the welcome news that Remy would meet me there.

I passed the phone back to Quincy and stared out the window.

The traffic picked up as we approached the highway's intersection with Interstate 95.

It was time to get the police involved. They would know how to contact the FBI.

Quincy turned off the highway and pulled over to the side of the road. He pointed out the window. "There's the Burger Barn. The strip mall is just beyond it."

"I'm very, very grateful for your help."

"Hey, no problem." He ran his hands through his mane of auburn hair. "Look, I could wait...make sure your friend shows up."

"I'll be OK now—thanks to you. I don't know what I would have done if you hadn't come by."

Looking embarrassed, he shook his head. "It's nothing."

I waved as he pulled away. In the Burger Barn, I went directly to the restroom: washed the grime from my face and hands, tried to blot the worst of the mud off my jeans, and ran a hand through my hair in an attempt to free the tangles. What I wouldn't have given for a comb and some make-up. *It will have to do.*

Buying a Surf Burger and a diet soda, I retreated to a corner booth where I could hide from the curious eyes of the servers who stared at my disheveled appearance.

I tried to remember what kind of a truck Remy had borrowed. It had been old, with rust patches.

A black car pulled into the parking lot. I scrunched down and peered out the window. A man dressed in a suit and tie, carrying a briefcase, got out.

My breath came out in a rush of relief. Next came

two pickups, one cardinal red and the other dark green. Finally, a rusty pickup pulled into the parking lot and drove slowly by the front of the restaurant. Through the driver's window I could see Remy.

I ran out and waved.

He backed up, opened the passenger door, and beckoned for me to hop in. On the far side of the lot, he drove into a slot between two cars, shut off the engine, and turned to look at me.

"Remy, I'm so glad to see you again."

For a minute he said nothing; just shook his head. "You're a living, breathing lightning rod."

"Sorry."

"You're sorry? Hey, I haven't had seen so much action since the Gulf War…but the important thing is, are you OK? You look like you've tangled with a gator. I don't mean you look bad, I mean…"

I wanted to throw myself at this man; feel his arms around me, hear him telling me everything would be fine. Instead, I said, "I know what you mean. On a scale of one to ten, I'm about a two." I paused. "In fact, I'm a mess and I smell like the swamp."

He grinned in that quirky way he had of lifting one side of his mouth. "And I smell like shrimp; so I guess we cancel each other out." His expression went serious. "What happened? I saw the broken lock, the busted out screen, I thought…"

"A black car came up the lane leading to the cabin. After grabbing your gun, I fled into the swamp." I shuddered. "I hate swamps…alligators…snakes." That's when the dam burst and tears began to pour down my cheeks. "They shot at me!" I hiccuped. "I waded through the swamp…stand of pines…ran…hid."

Remy reached over with a tissue and began to blot my tears. "Hey, hey, it's OK. You're safe now." His fingers felt rough, and yet, he was gentle.

The flutter I'd begun to feel in my stomach, whenever I was around him, intensified. *Careful, Ashlyn, don't lose control!* I took the tissue from him and blew my nose. "Sorry, I seem to be crying a lot lately."

"You have a right to cry all you want to. You're the gutsiest woman I've ever met."

I told him about jogging through the woods towards the distant sound of a chainsaw and meeting the woodsman character.

"Must have been Clete," Remy said. "Vietnam vet, bit of a recluse."

"He was a scary character; fired a warning shot at me. At first, I thought it was the Russians. He said I was trespassing on his property. But he gave me a drink of water and pointed me in the right direction. When I got to a gravel road, I hid again when the Russians came by in their black car. Then I flagged down a logging truck." I frowned. "I had to leave your rifle in the woods there. Sorry."

"You carried it all that way?"

"Yup."

"Don't worry about it. You could hardly flag down a truck while waving a rifle."

"Anyway, that's how I got here."

"I think it's time to go to the police." He looked over at me. "Don't you think so?" He scrunched up his face. "Mind you, I'm not partial to the cops. Us shrimpers seem to be always on the losing end of things whenever any law enforcement types come sniffing around. But this is different."

"Just drop me off at the sheriff's office. I have no

right to involve you in my problems."

"Young lady, ya'll is starting to get me riled."

Young lady? My mouth fell open as I stared at him.

His mouth was cracked in a smile and his gaze danced with mischief.

I couldn't help smiling in return. "But…"

"No buts. I haven't had this much excitement in a coon's age. Besides, I am involved."

"Excitement? I'd hardly call getting your truck bombed and having to move your mother excitement."

"Perhaps excitement isn't the right word." He rubbed the stubble on his face. "But it gives me something to occupy my mind instead of obsessing about the price of shrimp. Anyway, the police. You agree?"

"Yes."

"Since it's a matter of Russian mobsters, the FBI will need to be involved. If we go to the State Police, they'll try to deal with it themselves. They tend to be jealous of the FBI."

"The FBI is already involved." I said. "I think I told you about the two agents. Since then, they seem to be shadowing me. One agent, the woman, has checked on me a couple of times."

"Do you know how to contact them?"

"I had their card but left it with all my stuff."

"I think we need to go to the local sheriff. He'll know how to contact them, and he can provide the protection you need."

He started the truck and pulled out of the parking lot.

# 40

Remy drove to the Glynn County Sheriff's office on Newcastle Street. "Why don't you let me take the lead and tell the sheriff what happened. He'll want to question you, of course." Inside the station, Remy went up to the receptionist. "We'd like to see Sheriff Donner to report an attempted kidnapping."

"Kidnapping? Right down the hall, first door on the left. I'll tell the sheriff you're coming."

The door opened and a paunchy man in a short-sleeve khaki shirt leaned out and peered in our direction. He beckoned, and then indicated a couple of scarred chairs in front of his desk. He pointed a finger at Remy. "You're that troublemaker with the shrimp boat. Robert...no, Rembrandt, no, Remy. That's it, you're Remy Jeandeau."

Remy's voice took on a hard edge. "Sheriff, that was all a misunderstanding about a loggerhead turtle and a couple of dead dolphins. You know as well as I do that I had nothing to do with their deaths. Those sport fishermen make up all kinds of stories. They'd like nothing better than to see shrimpers driven out of business."

"Yes, well..." He turned to me. "Ma'am, you are?"

"Ashlyn Forsyth. And I..."

"Excuse me, ma'am, but before we hear your story, do I have your permission to record this interview?"

"Yes, of course. But it's not a story!"

This was not going well. The sheriff seemed to assume I was another hysterical female.

"I should have warned you," Remy whispered.

"I didn't mean to imply that whatever you're going to tell me didn't happen." The way he folded his arms and leaned back, told me that was exactly what he believed.

"On Friday, Ashlyn…"

The Sheriff broke in. "Let the lady tell us what happened, unless you were the one threatened with kidnapping."

"On Friday, I returned from jogging on the beach to be confronted by two men. They questioned me about the whereabouts of my husband…ex-husband. When I told them I didn't know where he was, they grabbed me and were about to stuff me into the trunk of their car, when—" I motioned towards Remy "—he showed up."

"Where did this take place?"

"At Mimosa Cottage," I said. "Right on the beach, north of the Lighthouse, oh, five or six blocks. I don't remember the number."

"I know the place. Can you describe the men?"

"They were Russian. One was thin—oh, about my height. Five foot five. Dressed in a dark suit that didn't fit well. He called himself Pavel. The other was big, heavy, at least six or seven inches taller. He wore khaki pants and a muscle shirt and had tattoos on his chest and shoulders. The short guy, who seemed like the leader, called him Gorya."

"They told you their names. Why would they do that?"

"At first, they tried to get information. They said they were business associates of my husband representing some Russian company."

"They were Russian? And your husband, what is his business?"

"He owns a financial services company. Invests for people."

"What happened next?"

Remy leaned forward and took up the story. "I was driving by, heard screams, saw them about to stuff Ms. Forsyth here into the trunk of their car. I stopped, grabbed my shotgun and told them to let her go. Fired off a shot to show them I meant business. They freed her and she ran to my truck. I fired a couple of shots into their tires so they couldn't follow."

"That was you? The shots fired over there on Friday?"

"Yup."

"Why didn't you report it then?"

"Kind of worried about our lives. The most important thing to do at that point was escape. Get Ms. Forsyth to someplace safe. We thought they'd leave her alone if she disappeared."

"You had a responsibility to report the incident." His voice rose. "To me!"

The muscles on Remy's neck corded as he leaned forward and tapped his fingers on the desk. "That's what we're doing now."

They were like two bulls pawing the ground. I rushed to defuse the confrontation. "I apologize. I should have reported the matter, but I was too frightened. I feared for my life. You should have seen those men. They were evil." I shuddered. "Evil! Remy here, he risked his life to rescue me."

"Now ma'am, I understand why you'd be afraid, but that's why we're here, to keep people safe."

"But we weren't safe. They fire-bombed his truck!"

The sheriff leaned back to look up at the ceiling fan. "Jeandeau, that truck was yours?"

"It was."

"Homeland Security has that cordoned off." He turned to me. "Why don't you fill in a few more details?"

I went on to tell him everything that had happened since Remy's rescue until we walked into his office. Remy added the occasional detail.

When I was through, the sheriff stood up. "OK, the way your jeans look certainly corroborates your story. If you'll give me a few minutes, I'll contact the FBI. They'll crucify me if I don't pass this on to them."

"That's why we came," I said. "So you could contact them. Two agents—Cutter and Tibbs—interviewed me about my husband's business a month or so ago. They'll know about those two Russians."

"Cutter and Tibbs? Know 'em. Maybe you should have told me they were involved when you first came in."

"Sorry," I said. "It just seemed right to tell you before we mentioned the FBI."

"And you're right about that. Local law enforcement needs to know the facts, facts the FBI often keep to themselves."

He led us out of his office and pointed to a couple of seats in the waiting room. "I'll get my secretary to type everything up. You can come back and sign your statement later. Can I get you something; a coffee, a soda?"

"No, thanks."

I sat down while Remy paced back and forth. The receptionist smiled at me over the counter. "Are you sure I can't get you something?"

I ran my hand through my hair. "What I need is a change of clothes, but I don't suppose you provide that unless you jail me."

"No."

I had cracked a joke! I must be getting used to living on the edge. Gallows humor?

"I forgot to tell you. Your stuff from the cabin is in the truck, behind the seat."

I felt like throwing my arms around him—again. Instead, I stood up and held out my hands. "You're a life-saver. Can I have the keys?"

He waved towards the door. "Not locked. This is a police station!"

In the truck, I rummaged around until I found what I needed. Returning inside, I went into the ladies' restroom, washed up, and changed into black jeans and a blouse. My sneakers would have to do. I reapplied my lipstick and almost felt presentable.

Remy had stopped his pacing and was munching on a candy bar. He pointed to the vending machine beside the bulletin board of wanted posters. "I didn't have my breakfast or lunch. Can I get you one?"

I shook my head and sat down beside him.

"Sorry," he said. "I should have realized you'd want to change. Been a long time."

The sheriff strode over before I could answer. "OK, I've arranged for you to meet Agents Cutter and Tibbs at the overlook park on Glynn Avenue where it meets Gloucester."

"I know the place," Remy said.

# 41

Remy drove to the park overlooking the inland waterway. "I'll circle back and we can pull in by one those picnic tables. No one in sight. The agents probably want to look us over before they show themselves. Make sure we're not followed."

"Can we pick up a coffee first?" I said. "If I'm going to be interrogated again, I'd like to have something to distract me."

"Good idea."

We returned to the park with a couple of coffees. When we were seated, I took a sip of coffee and looked at Remy. "I don't know what I would have done without your help, Remy. But with the FBI taking over, I think you should distance yourself as far as possible from me. I attract trouble like a magnet—or as you said, like a lightning rod."

"I don't think the FBI or those Russian goons are going to let me just fade into the sunset. We're kind of linked."

"But Remy, your shrimping…"

"The first time you refused my offer of help, I chalked it up as natural. The second time, I was offended. Guessed you were too highbrow to accept a ride from the likes of me."

"That's not true!"

"I know now, that's just your way." He leaned across the table. "But you'll just have to accept hanging around until you're safe again and I have some satisfaction for my burnt-out truck. Then, if you want, I can fade away." He looked down. "Not that I'll want to."

"Remy, you're amazing!"

A red sports car pulled into the parking lot as we were talking.

I looked up to see Cutter and Tibbs get out. Cutter wore blue jeans, a baseball cap, and a T-shirt. Agent Tibbs seemed more in character with her white blouse, dark trousers, black jacket and a pair of sunglasses perched on her hair.

Cutter extended his hand to Remy. "Ms. Forsyth, we know. You must be Remy Jeandeau. I'm Agent Larry Cutter." He gestured behind him. "And this is Agent Susan Tibbs."

"Can we join you?" Tibbs asked.

"Let me say, first of all, how appreciative we are for you coming to Ms. Forsyth's aid." Cutter said to Remy. "We know you've both had a very difficult time."

"But we don't understand why you took so long to contact us," Agent Tibbs said. "The sheriff informed us you were grabbed on Friday. We gave you our card."

"Your card? Rather thoughtlessly, I left it at the beach house...don't you realize I've been running for my life?"

"Yes, but..." Tibbs said.

"It's OK, Tibbs." Cutter held up his hand. "Let's catch up. Mrs. Forsyth, let's begin with you. The Sheriff only gave me the vaguest of details."

Tibbs pulled a tiny black recorder from an inside pocket and placed it on the table between us. "Do you mind?"

"I guess not." I took a gulp of coffee, and then

described being surprised by the appearance of Pavel and Gorya on Friday.

"Can you describe them?" Cutter took out a notebook.

"One, the leader, was short and thin, almost emaciated. The other was big, with tattoos; must have been two hundred fifty pounds, at least."

"Sounds like Pavel Kolodenko and Gorya Slotnikof; we've been after them for a couple of years. Nasty pair. Mrs. Forsyth, did they say why they wanted to kidnap you?"

"They said to force me to tell them where my husband was. They blame him for losing money, or something. But you know all about that. They didn't seem to believe me when I told them he'd filed for divorce and disappeared."

"They don't take lightly the loss of millions," Cutter said. "So what happened next?"

Remy took up the story. "I stopped, grabbed my shotgun and told them to let her go. To enforce my meaning I peppered the big guy in the foot, and then shot out their rear tires. I figured they'd never look for her on a shrimp boat, so that's where I took her. After shrimping all night Friday, a storm came up and we had to return to port Saturday morning. From there I took her to my mother's place, thinking she'd be safe there. But Sunday morning I found my truck fire-bombed. I knew my mother's place was no longer safe, so I warned Ma to leave, and took Ashlyn to our family fishing cabin. She can take it up from there."

"They must have enormous resources to find Remy's truck, and then me in an obscure fishing cabin. Anyway, this morning I heard a vehicle approaching on the lane to the cabin. It was a black car, so I panicked, climbed out the window and took off through the swamp." I shuddered at the memory. "It was the same two men. They shouted at me, threatened me by firing their guns, but I lost them." I paused. "So, what happens now?"

Cutter rested his chin on his fists and frowned. "That's a good question."

# 42

"Give us a few minutes to talk this over."

I walked to the shore where I could watch a couple of ducks bobbing for food.

Remy went over to the truck, pulled out his cell phone and called someone.

After ten or fifteen minutes, Cutter called us back. "First of all," he said. "We'll provide protection to keep you safe. The Bratva are not going to give up, unless they find your husband first. You've still no idea where he is?"

"No idea," I said. "He sent another short e-mail the other day, but said he was on his way out of town."

"Do you have the e-mail? There might be some clue in it."

"I think it's saved on my laptop."

"OK we'll look at that later." He turned to Remy. "Do you have a buddy where you can stay?"

"Sure," Remy said. "But I'm not going to let a couple of thugs intimidate me."

"I don't think you understand how ruthless they are. What about your boat? Can you dock it in another harbor?"

"The government has us regulated to death. We can't just go wherever we want to. But I wouldn't worry; my shrimping buddies will watch my back."

"They've burned your truck. They won't hesitate to sink your boat," Agent Tibbs said.

"The main question here is; what are you going to

do to prove Ms. Ashlyn's innocence, help her get back her life? You do understand your actions have turned her life into a nightmare."

I touched Remy's arm.

"Look," Cutter said. "We've got off on the wrong foot, somehow. We're here to help you. We're on the same side. Don't look at us as adversaries. And since we're going to be working together we may as well do it on a first name basis. I'm Larry and my colleague is Susan."

Susan looked from me to Remy. "As Larry said, we're here to protect you, as well as catch those guys. Kidnapping is a federal crime."

"If we're on a first name basis you should call me Ashlyn."

"OK, Ashlyn," Cutter said. "Let's be honest. We can't stop you from going back to New York or wherever, but as I said, the Bratva are going to keep trying to use you as collateral to pressure your husband. The sooner we find your husband the better. Alternatively, the sooner we catch Pavel and Gorya, the safer you'll be. And we have a plan on how to do that, but it requires your cooperation."

"What kind of a plan?" I said. "

"I'd like you to move back into your beach cottage."

Remy snorted. "What kind of a plan is that? You want her to be a decoy?"

"Hear me out." Larry took off his baseball cap, laid it on the table, and ran his fingers through his bristly black hair. "We'll settle Ashlyn in the cottage, install motion sensors and surveillance cameras all monitored from the cottage next door." He turned to his colleague. "Susan will stay with Ashlyn at all times, posing as a friend visiting from New York."

"And just wait for them to show?" I said. "Like I'm shark bait or something?"

"Mrs. Forsyth, Ashlyn, you'll be completely safe," Susan said. "As Larry explained, I'll be with you and we'll put together a team of other agents monitoring you 24/7."

Remy was shaking his head. "I don't like it."

"It's for Ashlyn to say yes or no. But just be clear, if we don't do something soon to flush Kolodenko and Slotnikof into the open, they'll go into deep cover and she'll never know when they may strike. It could be at the grocery store, on the Interstate, when she's back home—or anywhere. And they'll call in other members of the mob. As it is now, they're probably trying to hide their failure from the mob big-shots."

"But won't they suspect something is up and back off if I suddenly act as if nothing has happened?"

"They may," Cutter said. "But remember, you've humiliated them. They have to prove themselves to the mob. We'll increase the pressure; make it so tempting they'll have to act."

"How're you going to do that?" Remy asked.

"We'd like Ashlyn to go back to work at the Shrimpboat Café," Susan replied. "Act as if she feels she's in the clear. That the danger is past."

"Act...as if...?" I sputtered.

"Ashlyn, you've been incredible up to now," Cutter said. "The Bureau has given us leave to use our own discretion on how to proceed, but only for a few days. If our plan doesn't work, we're to bring you in for further questioning. I know what we propose won't be easy, but we're sure you can do it, and we'll have agents there all the way: several alternating as customers, another across the road, plus I'll be involved." He held my gaze without flinching.

I looked sideways at Remy.

"You don't have to do this," Remy said.

"I just want this to be over," I said. "I'll do it—on one condition."

"One condition?" Larry said.

"That you protect my daughter, Tiffany."

"Done," Larry said. "We've already taken care of that. An agent is tasked with shadowing her."

"When I arrive at the beach house," Susan said. "You need to act as if I'm a friend from New York. You'll call me...let's see...Nicole. I'll be Nicole Seagrave. You'll need to meet me on the porch, embrace me as if we're good friends. I know that won't be easy, but try. If you want, I'll take the lead."

"I'm not very good at acting."

"Just follow her lead," Larry said.

"I'll do my best."

Susan reached into a pocket and pulled out a wallet. She took out a plastic disk the size of quarter and handed it to me. "You'll need to clip this onto the inside your bra. Press it if you're threatened. It'll send out a signal which our surveillance team will pick up. Keep it on you at all times."

I turned my back, reached under my T-shirt, clipped the disk to my bra and returned to the table. "Let's get on with it."

Larry stood. "You'll need to give us an hour or so to install the surveillance equipment and get ready." He turned to Remy. "Can you drive her around or go to a restaurant or something for an hour?"

"I'll take her to the Flying Duck," Remy said. "But just so you know, I'm not very happy about this."

"It'll be OK," Larry said. "Another thing, Ashlyn. Where is your stuff?"

I pointed towards Remy's truck.

Larry pulled out a cell phone. "We can't have Remy drop you off. It'll just make him a target. We've got an agent working as a taxi driver. I'll call him. He'll pick you up at the Flying Duck in an hour."

# 43

When the driver left the beach house, I made sure all the doors and windows were locked, and then collapsed on the sofa.

How nice it would be to have this behind me. But then what? How much more of this could I stand?

A sporty blue car pulled into the driveway. The driver beeped the horn, jumped out, and waved.

Playing my part, I ran out onto the porch and shrieked, "Nicole!"

She'd changed from typical FBI agent dress into a pair of khaki shorts, a T-shirt and sandals. On the porch, she wrapped her arms around me in a hug.

I flinched.

"Just relax," she whispered in my ear. "You're doing good." She chatted away like a long lost friend while I helped her bring a couple of suitcases into the beach house. When the door closed, her agent persona reappeared. She marched from room to room inspecting the yard through each window. She tried the window latches.

"Not very secure, is it?"

"Don't worry," she said. "I'll set up motion sensors in each room monitored from here." She pointed to the guest room. "The signals will be relayed next door to the surveillance team. That way there'll always be two watching for intruders."

One of her suitcases held an array of electronic gadgets. She turned to me. "Could you please make coffee while I get set up?"

I kept glancing outside. Could the birdwatcher on the beach be from the agency, or the Bratva? Who was in the car that drove slowly by the house?

Agent Tibbs—it would take effort to learn to call her Nicole—came over to where I stood looking out the living room window. "You're as jumpy as a grasshopper—which is understandable. But for this to work, you need to relax, or act as if you are relaxed. Imagine yourself playing a part in a movie. Let's take coffee out onto the back porch and watch the ocean, pretend we're girlfriends catching up."

"OK. I'll try."

Nicole began to jabber about her kids and her loser of a husband.

I gave short answers.

She leaned over and touched me on the arm. "I know this is hard, but try to smile a bit. We're friends who are catching up after a long absence. Tell me about your kids."

I could do that. "Tyler is the opposite of his dad. He hates finance; dropped out of his business course in junior year to see the world. He already has a bucket list and he's only 21!"

"What does he want to do?"

"He's been hiking in the Australian outback and he wants to trek the Serengeti, canoe down the Yukon River, climb Everest, and explore the Amazon to its source. At least that was what he said before he left for Australia."

"What does he plan to use for money?"

"That's just what his father asked, too. He's grabbing jobs when he can."

"The idealism of youth," Susan said. "What about

Tiffany?"

"Oh, Tiffany is more like her dad. She's taking a business course with a minor in marketing." I paused. "You're sure she's all right?"

"We can check right now, if you want." Tibbs took an ultra-slim cell phone from the pouch clipped to her shorts, punched in a few numbers, and after a moment, said, "Connect me to team three...Mikos, can you talk to the mother? She's concerned about her daughter." She passed me the phone.

"Hello," I said.

A female voice came on the line. "Good afternoon Mrs. Forsyth."

"Good afternoon. How is my daughter, Tiffany?"

"Your daughter is doing fine, in fact, she's very impressive. I'm sitting here at the back of a lecture hall listening to her and three other students give a marketing presentation on some new digital device. I don't understand any of the technical mumbo jumbo, but I must say, your daughter is a natural. I'd buy it in a heartbeat."

Tears sprang to my eyes. "You don't know how good that makes me feel. Can you arrange for me to talk to her?"

"Well, I'm not sure that would be a good idea. I understand that she knows she is being watched, but not who is doing it. If we reveal ourselves, it will make it harder for her to act natural. Ask the agent there with you to see if there is any way they can arrange it."

"Thanks." I passed the phone back to Tibbs, who cut it off. "Susan," I said.

"Nicole. I'm Nicole Seagrave. You've got to forget you ever heard of Susan Tibbs."

"I'll try. Look, I need to contact my daughter. You

said not to use my e-mail program and my cell phone was smashed. Can you arrange a call?"

"Can you give it a couple of days? We need to get you back working at the café."

"She'll be so worried."

The phone trilled.

She flipped it open and listened, before motioning to go inside. She waved me towards the bathroom. "Wait in there until we check this out. Probably a false alarm."

# 44

I eyed the shower stall. It didn't look like it could stop slugs. What if I opened the bathroom door and found Susan, ah, Nicole, lying on the living room floor in a pool of blood?

Pavel and Gorya would grab me, stuff me in the trunk of their car and take off. They'd torture me to tell them Craig's location. I wouldn't be able to, so they'd kill me. I shuddered.

The door opened and I jumped up, smacking my head on the shelf over the toilet.

"It was a false alarm," Nicole said. "Hey, are you OK? You look pale."

"I'm fine, just nervous," I said as we walked back into the living room.

"I've been thinking about your daughter. We could send an e-mail through a secure FBI server. You could say that a friend let you use their computer. But first we need to get you back to work in the café."

"I like the e-mail idea. But do you think it's really necessary for me to return to work?"

"Yes, I do. You need to be out in the public eye where we can keep you safe, but lure them into showing themselves. This cottage is out-of-the way; they're unlikely to think of coming back here, unless they see you first. And it's harder to protect without giving ourselves away."

"But..."

"I know you feel like a decoy—very vulnerable.

But actually, you'll be safer. We'll have a team on you at all times. In rotation."

"I guess until you catch them, or they catch Craig, I'll never be safe."

Nicole grimaced in affirmation.

I stood up. "Let's do it. You'll have to loan me your phone if you want me to call Holly at the café."

"Before you call her, let's go over what you want to say."

"What's there to go over?" I asked. "I just ask for my job back."

"You have to be confident and cheerful. She'll be wondering how you can leave that episode behind you so quickly. Tell her you've gone to the FBI and that they've nabbed the guys who tried to abduct you. And you need the money."

"You mean lie to her?"

"A necessary fabrication."

Holly answered on the fourth ring. "Shrimpboat Café, the best home-cooked meals on the island. How can I help you?"

"Holly, it's Ashlyn. I…"

"Ashlyn! I've been worried about you. What's happening? Are you OK?"

"Fine. Just fine. Remy picked me up, took me to the sheriff, then to the FBI. They'd already caught the guys who tried to abduct me."

"Already caught? That's good news. But how…?"

"I…I don't know how. I'm just glad it's over. But I need to do something to get my mind off the last few days. I would really like to get my job back."

"Your job? Oh, Ashlyn, honey, shouldn't you take a few days to relax? Why don't you go to Myrtle Beach, sit in the sun, and get your mind off things?"

"I can't do that, Holly."

"Why not? A friend has a condo there you could use."

Tears came to my eyes. "Holly, that's so sweet, but it wouldn't work. If I sit around, I'll be a wreck going over everything again and again. I need to be doing something. Besides you must be run ragged with Lottie in the hospital."

"We are busy. Are you sure you can handle it?"

"You afraid I'll drop another tray of dishes?"

"No, nothing like that. I'm not worried about your abilities. A couple of our regular customers were asking if you were coming back. No, I'm just worried about you."

"So, when can I start?"

"Could you come in today and help with the dinner crowd? Say four o'clock?"

"Wonderful. I'll be there."

Shutting down the phone I handed it back to Susan...uh, Nicole.

"You did good," she said, smiling. "Are you sure you aren't an actor on the side?"

"I hate lying to Holly, but at least it was true that I need to be doing something and not sitting around." Suddenly, another complication popped into my mind. "What about Remy?"

"No problem. I'll have Agent Cutter fill him in. Are you and he...?"

"No!" I moved towards my bedroom. "I've got to take a shower, find something to wear, and get to the café by four."

# 45

When I appeared at the back door of the Shrimpboat Café, Holly gathered me in a bear hug. "Ashlyn, are you telling me everything?"

"Yes. Isn't it wonderful that the FBI caught them so quickly?"

"Wonderful." She cocked her head to one side. "Almost unbelievable."

Claude appeared from the kitchen. The perpetual frown on his face softened into something almost welcoming. "We could use your help."

I took it as a compliment and smiled at him. "Where do you want me to start?"

"You know the drill," he said, as he returned to the grill.

"He's a barrel of sunshine," I said.

"Deep down, he's really glad to have you back and so am I. When I called Lottie Jane about you coming back, she was more hesitant, but finally agreed."

I spent the first half hour prepping veggies. Were Scarecrow and his sidekick around somewhere? Or had they sent in another team I wouldn't recognize? The only customers were a couple of workmen and a family with two kids. About four-thirty more customers arrived.

I joined Holly out front and was kept so busy I had no time to stoke the fear. Still, every time a black car went by on the street, my stomach gave a lurch. A couple of regulars came in and beckoned me over.

Instead of opening the menu one of them, a burly truck driver, asked about Lottie. "How's she doing?"

"She came through the surgery well," I said. "But she's going to take some time to get back her strength."

"Well, you tell her we're rootin' for her."

"I will. Now, what can I get you guys?"

Larry—Agent Cutter—came in and sauntered to a table near the back. I breathed a sigh of relief. Dressed as he was in jeans and a loose sports shirt, no one would consider him a federal agent, a tourist maybe. He laid his cell phone and a newspaper on the table and glanced around.

I handed him a menu. "Can I get you a coffee?"

"Is it still as good as Lottie Jane used to make it?"

"Holly makes it just as well as Lottie Jane."

"Great. Bring me a cup, black."

His head was buried in the sports section of an Atlanta paper when I returned with the coffee. He looked up. "Thanks."

"Ready to order?"

"What do you recommend?"

"If you like shrimp, I'd suggest the shrimp platter. Best shrimp on the coast. The coleslaw is made fresh twice daily and the fries are cut right here."

"That's what I'll have, then," he said, returning to his newspaper.

The backfire of a truck reverberated through the café.

I jumped, dropping a couple of dirty plates. Every eye turned my way as I knelt to pick the pieces up.

Holly knelt beside me. "Honey, don't worry. That backfire startled me, too. I just about dropped a whole tray."

"Sorry, Holly."

"Do you need a few minutes? I can cover for you. It may be too much, you coming back to work so soon."

"I…I'm OK. This keeps me busy. I don't have to sit and think about what a dope I've been."

In the back, I dumped the fragments into the garbage, and then went into the staff bathroom. After scrubbing my hands, I stood for a few minutes gripping the sink. I stared at my reflection. I applied fresh lipstick and tried to compose myself.

When I returned to the café, I kept busy delivering orders, refilling coffee cups, clearing tables, and bantering with customers about being clumsy. My mishap had endeared me to the people. The tips were larger than I'd ever received.

Two men in dark business suits came in.

"Welcome to the Shrimpboat Café. The special tonight is either jambalaya with garlic toast, or the shrimp platter with coleslaw and fries. Can I bring you some coffee while you're looking over the menu?"

The older of the two, a balding man in his late forties, nodded his head. "Yeah, that'd be great. Two coffees."

I pondered his accent, slight though it was. Had to be European. I returned with the coffees and a saucer of creamers.

The younger one, with short black hair, pointed to the menu and asked about a couple of the dishes. There it was again. The slightly guttural accent. Eastern European?

The older man pointed to the menu. "I'll have the jambal…however you say it."

"And I'll take the shrimp platter," the other

replied.

I wrote down their orders. Outwardly calm, my heart was thudding so loud that I was sure they could hear it.

They were Russian—had to be. The older one had an accent just like Pavel.

I fled into the kitchen.

# 46

I loaded dishes into the dishwasher until I felt calm enough to look back at the two men with Slavic accents. Both had on business suits. Did the Russian mafia wear suits? Pavel had. The ties looked conservative, yet fashionable.

Could they be selling insurance or farm equipment? Surely, their accents meant they hadn't been in America long. But some people kept their accents for generations.

The older man was talking on a cell phone. He could be telling the gang they'd found me while his younger companion surveyed the restaurant to see if there'd be any interference when they snatched me.

The ding of Claude's bell interrupted my thoughts. *Smarten up, Ashlyn. Stop imagining things. Larry is not going to let anything happen.*

I took a turn around the café refilling glasses of iced tea. When their orders were ready, I delivered them, afraid to speak lest my voice break. Both smiled at me.

I detoured towards Agent Larry who was holding up his mug as a sign he wanted more. "Just half a cup. You were right about both the coffee and the shrimp platter. Excellent. I'm sorely tempted to get a piece of lemon meringue pie, but," he patted his waistline, "I don't have any room, besides I need to keep trim."

"It's made at Grandma's Bakery, down the street," I said haltingly. "Melts in your mouth."

"Another time." He took a sip of coffee and mumbled from behind the mug, "Those two men are ours. Relax. Try not to be so nervous. You're under constant surveillance." Aloud, he said. "When you get a chance, could I have my bill?"

How was I going to keep up a front until we closed at nine o'clock?

Remy come in with his two crewmen, Gaston and Ches. Remy exchanged greetings with other customers as he sauntered over to a window booth where they all sat down. He wore his usual captain's cap, a flannel shirt, and worn jeans.

My stomach gave a little lurch as I thought of him leaving again on his boat. He'd be gone for a day or more, and I'd gotten used to him being around. I felt safe when he was within call—and something much more.

I tried to catch Holly's eye to indicate she should wait on Remy's table. I needed to avoid adding fuel to the uncomfortable feelings Remy was arousing in me. With a smirk, Holly shook her head and pointed at me.

I proceeded to their table. "Good evening, gents. On your way out upon the bounding main?"

Gaston and Ches, frowned at the obscure pirate term, but Remy smiled at my reference to the ocean. "Yes, we're off shortly to hunt for white gold." Then his smile dimmed. "But how are you doing? Everything OK?"

"Oh, I'm fine," I said as I filled their glasses. "Everything's good. I'm so very thankful for all your help."

"Let me know if you need anything, now."

Gaston grinned as he looked from Remy to me. "Now this is interesting. I haven't seen Remy give any woman the time of day for years—that is, until you arrived."

Remy punched him hard on the shoulder.

"Ow, what'cha do that for?" Gaston rubbed his shoulder. "It's the truth."

"So what'll it be?" I asked, embarrassed and trying to diffuse the situation. "I'd list the specials, but I think you guys have them memorized."

About the time Remy and his crew left, Agent Tibbs came in. I introduced her to Holly as Nicole, a friend from New York.

After we closed, Nicole drove us home. "They've installed motion sensors all around the house. Someone will be awake all night watching the monitors. They've added security inside as well. Plus, they have night vision goggles in case anyone does approach."

"Sounds like I should relax. But…"

"But what?"

"Have you always been 100% successful? I mean, no security is perfect, right?"

"Nothing's perfect. But you are better protected than anyone I've ever seen."

That night, I slept fitfully and woke often to peer at the darkness. Wild scenarios invaded my imagination, scenarios in which Pavel and Gorya killed the agents and carried me to a secluded cabin.

By the fourth day back at the café, I was beginning to think that the worst was behind me. When Lottie Jane returned to work on Thursday, she moved me from afternoons and evenings to the morning and afternoon shifts. The need to concentrate on customers relieved my mind of my own worries.

Nicole stayed with me and picked me up after

work.

Larry alternated with other agents at keeping up surveillance at the café.

On our drive home I told Nicole I needed to shop. "I've got a splitting headache. I need to stop at the drug store to pick up some pain killers and a couple of other things."

"Just make it quick." Nicole pulled into the parking lot, scanned the cars parked in front and surveyed the adjoining stores. Finally, she spoke into her phone, giving our location. "Let's go. I'll go first. You follow."

Inside, I searched the aisles until I found the painkillers.

A shot rang out.

A hand grabbed me from behind, covering my mouth and nose with a wet cloth.

I kicked and struggled until I lost consciousness.

# 47

As I returned to consciousness, the first sounds I heard were those of heavy traffic. I lay on the hard floor of some vehicle with my wrists handcuffed behind my back and a rag around my eyes. An oily gag kept me from screaming but didn't stop the panic. The smell of tomatoes, overripe peaches, and the occasional whiff of rotten vegetables assailed my nostrils.

Had they chloroformed me? How much time had passed? An hour? Two? Had Nicole been shot?

I'd had no chance to activate the alarm clipped to my bra. Could I punch the alarm with my hands shackled?

I rolled onto my right side as I tried to find some position that would relieve the pain radiating from my shoulders and wrists, but I came up against a rough surface. By the smell, I concluded that crates of tomatoes surrounded me. I twisted onto my left side, but felt resistance. I must be concealed in the back of a grocer's delivery van. The drone of heavy traffic meant we were on I-95. But were we going north or south?

In an attempt to activate the alarm, I pressed my chest against the crates on my left, but only succeeded in scraping my face. I curled my legs so I could use them to push, but soon realized it was futile. My attempts to bite through the gag left only an oily taste in my mouth. When I tried to sit up, my head bumped against something.

Terror constricted my chest and I lay back trying

to calm down. Being bound, gagged, and buried beneath crates of produce dispersed whatever reserves of strength I had left. I began to kick at the crates and roll from side to side.

"Ah, our little swallow is awake." The muffled voice sounded like Pavel, the scarecrow. "Just keep still," he shouted, "Or you'll be buried in crates of tomatoes and peaches. Would you like that?"

All that came out when I tried to scream was a whimper.

"Just enjoy the ride. We'll soon be there. Then we can get better acquainted."

I lay on my side trying to breathe through my nose and still the shudders that racked my body. I tried to recite the Lord's Prayer, but kept getting stuck at *thy will be done*. Finally, I just pleaded with God to ease the black terror.

The whine of the tires on pavement slowed and the sound of traffic faded. The truck lurched, bounced a couple of times, and stopped. A vehicle door opened and closed, and then there was the metallic squeal of a garage door being raised. The truck moved inside and the door closed.

Someone dragged me along the floor of the truck and pulled me to my feet. I stumbled, but shrugged off the rough hands that reached out.

"Well, here we are, Mrs. Forsyth. Time for you to tell us how to find your husband." Bony hands untied my gag and blindfold.

Scarecrow…Pavel…stood in front of me.

Gorya was grinning like a gargoyle. He still wore a tank top that did little to hide his brawn.

I worked my jaw to relieve the pain the gag had inflicted and leaned over to spit out some of the oily taste in my mouth. Out of the corner of my eyes, I tried to take in my surroundings.

I was in some kind of a warehouse. Crates stood in erratic piles along one side. Dim light filtered in through dirty windows near the ceiling. In front of the produce truck stood their black sedan.

I took a couple of rasping breaths and motioned over my shoulder. "What about the handcuffs? I can't think of anything beyond the pain in my shoulders."

Pavel tossed a key to Gorya.

Gorya slid his hand down my back, touching me and making my skin crawl.

I screamed and tried to wiggle away.

Pavel backhanded me. "Shut up! Any more screaming and I'll turn you over to Gorya…right here on the floor."

"You won't get away with this," I whimpered, massaging my face and shoulders with tingling hands.

"Over there. Take her over there."

Gorya dragged me across the floor in spite of my kicks, and pushed me onto a metal chair.

I continued to work some feeling back into the strained ligaments of my shoulders. I had to be ready to escape.

Pavel turned on a radio. The sound of pop music blared from the speaker and echoed through the warehouse. He grabbed a chair, sat down, and motioned to Gorya.

Gorya seized a handful of my hair and forced me to look directly at Pavel.

Tears began to stream from my eyes.

With one of his spidery hands, Pavel grabbed my nose and squeezed until I shrieked.

"Do I have your attention?" he asked.

"Ye...s."

"She's given us a lot of trouble. Hasn't she, Gorya?"

Gorya gave my hair another yank and growled something unintelligible.

"Pulling my hair won't help me think more clearly."

Pavel nodded to Gorya, who released me.

Whatever happened, they wouldn't let me out of here alive.

Could I buy time by pretending Craig would be contacting me soon, or send them off on a wild goose chase? Could I escape by stomping on Gorya's foot where Remy had shot it, kick Pavel in the groin, or bite his hand? If I ran, where would I hide?

Through a window I could see a neighboring building, but nothing else. A glance at my watch told me it was after seven. Best to play along with them; stall for time, find some way to activate the alarm in my bra. But even if I did, would anyone be within range so they could detect it?

# 48

Pavel stared at me. "Start talking."

"I'll tell you what I know," I said. "But, like I explained, Craig has disappeared and divorced me at the same time."

Pavel nodded to Gorya over my shoulder.

I heard a click and felt a sharp prick. "Ow," I cried, shrinking from the knife Gorya pressed against my cheek. "What are you doing that for? I told you I'd cooperate."

"Just want you to be clear about the alternative," Pavel said.

Gorya waved the knife in front of my face.

I stared at the drop of blood on the tip of the blade. My hand instinctively went to my cheek. "A month or so ago my...my husband sent me an e-mail informing me about the finality of our divorce. I couldn't contact him back because it was sent from an Internet café and he was leaving for another city even as he sent it." My voice rose. "How could I possibly know where he is now?"

"Tell us everything about him. More than you told us at the beach house. His friends. His contacts. Where he travels. The car he's driving. Where he banks. Everything."

I told them about his trips abroad, the color and license plate of his BMW, and the names of our banks. I listed a couple of his favorite restaurants and gave them the name of the exclusive club where he golfed and worked out. I put off naming any of our friends as long as I could.

While I talked, I scanned the warehouse for any avenue of escape. It was about a hundred feet by fifty feet with metal shelving down one of the sides. Many of the shelves were empty; others held crates of what I assumed to be fruits and vegetables. In front of the shelves there were more crates and boxes of produce piled erratically. High above the shelving, a row of small, dirty windows let in weak light.

Three offices had been built against the opposite wall. Their partitions extended two-thirds of the way to the girders that held up the roof. Through the smeared window of the first office, I could make out a row of clipboards on hooks and a desk with a computer.

A corridor ran between two of the offices to a side door. There appeared to be one or two other rooms off that corridor. Parked in an alcove near the far end of the warehouse stood one of those machines used to manhandle crates.

"What about that bimbo your husband drove off with?"

"You know about that?"

"Yeah, yeah, he's been squiring her around for months. She drove him to one of our meets."

Anger began to vie with the terror that made me shiver involuntarily.

Gorya chortled. "Wife's the last to know, huh, boss?"

I rubbed my cheek where Gorya's knife had pricked it, and then peered at the smear of blood on my fingers. I trembled.

If they had no intention of letting me get out of

here alive, why should Marlee escape unscathed? A wave of hatred coursed through me, hatred so intense that I felt my face flush. I took a deep breath and tried to fight it with no success. Then I answered, "Marlee is one of the financial consultants in his firm. She drives a silver sedan, lives in White Plains; East 16th Avenue, I think. She's a member of the Oak Valley Golf Course."

"Good. Now tell us about your son and daughter. Has your husband contacted them?"

I jerked. "No! You leave them out of this."

Gorya griped my shoulder and ran the blade along my cheek. "I think you should answer Mr. Pavel, or…"

I slumped in my chair. "My husband hasn't contacted either of them since he disappeared. Tyler's been backpacking in the Australian outback where he has no phone or Internet connection." I couldn't tell them about his being in Melbourne.

"And your daughter, Tiffany?" Pavel asked.

I massaged my forehead trying to ease the throbbing headache that made me want to vomit. "She's on an exchange program in Scotland," I whispered. "Part of her business course."

"I don't know if I believe you," Pavel said, his mouth stretching into an evil smile. "Maybe you need a little persuasion to make sure you're telling the truth."

"I've told you everything you asked. I've been cooperative." I jumped up, only to have Gorya slam me back into the chair.

"Please," I said, "I have to use the washroom."

Pavel frowned, and then pointed towards the corridor between the offices. "Gorya will go with you. You'll keep the door open."

I slouched in the direction Pavel had pointed. I

searched the warehouse for some way to escape. What to do? Make up names for Craig's friends and associates? Send them on a wild goose chase to Seattle? They were too suspicious. Somehow, I had to get away.

Gorya pushed me. "Hurry up!"

I stumbled into the bathroom. The reek made my eyes water. Dirt smeared the floor and grime rimmed the washbasin and mirror. The heavy door hung a little crooked on its hinges. I sidled behind it and pinched the tracking device clipped to my bra. I pushed the door almost closed and eyed the toilet.

Gorya pushed the door back to its half open position.

"A little privacy!" I cried, as I eased myself onto the soiled toilet. My mind raced from one scenario to another. Were the agents too far away to pick up the signal? I looked around the bathroom for some kind of weapon.

A plumber's helper stood on the floor beside the toilet, along with a bucket and a jug of bleach. Could I blind Gorya with bleach? The ceramic top of the toilet had been removed and leaned against the wall on the other side. Could I use that to hit Gorya? But did I have enough strength to swing it?

Somehow, I had to get past him and try to reach the door at the end of the corridor. If I couldn't open that, maybe I could hide behind the cases of produce. No, they'd find me too quickly. If I could climb high enough, I could use the plumber's helper to break out a window. But would I break a leg jumping from so high up?

Something…I had to think of something, and fast. Under the sink, I spied a length of pipe.

Gorya would see me if I reached for it.

That's when a desperate idea formed in my mind.

# 49

I eyed the jug of bleach. It would be inhumane. But did I want to deprive my kids of a mother, or did I want to live? And the thought of Remy skated around the fringes of my mind. I was at the age old dilemma of many Christians…them or me? Evil…or good?

I flushed the toilet, reached over to unscrew the jug's cap, and gripped it tightly in my right hand. Somehow, Gorya had to be lured into the bathroom. But how? The minutes ticked by.

"Hurry up."

I braced myself against the tank of the toilet, lifted my feet off the floor and shouted. "No! I'm not coming out."

Gorya bellowed and charged through the doorway.

I slammed the door with all my strength, catching him square on. He fell with a crash, landing full length on the floor. I jumped around the door and dumped the bottle on him. His hands went to his face and he began to shriek like a wounded buffalo. I grabbed the pipe from under the sink and smashed him on the head before jumping into the hallway.

I raced to the door where I skidded to a stop. It was locked with a padlock.

Pavel appeared at the end of the corridor waving a gun and shouting at me to stop.

Looking around frantically for another avenue of escape, my gaze fell on a barrel beside the door. I sprang onto the barrel and scrambled to the top of the bathroom wall, kicking over the barrel. Several shots rang out. I heard a whine and felt something graze my head.

I rolled onto the flimsy metal framework used to create drop ceilings. It sagged, threatening to dump me back into the bathroom. One of the foam pieces popped loose, giving me a clear view of Gorya screaming and thrashing as he tried to wipe the bleach from his eyes and face. I felt a momentary flash of guilt.

Pavel appeared in the doorway. He stared at the overturned bottle of bleach, and then rushed to the basin, turned on the tap and began to splash water on Gorya.

"You witch, you can't get away. I'm going to catch you and take pleasure in hearing you cry for mercy."

Balancing on the metal grid, I worked my way towards the solid wood of the office partition. I caught my breath before tiptoeing across the front of the offices to reach the far end of the warehouse. One foot slipped off the partition. A piece of the dropped ceiling gave way and I almost plunged to the floor of another room.

A couple of shots rang out.

"I know where you are," Pavel shouted from the bathroom. "There's nowhere to go. This warehouse is locked up tight. I'm coming after you, and when I get you, I'll skin you alive."

My heart hammered as I pulled back up onto the partition wall. Oblivious to any noise I might be making and with outstretched arms for balance, I ran along the top of the partitions until I came to the end of the offices. There I slipped over the edge, dropped to the floor, and raced to the big sliding door, only to find it padlocked shut. There had to be another avenue of escape, or place to hide. My gaze fell on the forklift parked against the wall.

I ran over, climbed into the driver's seat, and stared at the controls. After punching buttons and pushing various levers, the engine started, the lift at the front began to ascend, and the thing lurched forward. Scrunched down in the seat, I pushed the accelerator to the floor and steered for the warehouse door. The beast gained speed with agonizing slowness. Would I have enough momentum to crash through?

A shot glanced off the steel housing of the engine compartment. Another ricocheted off the lift mechanism. I crouched lower and prayed. *Lord help me!*

With a crash, I hit the door. The flimsy sheet metal crumpled under the impact. Bouncing wildly, the forklift plowed through. I spun the wheel right to get out of the line of fire. Once out of sight, I took my foot off the accelerator. Should I jump off and run, or turn around and try to run Pavel down?

The black anger fueled by adrenaline clouded my judgment. I was tired of running; tired of being a victim. I spun the wheel and accelerated around the corner towards the shattered door.

The speeding forklift caught Pavel off guard. With a shriek he leaped to one side, but not soon enough to escape the extended fork which speared through his coat, leaving a bloody gash along his side. His coat tore and he fell as I raced by. I spun the wheel, turned the forklift in a circle and aimed it again in his direction.

Dazed, he let out a bellow, jumped to his feet and fired. The bullets pinged into the metal housing of the lift mechanism until the pistol went silent. Out of ammunition.

He stood there staring, looking more like a scarecrow than ever with his coat torn and his face a mask of hatred.

I felt a wild desire to crush him into a grease spot on the pavement, to pound his bones into powder, to hear his head pop like a dropped watermelon.

He leaped to one side as I careened by. He fumbled in his pocket for another clip.

Sanity kicked in. It was time to go, so I sped out of sight around the corner of the warehouse, left the motor going, and took off running.

I plunged through the fringe of bushes bordering the warehouse parking lot, leapt across a drainage ditch, and ran through a vacant field towards a neighboring warehouse.

Halfway across the field, the forklift cut off. The bellow of rage that followed spurred me on.

Escape? The parking lot of the neighboring warehouse was empty. I raced around the corner of the first building and jumped behind a planting of evergreens to catch my breath. Collapsing on the ground with my back against a brick wall, I took in great gulps of air and tried to stifle noisy sobs.

Pavel wouldn't give up until he found me.

I shuddered and tried to think.

# 50

I peered around the corner of the building.

Pavel was halfway across the field headed in my direction.

Leaping up, I raced across the front of the warehouse to the other side where I found a fenced enclosure piled high with crates. I climbed over the fence and slipped between two towering piles where I would be out of sight. The aisle of wooden boxes ended at the chain link fence where I could be spotted if Pavel followed the fence.

Partway down the corridor of crates, I saw an irregular cranny about a foot and a half wide between the containers. It continued right through to the next aisle, but widened out halfway through. I crawled in sideways, bumping my head and scratching my arm until I reached the cranny where I could sit up.

"I know you're here somewhere," Pavel yelled. "I've called for more men. We'll find you if we have to search all night and block off every road. You witch, there's no escape!"

I squeezed the disk clipped to my bra a couple more times. The FBI had to be looking for me. And surely, they'd have every police force within a hundred miles on alert.

*Bang! Thunk.* I ducked my head as a bullet hit one of the crates. *Bang! Thunk.*

His shouts faded as he moved away.

*Be still....just keep calm, Ashlyn. Wait. Be patient. It*

*will soon be dark. Be still…and know that I am God…*

I drew up my knees and took deep breaths to slow my racing heart.

Ten minutes, perhaps fifteen went by without any further shouts.

A distant police siren sounded. Help was coming! The sound swelled…only to slowly fade away.

I groaned.

Another eternity dragged by before I heard a vehicle approaching. I shimmied out and peered towards the road. A sedan with the insignia of a security agency emblazoned on the door crawled into view. I ran to the fence and waved my arms, but the car continued down the road until it disappeared from sight. With a sigh, I returned to my hiding place.

Crickets began to tune up their instruments for an evening concert. Sweat trickled into my eyes. A breeze blew in the stench of something rotten. The sound of a scampering creature sent chills up my spine. Every time I stretched, I banged my head on the corner of a crate and when I squirmed to work out the agonizing kinks, I scraped my arm or leg on the rough wooden surface of another box. The minutes ticked by as the light began to fade.

The sound of another vehicle moved me to crawl out. I peered out and ducked my head back in. A black sedan was driving down the road.

I held a hand over my heart to still its pounding.

The car came to a stop in front of the next building and another car joined them from the opposite direction. Car doors slammed and commands were issued in Russian.

I ran to the back of the fenced-in enclosure and, using footholds on nearby crates, climbed the chain-link fence and jumped to the ground. A hundred yards behind the building, a row of weedy bushes screened a ditch. Beyond it, all I could see were fields. No cover there, unless I crouched below the height of the bushes and used the ditch to slip away. No, they'd search that for sure.

To my right loomed another warehouse. Going that way would bring me closer to Pavel and his thugs. I could go left, back the way I'd come from. Beyond it, I could see other buildings. Would they have a guard stationed there? If not, they would never think of me returning that way.

I had to find a phone fast. Keeping the building where I'd hidden between the car and me, I dashed back across the field, forced my way through the bushes along the ditch, and paused to listen. Distant voices murmured and the car started up again. Had they let off one or two men?

Using the drainage ditch as cover, I worked my way behind the produce warehouse and peered through the foliage. No movement. The forklift stood where I'd left it. Beyond the warehouse loomed a two story building. Offices probably. Bound to have phones.

The streetlights came on as I slipped out of my hiding place and ran. The increased illumination cast light on a bulky lump of fabric by the forklift.

It was Gorya. A little black circle was in the middle of his forehead and his skin looked like raw meat. His black eyes, though sightless, seemed to stare at me accusingly from his inflamed face.

I stifled a scream and collapsed against the wall of the building, where I fought to control convulsions of nausea. Terror filled my heart as I considered the depths these men would go.

Pavel would be even more desperate to find me.

Finally, I stumbled for the office building next door.

Once in the shadows, I tried the door. Locked. Peering through the window I could make out a row of desks, each with phones and computers. At the back of the building, I tried every window. All were locked and revealed tell-tale white security tape indicating the presence of a burglar alarm.

I could throw a stone through a window triggering an alarm, and then hide until security personnel arrived. But how long would they take? Somehow, I needed to trigger a massive emergency. I must have a phone. But how to get one without setting off an alarm?

The office building behind which I hid was one of a cluster of three. All appeared deserted. Why couldn't there be some conscientious secretary working late? But no, every window was dark.

A daring idea popped into my mind.

# 51

Everything would depend on split-second timing. Could I pull it off?

All three buildings were serviced by the same alarm company. The buildings formed a 'U' shape around a parking lot that was landscaped with pyramidal evergreens interspersed with rhododendron and azalea bushes.

When I executed my plan, the Russians would assume I'd make for the area behind the buildings where there was less light and scattered bushes bordering fields. So I needed some place to hide in front of the buildings, a place where they'd never look.

The rhododendron and azalea bushes weren't dense enough to conceal me. The thought of hiding in a closet inside gave me the heebie-jeebies. Of course, that plan would give me access to a phone.

The parking lot contained an old pickup under the shade of a live oak tree off to one side. On the other side were a group of three black panel trucks whose logos I couldn't read.

I searched for ammunition. Sticks? No, not heavy enough. I needed some large stones or bricks. I finally found a pile of discarded bricks. I selected four and carried them near the corner of two buildings. I might need the extra one.

Now to find a place to hide. I had to find a spot where I could wait five, maybe ten minutes, until the authorities could get here. I flicked away a drop of sweat as I thought of the implications if they were delayed.

Time was running out. The panel trucks in the parking lot. The nearest one had been backed in so the passenger side was almost against a thick clump of rhododendrons. I could crawl under the truck.

I took a couple of deep breaths and looked around for any sign of Pavel and his thugs. I jumped up, grabbed one of the bricks, raced to the first window, and hurled it with all my strength. The window exploded and a siren began to wail.

I hefted another brick and hurled it through the nearest window of building two. It set off an undulating wail. I raced to the back of the third building, where I slipped on a patch of mud and dropped both bricks into some long grass. Frantically, I searched until I found one. I tossed it at a group of three windows.

By this time the shrieking alarms and the adrenaline had me shaking like a tree in a hurricane.

Incredibly, the brick bounced off one of the window supports to fall at my feet. I hurled it again at the recalcitrant window. The glass shattered and a third alarm added to the cacophony.

I shook my head to clear it and took off for the parking lot where I dived into the shrubbery. I lay there catching my breath and staring at my muddy hands and broken nails. I badly needed a manicure. This thought almost made me burst into uncontrollable giggles. I smothered my mouth to silence the convulsions of hysteria that threatened to break out.

The sound of a racing engine sobered me quickly. I rolled under the nearest panel truck. Wiggling into a position where I'd be screened on the back and on one side by shrubbery, and on the other by the rear tires of the truck, I collapsed.

Against the backdrop of wailing alarms, the screeching of brakes, the slamming of doors, Pavel's screaming reached my hiding place. I lay motionless, barely breathing while his men shouted as they ran from place to place.

The agony of lying on the pavement became unbearable. Every tiny stone of the asphalt was leaving a mark on my skin. The oily mass of the truck chassis was a few inches from my face. My scrapes and bruises began to sting unmercifully.

Time stopped. My world became compressed into a microcosm of torture: my head pounded, my skin crawled, my knee stung, my shoulders ached, my ears throbbed, and my breath came in gasps. Every time I heard the pounding of feet on pavement come near, my heart-rate sped up until I thought it would burst from my chest. I expected a fusillade of bullets at any minute. I began to pray desperately for help.

The sounds faded.

A siren screamed, and then the sound of a vehicle approached. It screeched to a stop across the parking lot. The smell of burnt rubber drifted in the air.

I crawled to the front so I could identify my rescuer. From beneath the front bumper I could see a security guard standing by the open door of his idling vehicle talking into a mike.

Without another thought, I crawled out of my hiding place and ran towards him waving my hands and shouting. "Help! Over here. I've been attacked."

He turned. A shot rang and he crumpled to the ground.

# 52

For a moment, I stood there staring at the dark stain spreading on the downed security guard's blue shirt, originating at his shoulder. Before my brain fully processed what to do, I bent down. His pulse was weak, but there. I couldn't pick him up, I'd have to leave him.

*Be with him, God. Help me get him the help he needs.*

Then, as if suddenly waking from a trance, I jumped into the driver's seat, slammed the door, punched the gears into drive, and mashed the accelerator. The wheels spun and the car careened towards the exit of the parking lot.

My mind processed one thought: escape. Get far away. Never let them catch me again. Adrenaline must have taken over, pumped into my system by the survival instinct, because when that hateful black sedan appeared ahead of me blocking the entrance I headed directly for it shrieking at the top of my voice. If I was going to die then I'd take that malevolent scarecrow with me.

The driver—by his bulk I could see it was not Pavel—jumped out and began to fire. I swung the wheel from side to side, but a couple of the bullets must have found their mark because the windshield cracked. I swerved to the right, clipping the front of the car before I mounted the curb, tore through a clump of azaleas, and lurched onto the road in front of the offices. Stomping on the gas, I drove erratically down the road.

As the wail of the alarms began to diminish with distance, I became dimly aware of another sound, a woman's urgent voice from the car's two-way radio which the guard had left on.

"Brody, Brody, Brody. Come in. What was that screaming? Come in. Report. What's happening? We heard shots."

"Can you hear me?"

"Who are you? Where's Brody?"

"If Brody is the name of your security guard," I said, "He's been shot. Do you understand that? Send an ambulance and police immediately."

"What? Brody has been shot? Is he seriously wounded?"

"He's unconscious and bleeding from a shoulder wound."

There was a pause as someone swore in the background, and then a man's voice came from the speakers. "This is Coastal Security. Are you sure he's alive?"

"I felt a pulse."

"Who are we speaking to?"

I glanced at the rearview mirror only to see a dark-colored SUV. "My name is Ashlyn Forsyth."

"Ashlyn Forsyth? What are you doing in Brody's car?"

"It's too complicated to explain. Just send an ambulance and police...fast. Do you understand? Brody needs help and my life...is in danger."

The speaker went silent as if the dispatcher was processing what I'd told him. Finally, he came back on. "We've dispatched the police and an ambulance. Now explain slowly what is going on."

My voice rose. "I'm being chased by the Russian mafia and you want me to explain?"

"What do you mean, Russian mafia?"

I shouted at them. "Contact the FBI! Use my name. They'll know what's happening."

"OK. OK. Keep calm."

"Keep calm? There's an SUV chasing me and they're shooting."

"Can you keep ahead it?"

"I don't know. I'm trying."

"We've got you on GPS heading north from Kingsland. The police will intersect with your road momentarily. Watch for them ahead of you."

I concentrated on driving, swerving from side to side to throw off the aim of those in the vehicle behind me. I passed several cars and a truck going the other way, all of whom blasted their horns at me as they passed on the left. A truck took to the shoulder in a cloud of dust.

I could feel the vehicle pulling to the left as I roared down the highway. I must have damaged something. Seeing a couple of teenagers ahead gyrating along the edge of the highway, I hit the horn. But instead of getting off the road, they shouted at me until a fusillade of bullets zinged by and they dove for the ditch.

The car behind was closing the gap. I looked for some avenue of escape, but nothing but pines alternating with fields met my gaze. I'd left the town far behind. Occasional crossroads seemed to only be dirt tracks.

Finally, I heard the faint sound of sirens coming towards me. Only a hundred yards separated me from the other car. I stomped on the accelerator but couldn't increase the distance. The rear window shattered, sending pebbles of glass raining through the car. I slid down in the seat.

An old farm market with a faded sign advertising peaches lay ahead. Waving my left hand out the window, I slowed down, allowing my pursuers to close the gap in hopes that they would conclude I was giving up. At the last minute, I jerked the wheel and flew off the road into the parking lot of the market. The other car shot past on the highway while I did a U-turn and raced back the way I had come.

"Mrs. Forsyth, did you just change direction? Two police cars are coming towards you. They're within a mile of your location. Are you there?"

"I'm here," I gasped.

"What's happening?"

"I tricked the other driver. I reversed direction. They shot past me. I'm headed back towards town."

"Is there any place you can hide until the police get there?"

"I don't think so."

Along the highway huge masses of kudzu vine draped the pines along the road, almost smothering them. When a forest track appeared, I veered off the road and drove behind a thick mass of the strangler vines. I jumped out and ran through the pines trying to put as much distance as I could between the vehicle and me.

From a dense clump of bushes, a few hundred yards beyond the hidden vehicle, I stopped to catch my breath.

The dark SUV sped by before screeching to a stop and reversing. They must have seen the dust.

I raced between the pines keeping hidden from

view by the screen of bushes along the roadway. When I heard sirens approaching, I peered back.

Two state police cars slowed as they approached the place where I'd hidden the car. Did they have the GPS coordinates?

My pursuers had reversed again and were heading north at a slow speed.

As the police vehicles approached my position, I jumped up, ran into the middle of the road, and waved my arms. Both cars screeched to a stop fifty feet from where I stood.

I ran towards them until an officer exited one of the cars, pulled his revolver, and pointed it at me. "Stop right where you are. And keep your hands in sight."

I lifted my hands waist high and shouted. "What are you doing? I'm Ashlyn, the victim here."

"We know who you are. You're Ashlyn Forsyth, and you stole the car of a security guard after you shot him."

I pointed behind them towards the SUV. "They shot him...would have killed me if I hadn't gotten away."

The SUV squealed away in the opposite direction. "Catch them. They're getting away."

"Ma'am," an officer said as he approached. "Put your hands behind your back." He handcuffed me and began to Mirandize me. "You have the right to..."

"No. Listen to me," I pleaded.

"Ma'am, you'll have lots of time to tell your side of the story. Now get into the back of the police car."

I stood my ground. "Call the FBI; agents Cutter and Tibbs. You'll be sorry if you don't."

He glowered at me as he pointed towards his car.

"Don't make me use force."

I eyed his six foot five frame from the top of his standard issue hat hiding closely cut blond hair to his light blue shirt, dark blue pants, and shiny black shoes. Everything about him indicated spit and polish, except the freckles on his unlined young face.

No wonder he didn't listen to me. I was a sight. My hair fell in greasy strands down my dirty face. My blouse and jeans were soiled with grime. I had cuts and bruises anywhere my skin had been exposed.

A momentary uncertainty flashed across his face before he grabbed my arm and marched me towards the cruiser.

# 53

From the back of the Georgia State Police car, I shouted at the young officer in the front seat. "You're going to be sorry."

He ignored me and sped towards the town where I'd triggered the alarms.

Why was all this happening to me, and why did I keep asking why?

A few months earlier, I'd been counseling couples on how to mend rips in their marital fabric. They'd been grateful, filling my file drawer with glowing thank you letters. My pastor had asked me to lead a weekend retreat for couples and I'd been in the process of convincing Craig to help me. The New England Council of Marriage Therapists asked me to give a paper at their next convention in Boston. I felt good—I was doing something constructive with my life. Now I was in the midst of a hurricane with no relief in sight.

I glimpsed a dark-colored SUV in the distance. It had to be a coincidence. There were millions of SUV's. At least I was safe in this police car.

With a screech of brakes, the officer stopped in the parking lot between the three offices. The alarms had fallen silent.

An ambulance followed us in, parking near the downed security guard. Two attendants jumped out and ran to him. They checked him for vitals, and then started working on him. After lifting him onto a stretcher, they put him in the ambulance, and took off.

*Thank You, God.*

Two more State Police cars stopped nearby. Half a dozen officers spilled out and scattered through the complex with their guns drawn.

My mind drifted into painful territory. *God, isn't this a bit extreme? I know You wanted to get my attention. OK, you've got it. But aren't there easier ways? You've taught me some painful lessons about practicing what I counsel others. About having more empathy for those going through divorce. And, Lord, You've shown me that I often approached my clients with a sense of superiority. I really felt I had it all together, that I was a model wife. How blind! If I get a chance in future to counsel others, I'll approach it more as a wounded healer, that is, if I ever get through this. Get me through this, please, Lord.*

The young officer returned to the car and got in the driver's seat. Another apparently senior officer joined him in the other seat. They turned to face me.

"I'm Captain Johnson," the new man said. "And this is Trooper Vogel. Have you been read your rights? You know you have a right to a lawyer."

"A lawyer? I haven't done anything; why would I need a lawyer? Have you called the FBI or the Brunswick Sherriff?"

"This falls within the jurisdiction of the Georgia State Police. Now, please answer. Were you read your rights?"

"Yes," I said, "but…"

The captain held up a brick. "Did you throw this through the window of The Great Blue Heron Finance Company?"

"Yes, but…"

"And bricks through the windows of the two other buildings?"

"I can explain."

"Did you, or did you not?"

"Yes, but I had to." I rushed on. "The Russian mafia was going to kill me."

"Oh, I see." He winked at the younger officer, and then turned back to me. "And did you lie in wait for the security guard, shoot him, and steal his car?"

"No! Well...yes, I took his car...but no, I didn't shoot him! Pavel did...or one of his thugs."

"Oh, Pavel. Is he one of those phantom Russians you mentioned?"

I kicked the seat. "Can't you understand? He's no phantom. Do you think I'd throw bricks through three windows if I didn't want to attract the attention of the police?"

Captain Johnson's eyes bored into me.

"If you'll look around the parking lot, you'll find shell casings from the Russians. Up there by the entrance. They shot at me when I drove away."

"Vogel," Johnson said. "Check it out. See if you can find any casings."

Trooper Vogel got out and headed towards the entrance.

I pointed in the direction of the building where I'd been held. "You'll also find bullet casings over there in that other building. It's a produce warehouse where they held me captive. I think they use it to store drugs...and behind the building is a body."

Johnson raised his eyebrows. "A body? Another body?"

"They shot one of their own men."

Captain Johnson muttered something under his breath as he got out of the car and beckoned to another officer. "Take a couple of men to that warehouse and check it out." He pointed towards the produce warehouse, and then glanced in my direction. "The lady says there's a body behind it. See if she's right...and look for any shell casings."

Johnson got back into the police car. "Now is there anything else you want to tell me?"

"If you'll have a trooper go back to the place you picked me up, you'll find the security company's car. It's riddled with bullets. I hid it behind some kudzu vines and ran. That should prove what I'm saying."

Johnson punched a key on the radio and began issuing instructions.

"Can you take these handcuffs off?"

"Sit sideways with your hands pointing towards the door. And don't try anything, you hear?"

My mind reeled through desperate options. Let him unlock the handcuffs, and then knock him over? Get his gun? But how? Run? Hide until I could somehow contact Tibbs and Cutter? Or jump into the front seat and drive off in the police car?

In the time it took him to open the door, I realized how stupid any attempt at escape would be. At least I was now protected from the Bratva. Soon the FBI would get here. Then I'd be free...wouldn't I?

Johnson unlocked the cuffs and shut the door. I sat on the edge of the stained seat, massaged my shoulders to restore circulation, and tried to block out the smell of disinfectant that permeated the rear seats.

As soon as Tibbs and Cutter show up, I would pick up the pieces of my life. I'd contact Tiffany and Tyler—tell them I was OK and have Tyler fly home from Melbourne. I couldn't think clearly beyond that.

Trooper Vogel loped over to Johnson. He pointed back towards the entrance to the parking lot saying something about the shell casings and not wanting to mess with the crime scene.

Good.

I heard the sound of a chopper overhead.

A dark-colored SUV turned in and sped towards us. Surely, not with the police here.

"Watch out," I shouted, before crouching down out of sight.

# 54

I waited for gunshots to ring out. The police were outgunned by the Bratva. My mind conjured up a scene of bloodshed with the corpses of officers scattered all over the parking lot. Pavel would pull me from the car and make good on his threats.

Just as panic began to squeeze my chest in earnest, instead of shots, I heard angry voices.

Agents Tibbs and Cutter were arguing with Captain Johnson in front of a dark blue SUV. Agent Tibbs had her left arm in a sling and a bandage on her head. Cutter was gesturing towards the patrol car.

A wave of relief swept over me.

Captain Johnson strode towards the patrol car and flung open the door. "I'm reluctantly turning you over to the custody of the FBI. Be sure you are available for further questioning."

"Thanks for the presumption of innocence! You could have believed me."

"Perhaps, but remember, you broke the law."

Tibbs, whom I'd begun to think of as Nicole, came over, reached out with her good arm, and touched my face. "Are you all right?"

"Beyond hurting all over, I think I'm OK...but I must be a sight."

"We'll get you cared for shortly," she said. "At least you're safe. I was stupid to let my guard down like that in the drugstore. As if I was a probie or something."

"I heard a shot."

"One guy distracted me while his buddy crept up and whacked me from behind. I tried to pull my piece as I fell, so they shot me. I just got hit in the muscle of the upper arm. Now, we want to hear what happened to you." She motioned over her shoulder. "Come on."

I followed her towards the group standing by the SUV.

Agent Cutter met us halfway. "You scared the life out of us. We're glad to finally catch up with you again." His brown eyes warmed with concern. "You look like you've been through the wars." He smiled. "And from what we've heard, you're tougher than the Bratva. Remind me not to cross you."

Instead of replying, I followed them towards the SUV where two men waited. My head throbbed and I ached all over. Oh, for a couple of pain killers, a shower, fresh clothes, and ointment for my cuts and bruises.

Cutter pointed first to an older man with short grey hair, and then to a muscled thirtyish African-American. "These are Agents Lee and McFadden."

"We're gratified you're safe, ma'am," said Lee, who seemed to be the senior officer. "Do you need medical attention?"

I fingered the bruises and scratches on my face. "Other than a couple of pain killers, all I need is some ointment and a long shower."

Lee turned towards Cutter. "See that she gets what she needs." Then addressing me, he pointed towards the SUV. "Cutter and Tibbs will take you to your beach house and debrief you." He raised his voice to be heard above the clatter of the incoming chopper. "McFadden and I will work with the forensics team then join you later."

⮞⮜

Back at the beach house I took a long shower and washed my hair, reveling in the sensation of being clean again. Stepping out of the shower, I eyed the pile of soiled clothes lying on the floor where I'd discarded them. A sudden spasm of fear made me shiver. I collapsed on the toilet, convulsed by shudders and floods of tears. I don't know how long I sat there before I could gain some semblance of control.

Finally, I grabbed my soiled clothes and tossed them into the waste basket. I dried my hair, dabbed ointment on my cuts and bruises, and applied foundation to my face. Nothing could be done about my broken nails.

After donning a T-shirt and jeans, I collapsed again and took a couple of deep breaths to stave off a bout of hysteria. If only I could erase the memory of Pavel's beady eyes and the feeling of Gorya's grip on my arm—and his corpse. I shivered.

Cutter and Tibbs had brought me up to speed. My kidnapping triggered a statewide manhunt. Although I'd been driven some distance from St. Simons—almost to the Florida State line—an FBI agent cruising the I-95 corridor picked up the distress signal I'd triggered.

They relayed that back to Cutter who assembled a couple of assault teams and set up roadblocks on all area roads. Cutter's team was in the process of zeroing in on my signal, when a flurry of calls came in about a three-point security breach at some local offices in Kingsland.

When Coastal Security informed the State Police

that one of their guards had been shot and they were in conversation with some hysterical woman who had stolen his car, Cutter knew it had to be me.

He and Tibbs raced towards where I'd been spotted. But before they could arrive, the State Police had me in custody.

I joined Cutter and Tibbs in the living room where I perched on the edge of a cane armchair.

Nicole…Susan smiled. "Feel better?"

"Yeah. Much better, thanks."

"I've made you some hot tea," she said. "I thought that would be better than coffee this late at night. And we've ordered a pizza. You don't have to eat any, but we thought you might be hungry." She pointed to her bandaged arm. "Larry, can you do the honors?"

"So is the charade over?" I said to her. "Do I go back to calling you Susan, or is it still Nicole?"

"Susan's good."

"And you can call me Larry," Agent Cutter said from the kitchen.

"Any progress on catching Pavel and his thugs?"

"You bet," she said. "They tried to run one of our roadblocks, but didn't make it. Another of their men is dead and Pavel is in custody. You can stop worrying about them."

"Black, foreign, expensive sedan?"

"Yeah, that's right."

Agent Cutter returned with steaming mugs of tea.

I sighed as I took a sip. So good. I thought of the irony of growing up on iced tea and not even knowing what a teapot was when I married. But I'd learned to love a cup of hot tea—somehow it seemed more soothing than coffee.

I frowned as a thought skittered across my mind.

What did I need to tell them? There was some fact they needed to know. What was it?

Cutter set down his mug. "Ashlyn, do you feel like telling us what happened? We don't want to add to your trauma, but it's best to get it all out while it's fresh in your mind."

I stared at the worn throw rug on the floor. It was fraying around the edges—just like my life.

Larry took notes while I haltingly went over everything that had happened, from my abduction in the drug store to their arrival.

I stopped my narration. "Two cars!" I said. "There were two vehicles. One was a black sedan and the other a dark colored SUV. They used two vehicles. Did you find the SUV?"

Larry flipped open his cell phone as he stood up. "Can you describe it?'

"Like yours, but darker, maybe black."

He listed different models but I didn't recognize any. I frowned as I tried to recall the SUV that chased me down the highway. "It was big. Lots of chrome. Some kind of hood ornament. I'm sorry, but I have no idea about makes or models."

He nodded as if he recognized a model from my vague description. Then, keying in a number on his phone, he left the room.

# 55

Larry returned to the living room. "I've sent out an APB for any dark-colored vans or SUVs seen in the general area. But I don't hold out much hope that it will be found. Popular model, plus it's dark, and they could have switched cars by now."

"I'm sorry," I said "I told the dispatcher from the security company an SUV was trying to catch me. I assumed she would have told you."

Susan reached across the coffee table to touch me with her good arm. "Not your fault."

A car turned into the driveway, followed by a door slamming and steps coming up to the veranda.

Susan reached behind to grab her weapon.

Larry went to the door as the bell sounded. He peered through the glass. "Just one of ours delivering the pizza." He stepped outside and talked with someone. He came in carrying the pizza. "There've been developments. We've found a huge stash of smack, angel dust, and cash in that produce warehouse, and agents are closing in on three men who make deliveries. Perfect setup to distribute drugs. And we've found the car you hid." He raised his eyebrows. "Back window blown out, riddled with bullets. I don't know how you survived."

"One resourceful woman." Susan agreed. "You'd be an asset in the Bureau. Anyway, the pizza is getting cold. Anyone hungry?"

"I'm starved." Between mouthfuls of pizza I

continued to fill them in on how I had eluded Pavel. "Did your men find the body of Gorya behind the warehouse?"

"Not there, but in the trunk of their car."

"After finding his body, I knew I had to do something desperate. That's when I came up with the plan of breaking windows in nearby offices to trigger an alarm."

"Brilliant," smiled Larry. "But three?"

"I didn't want to take any chances that one was disabled. I knew Scarecrow would show me no mercy if he caught me again."

"Scarecrow—Pavel Kolodenko?" Larry said, "Fits him."

"Anyway, you guys arrived. So what happens now?"

Larry ran a hand through his short, cropped black hair. "The Bureau is even now raiding the offices of four of Bratva's front companies, companies we've been watching for a long time, companies that laundered some of their dirty money through Forsyth Investments. Plus another company that owned the produce warehouse. Forensic accountants will go through their books with a microscope."

"Craig didn't know the source of the money he invested. I'm sure he didn't." I looked from one to the other. "What are you not telling me?"

Susan frowned. "I'm sorry Ashlyn, but your husband's actions don't look like those of an innocent man. We have surveillance photos of him dining with a Russian mob boss at the Chez Robert Bistro just the week before you and he came down to St. Simons Island. And now he's disappeared. Why hasn't he contacted us?"

The last mouthful of pizza tasted like cardboard. I swallowed it with difficulty as I stared at Susan. "He told me he was going to contact the FBI...and he will...but first he has to feel safe."

He had chosen a time to disappear while Tyler trekked in Australia, Tiffany was in college, and I was a thousand miles from New York on an island in Georgia. Could that have been his motivation? But why defend him when I'd become the target? He had to know his actions would plunge me into danger. It was time I faced reality.

Both of them were staring at me with what looked like pity in their eyes.

Larry broke the silence. "This is very hard, Ashlyn, but we know you can handle it. You've proven yourself to be very strong. You have to face the possibility that your husband bears at least some responsibility for his predicament. We have an unconfirmed report that he boarded a plane to Rio...with a woman. "

I jumped up and walked over to the picture window where I stood and stared out at the darkness. Tears began to leak from my eyes. I batted them away. The sound of waves breaking on the beach came to my ear. The fathomless ocean. Waves ceaselessly beating onto the shore, oblivious to my emotions. "So what's going to happen to me? Do I look over my shoulder for the rest of my life?"

"We're sure you're no longer a Bratva target," Larry said. "Catching Pavel, shutting down the produce warehouse, and raiding the Bratva's front companies will effectively gut their organization. They probably already know that your husband has left the country and they'll realize there's no profit in trying to make you tell them what you don't know. Still, Susan will stick with you for a while."

"And my kids?"

"They'll be protected, too," Susan said.

"So I'm left to try and pick up the pieces of my life with no house, no bank account, no credit cards, nothing?"

Larry rubbed his chin. "A couple of days ago, before the drugstore episode, our boss was in the process of arranging for the unfreezing of your personal and business accounts and your cards. I'm sure by now you can use them again. The car? Sorry, but there's nothing we can do there. It's in your husband's name."

"The house?"

"That's even more complicated," Larry said. "It was jointly owned. I'm afraid there's nothing we can do about that until this case runs its course."

"My personal stuff—clothes and the like?"

"We'll arrange for you to pick up what is yours." Susan winked. "That is, whatever you haven't got already."

A series of beeps sounded on Larry's cell phone. He pointed me towards the bathroom. "Wait in there until we see what this is."

As I hastened to the bathroom, I heard the crunch of gravel on the driveway and the slamming of a door followed by a raised voice. Remy! I let out the breath I'd been holding in a great sigh and waited for them to call me back.

"You can come out, Ashlyn," Susan said. "It's Remy Jeandeau."

Remy strode forward, his blue eyes probing mine. "Are you OK?"

I shrugged my shoulders.

Then we seemed to melt into each other's arms. I don't remember who made the first move, just that it felt so good. I was tired of being strong. The feeling of his muscular arms cradling me against his chest opened the flood gates.

I began to weep. Finally, I turned away, intending to find a tissue to mop up the tears.

He reached out, turned me back towards him, and began to brush away the tears with his fingers.

"I'm OK, now."

Susan moved towards the door out onto the back veranda. Larry reluctantly followed her. "We'll let you two catch up. If you need us we'll be on the veranda."

"What happened?" Remy said. "I kept calling Larry but couldn't get through so I turned the boat around and came back in."

"You interrupted your shrimp run?"

"I was worried. As I've said, you seem to attract trouble like a lightning rod...I'm sorry." He looked away. "It's not like you cause it or anything. I mean..."

"I do, don't I? I'm sorry you interrupted your shrimping."

"Don't worry about it. So what happened?"

My mind, usually sharp and incisive, seemed to flit all over the place like a butterfly chased by a shrike. Was that the effect of the trauma I'd been through—or was it the warmth I saw in his gaze?

His blue eyes looked softer, not a startling sapphire, more like the color of a lazy summer sky.

I filled him in on everything that had happened since the kidnapping in the drug store. When my account came to a close, he sat there shaking his head.

"What is it?" I asked.

"You're an amazing woman! I've never known anyone like you."

I felt a flush spread to my face.

"What will you do now?" he said. "Return to New York?"

"That's what I was asking Larry and Susan. I'm not quite sure what I'll do beyond seeing my kids. Even though the FBI has promised to restore access to my bank account and credit cards, I won't have a house to return to. Thanks to you, I have a car. I need to let my friends and patients know."

"Would it help if I went with you? Then once you get settled, I could disappear—take the train back. I've gotten kind of used to my role as knight-in-blue jeans."

I felt a lurch inside as I thought of Remy disappearing. That idea threatened to start me sniffling again. "That's very thoughtful of you, but I've already interrupted your shrimping enough...and...I don't want you to disappear...you've become a special friend. I don't know what I'd have done without you."

Remy flinched as he leaned back.

"Remy, what is it?"

"It's nothing."

"Was it something I said?"

"I guess I had hoped...imagined. Oh, what's the use? I know I can't expect a sophisticated, highly educated woman like you to feel more than friendship for a salty old shrimper like me. We come from two different worlds, but..."

I reached over to touch his lips. "Remy, I have feelings for you...you stir something in me that I haven't felt for a long time...it's just..."

He pressed my hand to his lips.

I wanted to throw myself into his arms and forget

everything. "Remy…I have to see this through, first, Get it all resolved, and then…well…then…"

He looked deep into my eyes.

I held his gaze, hoping he read the promise there.

He did.

## About the Author

Eric E. Wright has had seven other non-fiction titles published. See: http://www.countrywindow.ca and http://www.ericewright.com

Reach the author at his email address: wrightee@eagle.ca

Thank you for purchasing this Harbourlight title. For other inspirational stories, please visit our on-line bookstore at www.pelicanbookgroup.com.

For questions or more information, contact us at customer@pelicanbookgroup.com.

Harbourlight Books
*The Beacon in Christian Fiction*™
an imprint of Pelican Ventures Book Group
www.pelicanbookgroup.com

May God's glory shine through
this inspirational work of fiction.

AMDG